"Marti Green's look at the potential for abuse and corruption in the privatized, for-profit juvenile-justice systems across America is taut, edifying, and, at times, terrifying. The thought that some of the terrible things described in this book really happen to youngsters charged with minor offenses made my skin crawl. This is an important novel as well as a top-notch thriller. I'd recommend it to anyone."

—Scott Pratt, bestselling author of *Justice Redeemed*, on *First Offense*

"*Unintended Consequences* is an engrossing, well-conceived legal thriller. Most enjoyable."

—Scott Turow, *New York Times* bestselling author of *Presumed Innocent*

"This one will grab you by the neck from the very first page!"

—Steve Hamilton, Edgar Award–winning author of *Die a Stranger*, on *Unintended Consequences*

THE
GOOD
TWIN

OTHER TITLES BY MARTI GREEN

Help Innocent Prisoners Project Series

Unintended Consequences
Presumption of Guilt
The Price of Justice
First Offense
Justice Delayed

THE GOOD TWIN

MARTI GREEN

f THOMAS & MERCER

Published by Thomas & Mercer, Seattle

www.apub.com

Amazon, the Amazon logo, and Thomas & Mercer are trademarks of Amazon.com, Inc., or its affiliates.

ISBN-13: 9781503949850
ISBN-10: 1503949850

Cover design by Rex Bonomelli

Printed in the United States of America

*To my husband, Lenny, my biggest fan and
love of my life.*

PROLOGUE

"Push," the obstetrician told Sasha Holcolm. "You're almost there." Seventeen-year-old Sasha thought she'd never experienced such pain before. By the time she'd arrived at the hospital, been checked in, and rushed to the delivery room, she was too close to giving birth for the doctor to give her an injection to numb the pain. She'd waited at home for her best friend, Lauren, to arrive from Allentown, usually a ninety-minute drive to Scranton, but a traffic jam had stopped her cold. Still, Sasha had read that a first baby always took forever to deliver. She'd been expecting eight hours at least—maybe much more. Finally, the pains were coming too close. Sasha couldn't wait for her friend. She took a taxi to the hospital all alone, without a husband or a parent. A breathless Lauren arrived while Sasha was still being processed in the emergency room, and ten minutes after being admitted, she'd been instructed to push.

Lauren lifted up her back with each push and whispered in her ear, "You can do it. You'll have your baby soon."

Sasha gave one more thrust, and a baby slid out of her.

"You have a daughter," the doctor said, smiling. She clamped the umbilical cord, then cut it. A nurse took the baby, dried her off, then wrapped her in a towel. "The next one is almost here, too," the doctor said.

"Next one?"

The doctor looked up at her. She seemed so young to Sasha, almost like a coed, despite the white jacket.

"Didn't you know you were having twins?"

Sasha shook her head just as the pain started again.

"Here we go," the doctor said. "This one should do it."

She screamed at the pain as she pushed. Seconds later, the doctor held up another baby. "This one's a girl, also." Another nurse took that baby. When they were wrapped up, both were brought to Sasha, one in each arm.

"They're beautiful," Sasha said. She stared into their eyes and felt a rush of love for them. She hadn't known it would happen so instantaneously.

She didn't want to think about what she needed to do, now that there were two. She was too happy to worry about that now.

Sasha picked up her newborn daughter and cradled her in her arms. So pink, so soft, so beautiful. Silky strands of blonde hair covered her scalp, and she had eyes so blue, they looked like jewels. She'd known she'd love her child, but she was thunderstruck by how deep the connection was after just one day. She pressed her lips to her daughter's cheek and inhaled the fresh scent of baby powder. "I love you," she whispered, then placed her back in the bassinet and lifted up the second baby, just as pink, as soft, as beautiful. Tears ran down her face as she held this child. "I love you, too. I always will."

The middle-aged woman sitting on a chair in the corner rose from her seat. "It's time now."

"Just a little longer? Please?"

The woman nodded. "Two more minutes."

Sasha stared into her daughter's eyes. They were wide-open, staring back, as if she knew what was about to happen. Suddenly, Sasha couldn't bear it any longer. "Here. Take her." She handed over the baby to the woman and watched as her daughter was taken away. When she was gone, the young mother lay down on the hospital bed and curled her body into a fetal position. "I love you, too," she said, over and over again.

PART ONE

MALLORY

PART ONE

CHAPTER 1

September 2016

I picked at the meager offerings on my plate, and once again, as I had every day for the past thirty-one months, wished I could find a way to get out of this dump. That's what I called the place—The Dump. The most I'd been able to afford was a boardinghouse in East Elmhurst. I hadn't known they'd even existed when I'd left Scranton and moved to New York. Boardinghouses were the stuff of a Dickens novel, not modern times. Yet, here I was, picking at runny eggs and burned toast with three other lost souls living at Marlon Manor, a fancy-sounding name for a rundown, two-story home on Astoria Boulevard.

Lou Castro, the owner of the house, stood up from the dining table to retrieve the pot of coffee and, as he always did, squeezed my shoulder. He was a middle-aged letch with a stomach that rolled over his belt by at least six inches, and whose pants always seemed to display the crack of his butt every time he leaned over. He'd been trying to get in my pants ever since I'd moved in, despite his wife watching his every move. As if he'd have a chance, even without that nag around! Thank goodness my room had a lock on the door. Still, I never complained to him about his roaming hands. After all, this hovel at least gave me a roof over my head.

"Some coffee, Mallory?" Lou asked me.

"Sure." He poured some into my mug, then squeezed my shoulder again.

I finished breakfast, then retreated to my room. All I owned was contained in this ten-by-twelve space, with its barren walls and peeling paint. I couldn't even claim possession of the saggy twin bed, or the plain end table with a small lamp on top. I didn't report to work until noon, in time for the lunch crowd. I'd be busy waiting tables until past two. Then it would slow down until five, when the dinner patrons began to arrive.

I moved a chair over to the window, then pulled out my sketch pad and 6B pencil. I began sketching the street below, the stores already busy with customers, the same old woman walking her miniature dog that I saw every day at this time, the cars speeding past. The pencil felt like part of my body, an extension of my fingers. From the time I'd received my first box of crayons, I was hooked on drawing. "You're good," my high school art teacher had told me. "Very good. Speak to me after class, and I can point you in the direction of the right college for you. Where you can develop your talent. Your grades are so excellent, you can get in most anywhere, but I can tell you which schools have the best art departments." I had wanted to laugh at her, at the thought that I could go to college. I didn't, though. I was too polite to laugh at a teacher. Instead, I said, "That would be great," and I showed up after school, wrote down the names given to me, and pretended to be grateful.

Even if the money had been there for college—and it wasn't, not even close—I couldn't leave my mother. Not then.

The morning passed quickly, too quickly. I suddenly realized if I didn't rush, I'd be late for work. I hurriedly changed into a black skirt and white blouse, then put on my comfortable shoes, the ones I could tolerate standing in for ten hours. Dressed, I threw on my coat and ran to the bus stop. I arrived at Trattoria Ricciardi with one minute to spare.

"Cutting it close," Gus said as I walked in the door. Gus Richards owned the restaurant, and I knew he was fond of me. Even if I'd missed the bus and walked in late, he would have forgiven me. I headed to the kitchen in the back of the restaurant, grabbed my order pad, then returned to Gus. "Today's specials?"

He handed me a sheet. I glanced at it, then tucked it behind my pad. I was familiar with each of the items. "Anyone of note coming in today?"

Despite the restaurant being in Astoria, it had a 4.6 Zagat rating for food, 4.8 for service and, with its white brick walls, rich burgundy tablecloths, and a small candle on each table, a 4.3 for decor. In addition to the neighborhood regulars, customers from surrounding areas traveled to it. And occasionally, actors working at the Kaufman Astoria Studios came by.

"Not so far," Gus said. "But there's a group of eighteen from Steinway coming in at one. A birthday party. I'm giving it to you." The famous Steinway & Sons piano factory was nearby, and its executives often ate at the restaurant. Getting a party to handle was always desirable—a 20 percent tip was automatically added to the bill.

I leaned over and gave Gus a kiss on his cheek. "Thanks. I appreciate it."

The lunch crowd started to dribble in, and I got busy. I chatted with the regulars and worked quickly and efficiently. None of my customers ever needed to ask for their water to be refilled, or more bread for the table. I always watched over them to anticipate their needs. At a few minutes before one, the Steinway party began to enter. Most of them I'd waited on before, but there were a couple of men I didn't recognize. Once they were all seated, menus in hand, I came over to take their drink orders and tell them the specials. As I walked around the table, writing down the drinks, I felt the eyes of one of the new men staring at me with a laser-beam focus. When I finally got to him, he looked up and whispered, "Charly, what are you doing here?"

"Excuse me?"

"Why are you waitressing? Is this some kind of joke?"

I kept the smile pasted on my face. "I think you have me confused with someone else. My name is Mallory."

The man shook his head. "Come on, Charly, I know it's you."

"What would you like to drink, sir?"

The man hesitated, a confused look on his face. "I'll have a glass of the house cabernet."

I wrote it down, then continued around the table. When I finished, I handed in the order, then refilled the water glasses at another table. I walked over to the bar and waited while the bartender, Freddy, readied the drinks for the Steinway group. Suddenly, I felt a tap on my shoulder and turned around to find the man who had confused me with someone else.

"I'm sorry. I think I embarrassed you." His eyes looked me over. "It's just—you look so much like my friend. Your hair is a little darker than hers. She's more of a golden blonde. But your eyes . . . I've never seen anyone else with eyes that color. Like sapphires. And not just the eyes—everything else is so similar. Your mouth, your nose—the same. Charly's slimmer than you, I think. At least she was back at college. I haven't seen her since we graduated. I live in LA. I'm just here on a business trip, and they invited me to this party."

"Mr. . . . ?"

"Findly. Matt Findly."

"Don't worry about it. They say everyone has a double somewhere. We probably look somewhat alike. But I'm not your friend."

Findly chuckled nervously. "Apparently not." He started to leave, then turned back. "Her name is Charlotte Jensen. Or now it's Gordon.

10

She married Ben Gordon. He went to school with us, too. I've heard she owns an art gallery, somewhere in Chelsea, called Jensen Galleries. You should stop in sometime and see what I'm talking about."

"Sure."

Findly nodded and returned to his table. I promptly forgot about him as I went about my work, smiling at my customers, pocketing their tips.

CHAPTER 2

Ben Gordon checked his gold Rolex watch, saw it was past seven, and stood up to leave the office of Jensen Capital Management. As he waited by the elevator, Rick Jensen passed by, stopped, and glanced at his own watch.

"Leaving already?" Rick said.

Gordon bristled. Naturally, his father-in-law would catch his early departure. "Nothing pressing with my clients. Thought I'd meet some friends for a drink."

"Oh? Charlotte joining you?"

His father-in-law never used Charly's nickname. Probably thought it wasn't sophisticated enough. "She's flying back from an art fair in Toronto. She won't get in until later."

Jensen nodded, then walked away without another word.

Bastard, Gordon thought. He knew Jensen didn't like him, hadn't wanted him to marry Charly. Given his middle-class upbringing in Queens—his father was an electrician and his mother was a teacher—Jensen didn't think Ben had the right pedigree. Charly was expected to marry someone like her—a spoiled rich kid raised by nannies and educated in private schools. The only reason Ben was given a job at this hedge fund company was to ensure Charly continued to live in comfort without taking money directly from her father. It didn't matter that Ben had sailed through Princeton with straight *A*s. His major was politics, not economics, so it didn't count in Jensen's eyes. It didn't matter that Ben had been accepted to Harvard Law School and turned it down so he and Charly could marry. "You'll be so good at this," Charly had assured him when she'd urged him to turn down law school and work for her father. "You're so smart." Instead, he felt stupid. Stupid for rushing into marriage. Stupid for thinking that making money as an end in itself would satisfy him. Stupid for not walking away from both his marriage and his job.

Yet, in the end, he'd learned that money, once had, was hard to abandon. His goal in college had been law school, followed by a job at a Wall Street firm, with an eventual foray into politics. He'd earn a more-than-respectable living. But he now pulled in a seven-figure annual salary at a job he hated but didn't want to give up. If he left Charly, his father-in-law would certainly fire him. And then what? Go back to school six years after his Princeton classmates? No. He no longer had the appetite for that.

He exited his building on West Fifty-Eighth Street, then flagged down a taxi to take him to East Twenty-First Street and Second Avenue. He nodded to the doorman as he entered the twelve-story building on the corner, then rode the elevator up to Apartment 812. Lisa was waiting for him with a vodka martini in her hand. She greeted him with a long kiss, then handed him the drink.

"You look tired. Tough day?" she asked.

"No. I was ambushed by Rick at the elevator." He shuddered. "I hate that man."

"Well, I'm not crazy about him myself, since he seems more of an obstacle to our being together than your wife. I wish you'd leave his company."

"And live on what?"

"You have money saved."

"Not enough. And you can bet that Rick would put the word out to every other hedge fund to blackball me."

"You don't like doing that, anyway. Go back to school. Get your law degree. We can live on my salary."

Ben looked around Lisa's 520-square-foot studio apartment. Once, he would have been happy in this space, with its tiny kitchen and a mere alcove for a bedroom. It was the kind of apartment the newly graduated moved into along with their first grown-up taste of independence. It was the only kind of apartment a social worker like Lisa could afford. It wasn't the kind of apartment a man could live in after experiencing the luxury of his 3,600-square-foot, three-bedroom townhouse on East Sixty-Second Street, just east of Fifth Avenue, and right across from Central Park.

He sat down on the living room couch, then motioned for Lisa to join him. "I don't want to think about that now." He pulled Lisa into his arms, then began kissing her, running his hands through her thick, untamed brunette hair. She was so different from Charly, with her smoothly perfect blonde bob, cool blue eyes, and model's body, her slim but toned arms and legs from years of tennis and sailing. Lisa was soft, full-bosomed. She was formed from the earth, Charly from the sky.

After a few minutes, Lisa pulled away, then took his hand and led him to the bed. "I need you now," she whispered. "Dinner later?"

Ben nodded. He wanted her.

Shortly before ten, Ben returned to his townhouse. It couldn't be more different from the apartment he'd just left. Instead of mismatched pieces of furniture garnered from friends and family's discards, every inch of the space had been meticulously planned. Although Charly had worked with a decorator, Ben knew that his wife had been instrumental in choosing every piece of furniture, every item that went up on the walls or down on the floors and over the windows. Every lighting fixture was unique, and every decorative item was a showpiece. Ben didn't know one type of furnishing from another, but he'd been told their home was decorated in the Mediterranean style, in colors of the sea, mixed with terra-cotta and yellow. It felt comfortable to him, and that's all he cared about.

Fifteen minutes later, Charly walked in, just the time he'd expected her. She had attended Canada's international annual fair for modern and contemporary art the past few days, and her flight had been scheduled to land at 9:30 p.m.

"How was it?" he asked his wife after she'd gotten settled.

"Tiring. But I sold a few pieces, enough to make the trip worthwhile." Charly attended a number of art fairs throughout the year, although she didn't always attend Toronto's. She never missed Art Basel in Miami Beach, or Tefaf in Maastricht, Netherlands, though, and with their hip scene, she always returned from fairs energized rather than fatigued. At first, she'd encouraged Ben to take a few days off work and join her, but it quickly became clear to him that he just didn't fit in with that crowd. It was bad enough that he had to smile through their endless social events in New York; he didn't need to extend the forced socialization. Besides, it gave him more time with Lisa.

"That's great!"

"Dad said you met some friends tonight?"

Naturally. His father-in-law would *make a beeline to his daughter.* "A couple of old high school buddies. You don't know them."

"Have a nice time?"

"Actually, it was kind of boring. Not much in common anymore."

"I'm surprised you didn't tell me beforehand."

"Last-minute thing. One of them called me at work to say the old group was in the city. Invited me to join them."

Charly nodded. "I'm beat. I think I'm going to head to bed now."

His wife walked into their bedroom, leaving him alone. He took a bottle of Sam Adams from the refrigerator, then turned on the TV in the den to watch the last quarter of the Knicks game, wondering the whole time how his marriage had become so barren, so devoid of love and tenderness. They never talked about it, but Charly *had* to feel the same way. *When did it start?* he wondered. Was it because he didn't want a child? No, it preceded Charly's request that they start a family. Maybe it was when she'd opened the gallery? Yes, that was it. Before then, he'd been happy. At least, as happy as he could be working for a man he hated, at a job he loathed. But he'd been happy with Charly back then. He'd come in from work grumpy, and she'd never fail to cheer him up. That's why he'd been attracted to her in the first place—because she'd always been able to read his moods and know precisely what he needed.

Now, it seemed like he was an afterthought. That's why he hadn't wanted a child so soon. It would push him even farther down the ladder, in her eyes. First, the child, then the gallery—or maybe even the reverse; he couldn't be sure—and last, him. Being last had never been acceptable. Valedictorian in his high school class, top 5 percent in his college class. Marrying the beautiful and popular Charlotte Jensen was part of the plan to stay on top. Only it hadn't worked out that way.

He felt no guilt for his affair with Lisa. Like his previous liaisons, it hadn't been planned. This time, though, it had lasted longer. He'd bumped into Lisa at a Barnes & Noble as they browsed through the books in the history section. He'd recommended the biography she'd had in her hand, and from that, a conversation had ensued, then coffee. It had started so innocently, through their shared interest in historical figures. She knew from the start he was married—the wedding band on his finger announced that fact. They met there again the following week, at the same time. They hadn't arranged it, but both showed up. He'd been pleased to see her again, and once more, they'd finished their book purchases and then had coffee together. When he'd suggested a drink after work, she'd hesitated only for a moment before accepting his offer. Their affair had begun that night, almost a year ago. He would leave Charly in an instant if it didn't mean giving up everything he had. Everything he'd gotten so used to.

CHAPTER 3

Wednesday through Sunday were the days I worked. Noon to 10:00 p.m., with an hour off for dinner between 3:30 p.m. and 4:30 p.m. It was an absurd time for dinner, but that was the slow hour. Usually, I found a stool in the kitchen and sketched, then grabbed a bite just before 5:00 p.m. when it really started to pick up. Mondays and Tuesdays were the days I lived for. That was when I took art classes at the Manhattan Institute of Art, on West Twenty-Third Street in the Chelsea section of Manhattan. It was the reason I came to New York. It was the reason I lived in the boardinghouse. Every dollar I saved went for art classes.

I arrived ten minutes early for my class in portraits and set up my easel next to Brian Swann. Brian was fifty-two, with curly hair that had already begun to have sprinklings of gray and a face that looked like it had been sculpted by Michelangelo. More important, he had no interest in dating me, or any other woman, for that matter, which was just what I wanted. I wasn't going to let myself get distracted by a romance. I was in New York for one reason only—to study art, to become recognized as an artist. I'd put my life on hold for too long in Scranton. Now, I only focused on my goal.

"Hi," Brian said, as he leaned over and gave me a peck on the cheek. "You doing good?"

I smiled at him. "Just peachy." I went to the storeroom in the back and rummaged through the canvases until I found mine. The model for the past three classes had been a woman in her seventies, her face filled with creases, her hair a silver white, her eyes a pale green. She dressed the same for each class—a flowing emerald-green gown, a necklace dangling down her neckline that I assumed was rhinestones, a similar bracelet on her right wrist, and draped over her lap, a silk scarf in colors of magenta, turquoise, puce, and gold. I found my canvas, then returned to my space and set it up on the easel. The first two classes we'd focused on drawing her; then last week we'd begun to paint.

The remaining students straggled in over the next few minutes, a total of fourteen, ranging in age from early twenties to one woman, Clara, who proudly proclaimed at the start of the new class that she was ninety years young. When they were all settled at their easels, Professor Greenblatt strode in. He was thirty-two years old, with long, almost black, wavy hair that he wore pulled back into a ponytail. With his aquiline nose, full lips, and thickly lashed eyes, I thought he was dreamy. When I allowed myself to fantasize about a relationship, I pictured his face. I suspected every other woman in the class, except perhaps Clara, felt the same way.

"Come by for dinner tonight," Brian whispered. "Stan is making *boeuf bourguignon.*"

It was tempting. I liked Brian's husband, and he was a gourmet cook. Even if he weren't, just getting away from The Dump was a treat. I'd planned, though, to stop by the art gallery that Findly had mentioned. I'd looked it up, and it was only a few blocks away, near West Twenty-Seventh Street. I knew it was silly, but he'd made me curious. It was in the opposite direction from Brian's apartment, though. Still, I supposed I could go to the gallery anytime.

"Sure," I answered, just before the teacher began to speak.

When the class finished, I headed with Brian to his condominium in the West Village. As soon as I walked into the apartment, I was bombarded with the rich odor of beef cooking in a wine sauce. I headed into the brightly lit kitchen, where Stan stood over the stove. Stan's bulbous nose matched his bushy, carrot-colored hair. "Thanks for the invite. It smells yummy."

"Glad you could make it, sweetie."

It was funny, I thought. Whenever any other man called me *sweetie*, or another term of endearment, I bristled. But not with Stan. He was so affectionate with everyone—man or woman—that it never seemed offensive.

"I would have brought something if I'd known in advance."

"Oh, honey, I'm just glad to see you. You never need to bring anything."

I knew that was true. Stan worked at Goldman Sachs and earned good money. Yet, he never acted snobbish. He and Brian had talked about moving uptown, maybe an apartment near Central Park. But the West Village had always been their home. It was where their friends lived, where they felt comfortable.

Just as I asked, "Want me to set the table?" the doorbell rang. Stan raced to the front door. I glanced over at Brian, who quickly looked away. *This isn't good,* I thought. A moment later, Stan returned to the kitchen, another man by his side.

"Brian, Mallory, this is Adam Jordan. He works with me."

Adam smiled. "It's nice to meet you both."

Adam was about six feet tall, with a quarterback's build. He had dark, tightly curled hair and a dimple in his cheeks when he smiled. *Handsome.* He was no doubt invited to meet me. Brian and Stan were always trying to fix me up, and I always rebuffed them. *At least they have good taste.* I would be pleasant to him, get through the evening, but nothing more. I knew from my mother where romance led—the death of dreams and saddled with a child. That wouldn't be my life, no matter how handsome Adam was.

CHAPTER 4

"Mallory? This is Adam Jordan. We met last week at Stan's."

Of course I remembered him. I'd half expected him to call, even though I hadn't given him any signals that I was interested in him during Stan's scrumptious dinner. I'd been polite, though, paying attention to his stories, smiling when he was amusing, serious when he touched upon matters that concerned him. I knew guys thought I was pretty, maybe even beautiful, if I believed the high school boys who had always tried to get in my pants.

"I was wondering, would you like to go out to dinner with me, maybe Saturday night?"

"I'm sorry, I work weekends."

"When are you free?"

"Adam, you seem very nice, but I don't want to get involved with anyone right now."

"It's just dinner, not a marriage proposal."

I laughed. Maybe it wouldn't be so terrible to go out to dinner, to be served by someone else. As long as he understood it wouldn't lead anywhere. "How about next Tuesday? I have an art class in Manhattan but finish up at eight."

"Perfect. Do you like French food?"

"I'll eat anything but Italian. That's all I eat where I work."

"I'll book us a table at La Grenouille for eight thirty. It's on Fifty-Second, just east of Fifth Avenue. Is that okay?"

"Sure." I'd heard of it, of course. It was one of the best restaurants in Manhattan, serving top-rated food, with prices to match. It was a place I'd never go to on my own. Jeans and a peasant blouse—my usual attire for class—wouldn't be seen there, where men were required to wear jackets and women dressed to show off. I had one decent dress and one pair of drop-dead-gorgeous heels, my only big splurge when I'd moved to New York. I'd have to tote them to art class and change afterward.

We chatted a few more minutes. Adam was easy to talk to, surprisingly low-key for someone who worked in a high-pressure job. When I hung up, I couldn't help smiling. I was pleased that I'd agreed to dinner. Although my resolve to refrain from romantic attachments hadn't changed, I could easily see him becoming a friend.

For the first time, I had difficulty concentrating during class, so I was relieved when the teacher announced he needed to end fifteen minutes early. I gave Brian a peck on the cheek before heading to the bathroom to change clothes. When I finished dressing, I stepped over to the mirror to see how I looked in my black jersey knit dress, with its deep vee neckline. *Not bad.* The knit fabric clung to my curves, and the neckline showed just the right amount of cleavage.

I stuffed the discarded clothes and shoes into a tote, then headed out of the building and walked toward Eleventh Avenue, then north up to Thirty-Fourth Street, where I could catch a series of trains to East Fifty-First Street. Manhattan never ceased to amaze me. Not just the buildings, crammed into every inch of space, but the hordes of people, any time of day or night. It suffused me with energy, just watching them rush to their destinations.

Chelsea was lined with art galleries, but I walked briskly past them, not wanting to be late, or at least not more than fashionably so. *A man should always wait for a woman,* my mother had often said. I'd just been casually glancing around me as I walked when I realized that right across the street from me, between Twenty-Seventh and Twenty-Eighth Streets, was the Jensen Gallery. It was in a two-story brick building that had been converted from a warehouse. The street level had no windows, just roll-up garage doors. I looked up to the row of windows across the second floor and saw that the lights were on. I was interested in seeing what artists they displayed. And, to be truthful, a little curious about the owner of the gallery, my supposed look-alike. The evening had turned chilly, and I pulled my lined trench coat closer around me as I started to cross the street, then suddenly stopped.

A man and a woman had walked into view. My breath caught, and I could feel palpitations in my chest. The woman's blonde hair was both lighter and shorter than mine, and she wore a dress that looked like it came from the window of Saks Fifth Avenue. But for those differences, I was looking at myself.

My hands were still shaking as I sat across the table from Adam Jordan at La Grenouille. I held them below the table, between my knees, in an effort to still them. Dimly, I could hear the sound of Adam's voice but scarcely comprehended his words. Instead, I couldn't shake from my mind the image of the woman I'd seen inside the gallery. As soon as I'd glimpsed her face, I'd jumped back, away from the window. I hadn't wanted to be seen. Not yet. So, instead of going inside, I ran from the building, confused and frightened. Now, sitting across from Adam, I tried to will my heartbeat to slow down.

"So, what do you think?"

I suddenly realized Adam expected a response from me. I felt myself blush and shook my head slightly. "I'm sorry. I was lost in thought about something. What did you ask?"

"You seem like something's bothering you. Want to talk about it?"

Did I? Should I just come out and say I'd seen my doppelganger? But the woman I saw through the window wasn't a ghost. She was real. And before I told anyone what I'd seen, I needed to first find out more about her. I smiled sweetly. "Sorry. I'm all yours now."

"I asked if you thought we should order a bottle of wine."

"I'm probably good for two glasses."

"Any particular likes?"

"You choose."

Adam motioned for the tuxedo-clad waiter to approach, then ordered a bottle of Puligny-Montrachet. I knew from my waitressing jobs that the bottle retailed for around sixty dollars. That meant the restaurant was charging at least $300. The prix-fixe dinners were $154 each. Briefly, I wondered if Adam was trying to impress me with how much money he had, then thought no. He was single, with no family, and earned enough on Wall Street that he didn't have to think about the cost of a meal out. I looked around the restaurant, fully taking it in for the first time. Each table was covered with a white linen tablecloth, and heavy mirrors hung on the walls. The room we were in, the main room, contained a profusion of flowers, each table with its own bouquet, and along the walls were tall vases with flowering branches reaching up to the ceiling. The lighting cast a golden glow over the patrons.

"Is this like a busman's holiday for you?" Adam asked.

"Hardly. Being served in an elegant restaurant is a far cry from waiting on others."

"Still, you're in a restaurant five nights a week. Maybe next time we can go to a play."

He's thinking next time already. I reached over and placed my hand on his. "Adam, I enjoy spending time with you, but as a friend, that's all," I reminded him.

Adam leaned over the table. "I came to New York two years ago, after I finished my MBA. I work six days a week, often till midnight. Sometimes straight through the night. It hasn't left me much time to make friends. If that's all you're looking for, then I'm grateful for that." Adam looked up and saw the sommelier standing by the table, a bottle of wine in his hands.

"Your Puligny-Montrachet, monsieur."

Adam nodded, and the sommelier poured a small amount into his wine goblet. Adam twirled it around in the glass, sniffed it, then took a sip. "Perfect," he said.

The sommelier filled my glass, then filled Adam's, and quietly retreated.

"There's no one at your job? Someone there you like?"

"Stan. He's been great." He chuckled. "Not exactly my type, though."

"How about one of the online dating sites?"

"I've tried. Met one or two that seemed promising, but then I'd keep breaking dates because something would come up at work, and they lost interest."

"I'm sorry."

Almost out of nowhere, a waiter appeared at our table. "Are you ready to order?"

Adam looked at me, and I nodded. "I'll start with the *Salade de Chèvre Chaud, Fondant de Poires Épicée*, and then the *Sauté de Homard et coquilles Saint Jacques a la sauge.*" I had studied French in high school, although by now I'd forgotten most of it. Still, I'd always been told my accent was perfect, so I ordered the warm goat-cheese salad and sautéed lobster and scallops in the language printed on the menu.

"And for dessert, mademoiselle?"

"Tarte Caramélisée à l'Ananas. Glace à la Noix de Coco au Rhum." Caramelized pineapple tart with rum coconut ice cream.

The waiter turned to Adam, who told him, "I'll have the mushroom and truffle soufflé, the Chateaubriand, and for dessert, the assortment of mini soufflés."

"Very good." The waiter gathered up the menus, then left.

Once again, I looked around the restaurant, each table filled with customers. They reeked of money, I thought, eyeing the ultrathin women who were all draped in expensive jewels, and dressed in silks and linens that looked like they'd come straight from a designer's showroom. Although I looked forward to my meal, I preferred the warmth of Trattoria Ricciardi, where the diners looked like real people.

I turned back to Adam. "So, tell me about your family."

As he spoke, I half listened. The other half of my brain kept returning to that gallery on Eleventh Avenue, and the woman inside who looked like my twin.

CHAPTER 5

Ben walked into Crown Fitness with just five minutes to spare. Every Tuesday he skipped lunch and played two rounds of racquetball with his oldest friend. He'd been best friends with Graham Deaver ever since they'd both lived in the Electchester housing development in South Flushing. Ben was three when they'd met; Graham, four. Electchester consisted of a group of low-rent apartments mostly occupied by members of the International Brotherhood of Electrical Workers union. Both of their families had moved to their own homes by the time Ben was seven, but they still had remained friends over the years.

Ben flashed his membership card at the front desk, then headed into the locker room to change. Crown Fitness was one of the top gyms in the city, with a membership initiation fee of $100,000. Inside were all the bells and whistles expected—a massive open space with rows and rows of machines, an indoor swimming pool, racquetball and basketball courts, fully stocked private rooms for personal training, larger rooms for fitness classes, and, of course, sauna and steam rooms. A nursery was set up for parents to drop off their toddlers when they weren't with their nannies or in nursery school. A small café served sandwiches and drinks.

When Ben reached the racquetball court he'd reserved, Graham was already there, hitting balls against the wall. Graham, an advertising copywriter, couldn't afford this gym. He was there each week as Ben's guest.

"I was starting to think you wouldn't make it," Graham said as he turned around.

"Yeah, I got stuck on a phone call with a nervous client."

"Need to loosen up first?"

"Nah. Let's just start. I can whoop your ass even coming in cold."

They began their first game, fast-paced and aggressive. They'd always been competitive with each other, hungry to be the best. Ben loved the sport, loved the sound of the ball bouncing off the walls, the sweat he worked up rushing to return each volley. When he played, he forgot about his job; he forgot about his marriage. It was just him and the ball. He won the first game, beating Graham by four points.

Graham plopped down on the bench, catching his breath. "You're on fire today."

"Yeah, well, I'm picturing my father-in-law's head as the ball."

"He still riding you?"

"Not anymore. He's sick. Liver cancer. He's been working from home."

"I keep telling you, leave there."

Ben just bowed his head and said quietly, "That's not going to happen." He knew Graham would never stay in a job he hated just because he feared what would happen if he walked away. Even as a young child, Graham had always been a risk-taker, willing to take chances and live with the consequences. Ben had always admired him for that.

Ben felt a push on his shoulder and looked up.

"Are you off in dreamland?" Graham asked. "Aren't you up for another game?"

Ben smiled. "Sure. Ten bucks says I beat you again."

They played two more games, Ben winning both. When finished, they headed to the locker room. Ben was chatting with Graham about the stock market when he turned the corner and bumped into a leggy redhead. He looked up and winced, then quickly caught himself. "Hi, Caryn."

"Oh, God, you're here. I should have asked to see the membership rolls before I signed up."

"Been coming here for years. If you don't want to run into me, stay away at lunchtimes."

Caryn harrumphed, then stormed away.

"What was that all about?" Graham asked.

"Just someone on the side before I met Lisa. A real bitch. She wasn't too happy when I dumped her."

Graham just shook his head.

After they showered and changed, they stopped at the gym's café and each ordered a smoothie, then sat down at a table.

Graham handed Ben ten dollars. "Something's up with you. I haven't seen you this intense in a long time."

Ben sighed deeply. "It's Charly. We haven't been getting along lately."

Graham smirked. "Gee, you think maybe it's because you're screwing another woman?"

"You're the only one who knows about Lisa."

"You sure?"

Was he? Charly had been cool to him for a while, but he'd assumed it was due to the demands of the gallery. She'd just opened it less than three years ago, and because of her father's connections, it had done well. But it wasn't just the hours at the gallery. There were the seemingly endless social events to build relationships with clientele, the dinners spent wooing artists, the travel to art fairs nationally and internationally. It seemed he hardly saw her anymore, and when he did, she was petered out. Still, he'd been careful about his trysts with Lisa. They were never together in public, not even at small restaurants near Lisa's apartment, where he was unlikely to run into Charly's crowd. There simply was no way for his wife to know.

"I'm sure."

Graham leaned back in his seat and was quiet while he finished his smoothie. When done, he said, "We've been friends for a long time, and I've never seen you this unhappy. Why can't you chuck it all? Leave Charly, leave your job, go to law school, which is what you'd always planned on. There aren't any kids holding you back."

How could Ben explain to Graham that marriage to Charly had changed him? He'd been brought into a world of wealth that had been foreign to him. It wasn't just the money; it was the access money bought. Access to gala openings at the Met, prime seats at the theaters, dinners with mayors and governors and senators, black-tie charity events, parties at the homes of New York's wealthiest families. As much as he complained about being dragged to the social events Charly needed to attend for the gallery, he was making invaluable connections if he ever went into politics. He couldn't walk away from that. No matter how much he wanted to.

CHAPTER 6

The following Tuesday, I headed to the Met. I often visited one of the many museums in the city before my art class began, but I was particularly excited today. The Metropolitan Museum of Art was exhibiting the work of Valentin de Boulogne. Relatively unknown to the casual museum visitor, the seventeenth-century artist was much admired for his naturalistic painting. Once I arrived at the massive Gothic Revival–style building on East Eighty-Second Street and Fifth Avenue, I paid the suggested fee and placed the sticker I was handed on my blouse. The museum, one of the largest in the world, contained more than two million works of art from antiquities to modern, gathered from every part of the world. Today, though, my only interest was de Boulogne. I headed to the rooms containing his paintings and slowly walked past each one, spending extra time at the portraits, studying his technique. After I'd walked past each one twice, I picked a spot, then sat down and began sketching. The hours flew by, and soon it was time to head downtown to art class.

We had finished with the elderly female model yesterday, and now a strapping man, shirtless, with bulging chest muscles and dressed in the pants and cap of a police officer, was in her place. The class had started out with nude models, focusing on learning to draw the contours of the human body, before moving on to clothed models. Now, the teacher wanted the students to gain experience utilizing both skills.

Five minutes later, Professor Greenblatt entered the classroom and walked to the center, next to the model. "Good afternoon, everyone. Clara's grandson, Detective Saldinger, has offered to sit for us."

There was a chorus of muted giggles around the room. "Yes, ladies, he really is a police officer. He didn't dress this way just to titillate you." The teacher cast his eyes around the room, glancing at each of the fourteen students standing in front of their easels. "Today, we're going to concentrate on the male upper body. I want you to focus on the definition in his muscles, and using light and shadow to delineate its three dimensionalities."

I studied the man before picking up my pencil. The sides of his brown hair that peeked outside his cap were clipped close to the scalp, causing his bushy eyebrows to pop. He had a slim face, with a nose a bit too large, and full lips. I didn't consider him handsome, but his face seemed welcoming. I suspected his muscles came from long workouts at a gym. I began sketching him. As with all our live models, after twenty minutes of sitting motionless, Saldinger took a break. He'd be off for ten minutes, then on again for another twenty.

I continued to work on my sketch until I felt a tap on my shoulder. I turned around to see Clara, her grandson by her side.

"Mallory, I wanted to introduce you to my grandson, Kevin."

I shook his hand. "Thanks for doing this for us. It's nice once in a while to get a real person, not a model."

"My grandmother insisted. She didn't give me a choice."

"Well, dear, I wanted you to meet him, and I know you wouldn't allow me to set you up."

Saldinger's face turned red. "Grandma!"

"What? You're divorced; she's single. You both need to get out."

I laughed. I gave Clara a quick hug, then looked at Saldinger. "Your grandmother's right. I wouldn't have allowed it. I'm sure you're very nice, but I'm off the market."

He smiled at me. "Well, that's a loss for the market." He scowled at his grandmother, then said, "Break's up. I've got to get back."

After he left, Clara shrugged. "You can't blame me for trying. He's such a nice boy, and you know what they say. All work and no play makes—"

"Makes me a better artist. I meant it when I told you I'm not interested in dating."

"Pshaw! I'm ninety years young. You think I'm going to listen to you?" She shoved a business card into my hand. "In case you change your mind."

I saw it had her grandson's name and the phone number and address of his precinct. I turned it over, and on the back was handwritten his cell phone number. "Clara, really, I'm not interested."

She started to return to her easel, then turned back and winked. "You know, I have other grandchildren. I'll find someone for you yet."

I had mulled it over for seven days, going back and forth. Did I want to speak to the woman at the art gallery? The thought frightened me. What if, somehow, we were related? My parents' pasts were a mystery to me. It was possible I had a cousin somewhere that I didn't know about. A cousin who bore an eerie resemblance. I welcomed that idea. With my mother gone, I had no family. But—the big *but* that held me back— what if she was more than a cousin? What if she was my sister? That would mean my mother had lied to me. And if that were true, maybe she'd lied about other things as well. Maybe she'd lied about my father.

I decided to go back and speak to the woman. As soon as class ended, I gathered up my belongings and headed over to Eleventh Avenue. As I neared the building, I saw it was dark inside. I glanced at my watch: 8:25 p.m. It was supposed to be open until 9:00 p.m. I had checked the gallery hours online earlier today. Open until nine on

Tuesday, Thursday, and Friday. My heart was beating rapidly. It had taken all my courage to return. I wasn't sure I could summon it again on another day.

I pulled out my cell phone and clicked on Safari, then typed in the website for Switchboard.com. When it opened, I typed the name *Charlotte Jensen Gordon*. Seconds later, a list of people popped up. Below each name were names of people each Charlotte Gordon knew. The second Charlotte Gordon knew a Ben Gordon, the man Findly had mentioned. It had to be her. I clicked on the name and a phone number, and an address on East Sixty-Second Street came up. I knew it was wrong to bother this woman at home. Maybe the closed studio was a sign I should walk away, go home, and forget about her. I also knew, if I did, I'd likely never come back. I tucked my phone back in my purse and started walking to the subway.

CHAPTER 7

It took a while for someone to answer the doorbell, and when the door finally opened, a tall man with brown hair and an athlete's body stood before me. He was dressed in neatly pressed jeans and a Knicks jersey. "Is this the home of Charlotte Gordon, the owner of Jensen Gallery?"

The man stood mute, his face drained of color. When he finally spoke, he said, "Who are you?"

I understood his reaction. It was the same feeling I'd experienced a week earlier when I'd first laid eyes on Charlotte. "My name is Mallory Holcolm."

"Are you related to Charly?"

"I don't know." I fidgeted with my fingers. I felt just as uncomfortable as the man standing before me looked.

He hesitated, then opened the door wider. "Charly's not home now. That's what everyone calls her. Not Charlotte. My name is Ben. I'm her husband. Why don't you come in?" He led me inside a marble-floored foyer, then into the den, and gestured for me to take a seat. The room was bigger than my whole apartment back in Scranton. The largest television I had ever seen was affixed to one wall, with a basketball game paused. Ben picked up the remote and turned off the TV. He sat down, then asked, once again, "Who are you? I mean, not your name. But you look so much like my wife, it's uncanny."

"I know. I work at a restaurant, and a few weeks ago, a guy—he said his name was Matt Findly—confused me for your wife. He told me about her gallery, and I passed by it last week. I thought I was looking at myself."

"Matt went to college with us. Did you talk to Charly? What was her reaction?"

I shook my head. "I was so startled, I walked away. Well, *ran* is more accurate. It frightened me."

"Charly was adopted. Were you?"

All this past week, when I'd run through possible explanations, that was the thing that had terrified me most: the possibility that my whole life had been a lie. That the mother I'd known hadn't given birth to me. "I don't think so. At least, my mother never told me I was."

Ben stood up. "I'm going to get a glass of wine. Would you like one?"

I nodded. It was exactly what I needed right now. Ben disappeared into what I assumed was the kitchen, then returned a few minutes later with two wineglasses, filled to the top. He handed one to me.

"Has Charly ever tried searching for her birth parents?"

Ben shook his head. "She's never seemed to be interested in that."

That surprised me. If it were me, I'd want to know. I'd want my family to be as big and inclusive as possible. I took a sip of wine, then glanced around the room. "You have a beautiful home."

"Would you like a tour?"

"Sure."

Ben took me from the den into an even larger room. The ceilings in each room were twelve feet high. "Our living room. More like a museum, if you ask me."

Although the furnishings were appealing and, I assumed, expensive, my eyes were drawn to the paintings hanging on the walls. Ben was right. It *was* like being in a museum. Most were contemporary or modern style, and all were breathtaking. I didn't need to look at the signatures on the paintings. I recognized the work of Gerhard Richter, Jasper Johns, and Richard Prince. Others I was less familiar with but were just as exquisite. I wondered what it must be like to have such masters at one's fingertips, to be able to gaze upon their beauty every day. I briefly felt a pang of jealousy, then pushed it away.

"Ready to see the rest of the apartment?"

I tore myself away from the paintings and followed Ben into the dining room, where more artwork hung than in the kitchen. It was bigger than the kitchen at Trattoria Ricciardi, with off-white cabinets, the top names in stainless-steel appliances, and a grayish-black soapstone countertop. The light wood floors in the other rooms continued into the kitchen. I had learned to cook out of necessity—when my mother worked, she often wasn't home to prepare dinner, and later, when she became ill, she was too weak to cook. At first, I popped frozen dinners into the oven but quickly grew tired of them. I began by making simple foods—scrambled eggs, hamburgers, spaghetti. But gradually, I started to experiment. When I had time, I watched the cooking shows on cable TV and soon became quite proficient. I missed cooking. There was no opportunity for it, living in one room in a boardinghouse. Cooking in a kitchen like this would be a dream.

Ben took me into the other rooms: three bedrooms, each with its own bathroom, and an office. When finished, we returned to the den.

"What was your home like, growing up?" Ben asked.

A hard laugh escaped. "Imagine the opposite of this."

"You were poor?"

"I had a roof over my head, food to eat, and clothes to wear, so I wouldn't say I was poor. But we always scraped for money. My mom was always behind on the bills. I'd wear the same clothes long after I'd outgrown them because we couldn't afford new ones. Instead, my mother would undo the seams and sew them back up a little longer, a little looser. Just shoes—they were always new. She didn't want my feet to become deformed by squeezing them into ones too tight."

"Would your mother tell you now if you were adopted?"

"She passed away a few years ago."

"I'm sorry. From what, if you don't mind my asking?"

"My mother had a three-pack-a-day cigarette habit by the time she graduated high school. Eventually, it led to stage three emphysema. I couldn't go off to college. I had to earn enough money to pay the rent, to buy food and medicines."

"That had to be tough."

"I found a waitressing job easily enough. I was young and pretty, and the customers liked me, so they tipped me well. Any money that was left over, I used to take one art course a semester at the local community college."

"Here, in New York?"

"No. I grew up in Scranton. As soon as my mother died, I packed up my things and moved to Queens."

"Where's your father?"

"He was killed in the Gulf War, before he and my mother married. Before I was even born."

"How about grandparents?"

I shook my head. "My mother was estranged from her mother. She didn't know her father—he split when she was a baby. I'm determined not to make the same mistakes they did." I took a sip of wine, then leaned back in the chair. "It doesn't make sense that I was adopted. I'm the reason my mother left her home, because she got pregnant before she graduated high school." I didn't tell him that whenever my mother felt overwhelmed, which was frequently, she blamed me for ruining her life. I tugged on my ear, a habit I'd had since elementary school when I was trying to figure something out. "Maybe my mom got pregnant before she had me? Maybe she gave that child up for adoption? Charly could be my sister, or half sister at least."

"When's your birthday?"

"September 24, 1990."

"That's Charly's birthday."

My hands began to shake. None of this made sense. I lifted the wineglass and took a large gulp.

"She has to be your twin." Ben moved closer to me and placed his hand over mine. "There's only one way to know for certain. DNA." He stood up and walked into the kitchen. I heard a drawer open, then a rustling sound. When he returned to the den, he had a plastic baggie in his hand. He handed it to me. "Hold it open," he said, then, leaning over me, yanked out a hair from the top of my head.

"Ow!"

He looked at it, then dropped it in the baggie. "It's good. The root is attached."

I rubbed my head. "You'll tell Charly? She'll put in a sample, too?"

"Charly's going through a hard time. Her father was just diagnosed with liver cancer. It's at a late stage. That's where she is right now. I don't want her to be distracted by this until we know something for sure. She's in too fragile a state. I can get her DNA sample without bothering her. I'll let you know when the results come back. Figure at least four weeks, maybe six." He took his cell phone out of his pocket. "What's your phone number?"

I gave it to him, and then he walked to a sideboard in the room, opened the top drawer, and pulled out a card. He handed it to me. "Here's my phone number. If you need to speak to me, use the cell phone."

I nodded, then slipped the card into my purse.

As I walked to the door, I glanced back at the apartment once more. I wondered if Charly lived like this because she'd married well, or because she'd been adopted well.

As Ben closed the door behind his unexpected guest, his mind was whirring. Charly had a twin! An identical twin, surely. There were surface differences—the hair color and fuller face, but that could be explained by a few pounds' difference. He'd seen the way she'd gawked at the opulence of the apartment. She'd told him she'd grown up wanting. She couldn't have much now, working as a waitress. He felt his excitement rise. This could be his chance. He had to approach it carefully. And, most important, he couldn't let Mallory meet Charly.

CHAPTER 8

The next morning, as soon as breakfast was finished, I retreated to my room and began making a list. That's my standard fallback whenever I feel stressed or confused. Write down the steps I need to take. First: track down any relatives. My mother had rarely spoken about her family. Whenever I'd asked about grandparents, she'd said there were none. When I'd asked about aunts or uncles, I'd gotten the same response. My mother had worked her entire life cleaning homes, at least two every day, sometimes three. She'd had friendships over the years, but they rarely lasted more than three or four years. If it was a man, usually less than a year. There was only one person who'd been a constant in my mother's life—her best friend, Lauren. I hadn't seen her since my mother's funeral.

I pulled out my cell phone and did a search for the phone number of Lauren Kurz, in Allentown, Pennsylvania. That's where my mother had grown up. That's where she'd first met Lauren. Nothing. No listing. In the years before my mother died, Lauren would usually come to Scranton to visit. Less often, we'd go to Allentown. I vaguely remembered once overhearing Lauren tell my mother that she was marrying again, but I didn't pay it much attention. I was busy working to pay for food. Now I realized Lauren's last name would be different, and I hadn't a clue as to what it might be.

I needed to drive to Allentown. Maybe Lauren was living in the same house. I'd visited it enough with my mother to remember how to find it. And if not, maybe a neighbor would know where she'd moved, or at least her married name. I didn't own a car, but Brian did. He'd lent it to me in the past, and I was certain he would now. Next Monday, I'd skip art class. I needed answers, and Lauren was probably the only person who could provide them.

I flipped through the stations on Brian's car radio as I headed west on Route 78. I didn't like any of the preset stations he had chosen, and I needed some distraction from the monotonous highway. I'd crawled through the Lincoln Tunnel, but that was no surprise. I didn't want to arrive in Allentown before 7:00 p.m., to make sure Lauren or her neighbors were home from work. That meant leaving Manhattan during rush hour, which was anytime after 3:00 p.m.

I found a classic-rock station and settled in. I supposed most people would think I was too young to appreciate classic rock, but it was the music my mother always had listened to in our apartment. At 7:15 p.m., I pulled up to what I hoped was Lauren's house. It had been years since I'd visited her with my mother, but I'd always had a good memory. I parked in front of the semiattached two-story brick house and rang the bell. Moments later, an unfamiliar woman answered the door.

"Does Lauren Kurz live here?"

The woman shook her head. "I don't know anyone by that name." She hesitated. "Wait? Do you mean Lauren Walker?"

"That could be her name. I know she remarried."

"That's the woman who sold me this house. Almost two years ago."

"Do you know where she's living now?"

"Sorry, dear. Don't have a clue."

I thanked her and left. At least I had her last name now. Unfortunately, it was a pretty common one. I retreated to the car, then entered the name *Lauren Walker* into a telephone app on my phone. There were too many to count. At least a dozen in the right age range residing in Pennsylvania, New Jersey, and New York. I got back out of the car and walked up to the other half of the semiattached house and rang the bell. A white-haired man leaning on a cane opened the door and smiled when he saw me.

"Well, you're a pretty girl. How can I help you?"

"Do you remember the woman who used to live next door?"

"Lauren? Of course. She was a pretty girl, too."

"Do you happen to know where she moved to?"

The man held the door open wider. "Come on in. I think I saved her Christmas card from last year."

I hesitated a moment. I already felt uncomfortable from his comments about my looks. Even though he appeared frail, maybe he wasn't. Maybe he was someone to be afraid of. As soon as I thought it, I felt silly. Twenty-four-hour news coverage on multiple cable channels had made the world seem like a frightening place. It was far more probable that he was a harmless old man, one who could possibly lead me to Lauren. I stepped inside.

"Go, sit down. Make yourself comfortable," he said. "Want some coffee?"

"No, thanks."

"I'll just be a minute."

The living room looked like it had been decorated in the seventies and never updated. The couch I sat on was frayed along the seams, and the fabric of the two slipcovered chairs looked faded. There was nothing homey about the room, and I suspected he lived alone.

"Found it," he said as he walked back into the living room. "I always keep the holiday cards, so I know where to send them the next year." He handed me an envelope. The return address had the name of Walker and listed a street in Philadelphia. I took out my phone and entered the address into a Notes app.

"I really appreciate this, Mr.—"

"Gunderson. Felix Gunderson."

"Well, thank you again." I stood up to leave.

"Are you sure you wouldn't like some coffee?" His voice had a pleading tone.

I bet he's lived by himself for a long time. I bet he's lonely. I gave him a bright smile. "Sure. I'll have a cup."

It was 8:00 p.m. by the time I left Gunderson's house. Over the half hour I spent nurturing one cup of coffee, I learned his entire life story. I was glad I'd stayed. He'd been retired and widowed for almost a decade, and he needed someone to talk to. But now it was getting late. It would take me a little more than an hour to get to Lauren's house. As soon as I got into the car, I checked online and came up with a phone number for Lauren Walker in Philadelphia. I dialed it, and a woman answered.

"Lauren? It's Mallory Holcolm."

"Mallory! My God, it's been ages. How are you doing, sweetheart?"

"Good. I'm good. Listen. I need to see you. Is it too late if I get to you around nine-ish?"

"What's wrong?"

"Nothing. I just need to see you, and I can't explain over the phone."

"You have my address?"

I repeated it to her.

"Then, sure. Come over. I'll be awake."

At 9:20 p.m., I pulled up to Lauren's apartment in Center City. I gave my name to the concierge, and he pointed me to the elevators. The door was already open when I reached 12G. I hadn't seen Lauren since my mom's funeral three years ago, yet somehow, she seemed even younger than she had then. Maybe it was because she'd dyed her hair a rich auburn, covering up the loose strands of gray that had popped up. Maybe it was because she'd lost some weight, and her tight jeans showed off her figure. Or maybe it was just because she was happy in her new marriage. If so, I was pleased for her. Yet, at the same time it saddened me that I'd never seen my own mother with the glow that radiated from Lauren.

Lauren threw her arms around me, hugging me tightly. "I'm so happy to see you. I sent you a Christmas card after Sasha died, but it was returned, marked *Moved*. I didn't know how to get in touch with you, you know, to see how you were holding up."

"I moved to New York City. Queens, actually," I said as Lauren led me into the living room. "I had to get away from Scranton."

"Are you studying art there?"

"I am. I'm really learning a lot."

"Good. Now, tell me—why are you here?"

On the drive over, I had thought of little else than how I would raise the subject. Ease into it, I'd told myself. Just ask about my mother's life, about her family, general questions. Get Lauren comfortable talking. All that advice evaporated in an instant. Instead, I blurted out, "Do I have a twin sister?"

Lauren's posture stiffened, and her voice, now shaky, said, "Why are you asking that?"

"I saw someone who looks just like me."

Now, Lauren's shoulders relaxed. "Oh, honey, I guess we all have someone who resembles us."

A feeling of anger arose, and I tried to push it away. I felt certain Lauren knew something and was holding back. "Not resemble. Exactly like me. With the same date of birth." I stared hard at my mother's friend.

Lauren stood up. "Let's go in the kitchen. I need a cup of coffee. How about you?"

Reluctantly, I followed her into a kitchen that looked like it had recently been updated. Although the apartment building was old, the kitchen shined with stainless-steel appliances and gleaming granite countertops. A round table with four chairs was tucked in the corner. I took a seat while Lauren went to the Keurig sitting next to the refrigerator and put a cup in place.

"Decaf or regular?"

I was already too wired. "Decaf."

"Milk and sugar?"

I shook my head. "Just black."

When both cups were filled, she brought them over to the kitchen table, then sat down. "Your mother loved you very much."

That was news to me. Growing up, my mother could be affectionate to me, or as cold as ice, depending on her mood. Mostly, though, she'd seemed indifferent toward me. "Was she really my mother? Or was I adopted?"

"She gave birth to you." Lauren sighed deeply, then dropped her head into her hands. After a minute, she looked up. "When she got sick, when it was clear she wouldn't recover, I begged her to tell you her story. She was terrified that you would hate her."

Suddenly, I wasn't certain I wanted the answers I'd come searching for. *Just get up and leave. Tell Lauren to keep Mom's secret.* But I knew it was too late for that. From the moment I'd spied Charlotte Gordon through the window of the art gallery, I knew that my life was going to change.

CHAPTER 9

"Your mom met your father when she was sixteen," Lauren began.

My arms were wrapped tightly around my body, a protective armor. Despite the sips of coffee I'd taken, despite the warmth in the kitchen, I shivered.

"He was eighteen, finished with high school, and working in his father's construction business." Lauren stopped and smiled. "My, he was handsome. Just about the most handsome boy either of us had ever seen. Wavy blond hair and the deepest blue eyes."

"Like mine?"

"Exactly like yours."

"Mom told me he was killed in the Gulf War. Is that true?"

Lauren nodded. "Sasha didn't know she was pregnant when he entered the army. If your father had known, maybe he wouldn't have enlisted. Then, your grandmother probably wouldn't have kicked her out."

My eyes widened. I'd known that my mother had cut ties with her own mother, but I didn't know she'd been kicked out of her home, pregnant and alone. "How could her mother do that?"

"Your grandmother's name was Millie. Your grandfather, Kyle, walked out on her when Sasha wasn't even a year old. Left her with nothing. She'd struggled raising Sasha, all on her own. She just wasn't willing to start all over again, raising her granddaughter."

"But still—"

"Millie was resigned to the pregnancy while your dad was off fighting in Kuwait. Sasha had written to him, and he wrote back that he wanted to get married."

"But then he was killed?"

"That's right. Millie insisted that Sasha put you up for adoption. But Sasha wouldn't think of it. So Millie threw her out."

"She's horrible! I'm glad I never knew her."

"Don't judge so quickly. Life decisions aren't always black and white."

I looked at Lauren incredulously. "She abandoned my mother when she needed her the most. There can't be any excuse—"

A wailing sound coming from down the hallway stopped me. "What's that?"

Lauren smiled. "Be back in a minute."

Five minutes later, she returned with a sleepy toddler in her arms, his head resting against her chest.

"Meet Tyler."

My mouth dropped open. Lauren was the same age as my mother would have been—forty-four. "Is he yours?"

Lauren laughed. "You think I'm too old?"

"No, I . . . I mean . . ." I could feel my face turning red. "I didn't even know you were pregnant."

"I wasn't the last time I saw you. Tyler was my happy surprise. I got pregnant soon after your mom died. Sometimes I think Sasha pulled some magic strings from the grave to bring him to me. He's twenty months old now."

"Can I hold him?"

Lauren handed him to me, and immediately Tyler wrapped his arms around my neck. I'd never thought about having a child myself, but I suddenly felt overwhelmed with the desire for a baby. I didn't understand how my mother could have given one away.

Lauren poured some milk into a sippy cup for Tyler, and he grabbed it in his soft, pudgy hands, then leaned back into my body as he began to drink.

"You okay with him? My husband won't be home until midnight, so he can't take him."

"More than okay," I answered.

Lauren sat back down. "So, where were we? I remember. Your grandmother. She had a difficult life. After your grandfather left, she had no money and no skills. She tried to track down your grandfather, make him at least pay child support, but he'd disappeared completely. After five years, she had him declared legally dead. That way, she'd be free to remarry. Although no man was ever good enough. I think she was afraid to trust someone again.

"Millie began cleaning homes to support Sasha and herself. When Sasha was nine, Millie was at a job. She tripped and fell down a flight of stairs, broke her leg and a few ribs. She couldn't work and had no money in the bank. Her landlord kicked her out when she couldn't pay the rent. She and your mother lived in her car."

My hand flew to my chest. The thought of my mother living in a car, even for a short period, made my heart ache. "Oh, no!"

"We were already friends then, me and Sasha. At first, she didn't tell me. She was too ashamed, but after a week, she did. My parents took them both in. We lived in a one-bedroom apartment ourselves. My father had turned the dining room into a small bedroom for me, and Sasha shared my bed. Millie slept on the couch."

Tyler began squirming on my lap, and I hugged him tighter.

"When the cast finally came off and your grandmother could go back to cleaning houses, they stayed another month, so Millie could save enough money for her own apartment. She promised my mother that she'd clean our apartment for free every week for two years, and she kept her word, even though it meant turning down another job for

48

that time period. So, you see, she just didn't want that kind of life for her daughter. Living hand to mouth."

"Kicking her out almost guaranteed that would happen to my mother."

Lauren's face took on a grave expression. "Millie thought that if she threw Sasha out, then she would learn that she couldn't take care of herself, much less a child, and realize that she needed to give the baby up for adoption."

"But that didn't happen."

"No. Instead, Sasha dropped out of school and fled Allentown. She arrived in Scranton with less than a hundred dollars that she'd saved over the years. She found a room for rent in someone's home and then started doing the only thing she knew—cleaning houses, just like her mother. She saved every spare penny so that when she gave birth, she could stop working for a month."

"Mommy, I sleepy."

Tyler had finished his milk and held up his arms. Lauren picked him up from my lap. "I'll just be a few minutes. He falls back asleep quickly."

Lauren left to bring him to his bedroom while I digested everything I'd just learned. My mother had never told me any of this. I slumped down in my chair and stared at my hands. The ache in my chest deepened, and I struggled to hold back tears. After a minute or two, I realized that I still didn't have an answer to the question I'd come here for.

When Lauren returned, I asked, "Do I have a twin sister?"

Lauren turned her head away from me, and she squeezed her lips together.

"Tell me."

She looked back at me. "She never went to a doctor. She had no money. When she went into labor, I drove from Allentown and met her at the hospital. She hadn't realized the stomach discomfort she'd been experiencing all day was actually labor pains, and so by the time I got there, they rushed her to the delivery room. They didn't even have time to do a sonogram, and so she didn't know she was having twins until your sister was born."

So, it was true. I had a sister. A twin sister. I opened my mouth, but no words came out.

"Sasha never wanted to give her baby up. But she knew she couldn't handle two. It was all too overwhelming for her. When the social worker came by, your mom agreed to let one be adopted. The social worker tried to convince her to give up both—they were identical twins; they should stay together, she said. Your mom was barely seventeen and lived in one room, but she was adamant. She wanted her baby."

My head spun. I wondered if I should feel angry at my mother for giving away my sister, for never telling me about her, but all I felt was great sadness. Sadness for what my mother must have gone through in making that decision. What she must have gone through all those years not knowing where her other daughter was, and how she had fared. How every time she looked at me, she had to have been reminded of her other child. I thought of those times I'd catch my mother staring at me with an odd look, until I'd turn and demand, "What!" with an edge in my voice. I understood now that at those times, she was thinking about my sister.

"How did she choose me?"

"You were the first," Lauren said. "Your sister was born two minutes later."

Two minutes. That was the difference between a childhood spent in poverty or one lavished with wealth.

CHAPTER 10

Ben could barely contain his excitement after he'd hung up the phone. Mallory had discovered last night that her mother had given birth to identical twin girls and turned one over for adoption. He'd wait, of course, until the DNA results confirmed what he now knew was a certainty. His wife, Charlotte Gordon, had an identical twin sister no one else knew about. He'd put Mallory off contacting Charly right away, saying she was too absorbed with her father's health right now. That was true, actually. The old man *was* going to croak—within the next few months, if his doctor was to be believed. Ben wished he could tap into some sympathy for the guy, but the truth was, he hated the man.

He turned back to his computer but had difficulty concentrating. Rick hadn't been in the office since his diagnosis, and that was good. When he was around, it felt claustrophobic, as though Rick's presence down the hall somehow crowded Ben's own space. He'd taken off early last night to spend the evening with Lisa and hadn't had to worry that his father-in-law would report it to Charly. That felt good, also. Charly had rearranged the gallery hours, closing early on Tuesdays now. Her assistant had agreed to cover for her on the Thursday and Friday late nights so Charly could spend each evening with her father.

When Mallory Holcolm had left his townhouse last week, the seed of a plan had begun to germinate. Over the past few days, he'd thought about almost nothing else. He was convinced it could work, but first, he'd have to persuade Mallory. That wouldn't be easy, he realized. Without knowing very much about her, he suspected she'd be shocked by his proposal. Still, he could tell she was impressed by their home, by the money it represented. She'd grown up poor; that much he knew. That was the card he needed to play with her. That, and how her twin sister had been raised to become a cruel and unlikable person. An unworthy person. Yes, his plan could work. It had to work.

Ben looked once more at his computer screen. The numbers all seemed jumbled together. He rubbed the back of his neck, then stood up. *I need some java to clear my head.* He left his airless interior office, and as he walked to the coffee room, he passed Rick's large, windowed corner office. He smiled to himself. If things went as planned, by next year that office would be his.

CHAPTER 11

I'd been in a daze ever since I'd learned I had a sister. Over the years, I'd read accounts of identical twins who shared such a strong bond that when one got hurt, the other felt it. Or twins who'd been separated at birth and always felt something was missing. None of that was true for me. I'd never had any inkling that there was someone in the world I'd shared a womb with, someone whose DNA matched mine.

Every few days, I checked in with Ben. "Do you think I can meet Charly now?" was always my opening question. Each time he'd answer, "Not yet." This morning was the third time I'd called.

"Don't you think she'd want to know she has a sister?" I asked, hoping he'd pick up on the frustration in my voice.

"Look, you don't know Charly at all."

"Of course I don't. That's the whole point of wanting to meet her."

"She goes straight from the gallery to her father's apartment each evening. Doesn't get home until close to eleven."

"What about at the gallery? I could stop in there?"

Ben laughed loudly. "Oh, that would be a treat. I'd pay to see that."

"Why?"

"She's generally tense all the time now, with her father dying. But ratchet that up ten times when she's at work. Then her true colors come out. Unless she's with a client."

"What do you mean?"

"Look, you're going to discover this on your own, when you finally get to meet her. She's not a very nice person."

I was stunned. This was her husband, talking about his wife. They couldn't have been married very long—certainly less than seven years. Shouldn't they still be in the honeymoon phase? All goo-goo eyes and lovey-dovey with each other? Granted, I didn't have much experience with married couples, having been raised by a single mother and without close friends whose parents I could observe. But certainly love had to last longer than seven years. Or had I been reading too many romance novels?

"We're identical twins. Shouldn't we be alike?"

"Maybe if you were raised together. But Charly was brought up as a princess whose every wish was granted. She means the world to her father. He always doted on her, but especially so after her mother died."

"Her mother's dead?"

"Yeah. When Charly was nine, her mother was hit by a drunk driver. Died instantly."

"How awful."

"Don't pity her too much. She's used to getting everything she wants, when she wants it, and has no patience for anything—or anyone—who doesn't provide that. Her assistant at the gallery is terrified of her. She probably won't last. None of them do. In the three years she's had the gallery, she's gone through four assistants."

Is that what money does? I wondered. I knew what *not* having money did. It meant wearing clothes long after they were outgrown, never having enough to eat, always wanting what other kids had but never getting it. It meant having a mother who was never home when I returned from school and starting a part-time job as soon as I turned fourteen. It meant living in a roach-filled apartment that stopped me from ever getting out of my bed in the middle of the night for fear of what I might find crawling around in the dark. Despite those deprivations, I couldn't imagine not being courteous to people I worked with. How could money change that?

"It's hard for me to believe she's like that."

"You'll find out soon enough." He paused for a beat. "Have you ever thought about what it would be like to be rich?"

I couldn't stop myself from laughing. Never once had I imagined that. My fantasy was for fame as an artist, and sufficient money to have my own apartment, one with enough space for a studio. That's what luxury was for me. "No. Not once." As soon as the words left my mouth, I knew that wasn't entirely true. As a child, I'd often dreamed of what it would be like to own the clothes my schoolmates wore, to have the tech gadgets that they possessed, to be able to travel to the ocean, or Disney World. By the time I entered high school, I'd buried those dreams. They were for other people. Instead, I focused on what I hoped was achievable.

"That's all Charly thinks about. Accumulating as much money as she possibly can. She loves her father, but she's already talking about how much she'll inherit when he's gone."

I shook my head. I hated the picture he was painting of my sister. But . . . she was still my blood. The only relative I had.

Two days later I called again, and was again put off from contacting Charly. I was starting to wonder if there was another reason Ben didn't want me to see her, so I asked him.

"Of course not. I just don't want to increase her stress level."

"But wouldn't she think it's a good thing to find out about me?"

"I know my wife. Her first thought will be to wonder if you'll try to get some of her money."

"That's ridiculous!"

"But that's what she'll think. And then she'll stress over it."

It was almost funny. I had nothing, yet Ben painted such an unflattering picture of Charly that I began to feel sorry for him, who had so much more.

When I'd called Ben this morning, he'd said he had something important to tell me and suggested we meet for lunch. It was a Monday, and because I needed to be in the city for my art class, I offered to meet him somewhere near his office. Instead, he wanted to come out to Queens, so I met him at a diner near The Dump. It looked like every other diner in the Northeast—a long rectangle, with an extra room added toward the rear of one side forming an L shape. Its large and varied menu kept it busy for breakfast, lunch, and dinner.

Ben was already waiting for me when I arrived. Although I'd only met him in person once, I felt like I knew him after several phone conversations. "How's my sister doing?" I asked as soon as I sat down.

"You're not going to like this, Mallory. I finally told her last night about you. She doesn't want to meet you."

"What! What did you say about me?"

"Just that you'd recently discovered she was your twin and wanted to get to know her. She asked me what you were like, and I told her you seemed very nice and genuine. She wanted to know what your family was like, and, well, I had to be honest. I told her you'd grown up poor. Were still poor. Just as I'd feared, right away she started saying that you probably think you struck gold having a rich sister. I told her you weren't like that, but she was adamant. I'm sorry."

I was stunned. How could she not want to know her identical twin? I felt my chest tighten up and knew, if I spoke, my voice would be choked, and so said nothing.

"She's a bitch!"

My mouth dropped open, shocked at Ben's outburst.

"Sorry. I didn't mean to blurt that out. It's just . . . the poor guy's not even dead yet, and she keeps talking about her inheritance. And then she shuts you out in case you wanted some of it. Frankly, if you were my sister and I had as much money as Charly, I'd want you to have some of it. Enough at least to make your life a little more comfortable."

I didn't know what to say, so I just shook my head.

"Sorry. I didn't mean to burden you with this. It's just . . . you seem so different from her. Softer, somehow. Charly's always had a mean streak, but it's gotten worse over the years. She's not like you. She's selfish and a bully. She takes pleasure in humiliating me in front of our friends. I can't count the number of times she's told them I would be a civil servant if her father hadn't given me a job." Ben's face began to redden. "That's so not true. I would have gone to law school. I would have had a career I enjoyed if she hadn't pushed me into her father's company."

I put my hand on Ben's arm. "I'm sorry. If she's so terrible, why don't you get a divorce?"

"Because her father would fire me, and I'd have nothing. I signed a prenup."

I couldn't help but think that his was the problem of the wealthy. When you don't have money, you don't care about prenuptial agreements. If the marriage goes sour, the parties split whatever they have and move on.

Just then, the waiter came to take our order. I was glad for the interruption. When he left, Ben bent forward on the table and leaned his chin into his hands. "Charly's very smart, so you must be, too. It had to hurt you, not to go on with your education."

Of course it hurt. I'd wanted desperately to study art. I'd watched my fellow high school seniors—even those who hadn't had grades nearly as good as mine—head off to college while I stayed back home, working sixty hours a week. I'd tried not to be angry at my mother for her illness—most of the time, I understood the feeling was irrational—but sometimes it was too hard to hold back my resentment. At those moments, I'd snap at her and say, "You think I ruined your life? Well, you're ruining mine!" Now, with the new information Lauren had given me about my mother's life, I wished I could take those words back, tell her that I loved her, how she was more important than art. But that pain I now carried was mine. It wasn't something to share with Ben.

"I care about art, about painting. I'm taking classes now. That's what matters. Not the past."

"Still, if you were the one who was born two minutes later, you could have had anything you wanted. Doesn't seem fair, does it?"

Did it? I'd thought about that a lot over the past few weeks. Our mother had chosen one of two identical babies to raise as her own. Growing up, I was often on my own while my mother worked to pay the bills. Other girls my age would go to each other's houses after school, but I could never have someone back to my house, because no parent was there to supervise. And because of that, I didn't go to their homes. Other girls would join clubs after school, or go to gymnastics or swimming or Girl Scouts or anything else they wanted. I always had to head straight home. I was lonely growing up. But that experience helped me endure my current, self-imposed, solitary life.

If my mother had chosen Charly, I would have had two parents who loved me. I would have had friends and clubs and my choice of colleges. I would have my own art gallery and rub shoulders with the most accomplished artists. Maybe one would have taken me under her wing, mentored me. I would never have to worry about paying my bills. I wouldn't be living in The Dump.

My reverie was broken by our waiter bringing our meals.

"So, anyway," Ben said, "I also wanted to tell you the DNA results have come back. You and Charly are definitely identical twins."

"That's no surprise." As soon as Lauren had shared my mother's story, I'd known.

"Well, it's clear you were twins. But sometimes same-gender fraternal twins can look very similar. So, the DNA confirms you're identical."

"Does Charly know that?"

"She does."

"And she still doesn't want to meet me?"

Ben just shook his head.

The sadness I'd felt just moments ago began to turn to anger. I folded my arms across my chest and tried to calm down.

We finished our lunch in relative silence. I kept thinking about Charly and what Ben had said about her. I knew that studies had shown some personality differences between identical twins, but how could they be so dramatic? I'd never thought much about money because I didn't have any. Maybe it was different for someone who grew up wealthy. Maybe money was always on their minds. Much as I tried to square Ben's description of Charly with my own sense of myself, it just didn't add up. I couldn't ever see myself caring about how much I would inherit from a parent I loved as he lay dying. And I would never cut off a sister because I feared she wanted my money. I wondered if that's why Charly had never searched for her mother. Was she worried that her birth mother was poor and would look upon Charly's wealth as a gold mine to tap?

When we were done, Ben paid the bill—turning down my offer to pay my share—and we walked outside. Ben had called an Uber, but it wasn't there yet, so I waited with him for it to arrive.

"She's ruining both our lives, you know," Ben said.

"Well, she's certainly made me feel miserable."

"I asked you earlier whether you thought it was unfair that you had to struggle while Charly always had it easier. I'd like you to answer that," Ben said.

"It is what it is. My mother made a choice. That can't be undone."

"What if it can be?"

I stared at him, an uncomfortable feeling starting to spread through my body.

"What if you could have more money than you ever dreamed possible? What if you could study art at the Sorbonne? What if you could travel to every museum in the world and study the paintings of the masters up close?"

I shook my head. "I don't believe in what-ifs."

"Charly's been cruel to both of us." He looked around to make sure no one was near us, took my arm, and pulled me closer to him, then whispered in my ear. "I was thinking over lunch: What if Charly died?"

That uncomfortable feeling spread to my chest, and it began to tighten. "Is she sick, too?"

Ben shook his head. "What if someone killed her?"

I pulled away. Despite the brisk air, I could feel my face become flushed. I had no idea what to say to him.

"You could take her place," he went on. "We'll split her father's inheritance. He's worth over two billion. That's one billion dollars for each of us. Just think what you could do with that money. Your life would completely change."

He has to be mad, I thought. *Completely and utterly crazy. I can't be involved in this.*

"No one knows she has a twin sister," he continued. "We'd need to wait until her father dies. Then, after the killer makes sure her body can never be found, you step into her place and pretend you're Charly. First, you'd revoke the prenup. Then, maybe six months later, a year at the most, we would divorce. Split the assets down the middle. You'll go away then, wherever you want. Anywhere in the world."

I could feel a rising panic and was having difficulty breathing. His proposal was terrifying and so very, very wrong.

"Just think about it. A billion dollars."

I wanted to slap him, spit in his face, tell him how horrid he was. I wanted to run as far away from him as I could. Then, I thought about Charly's rejection of me. She'd put money before me. Why shouldn't I do the same? Why should I have to keep waiting on tables just to finance my art education? Why shouldn't I have renowned artists' paintings adorn my walls? I stepped closer and asked, "Just how would this work?"

CHAPTER 12

My heart raced the entire walk back to my claustrophobic room, and once I reached it, I locked the door behind me and lay down on the bed. *Calm down, calm down.* I hadn't committed to anything, yet I felt as guilty as if I had.

I'd had so many questions of Ben, but he had to get back to his office. "We'll talk again, soon," he'd promised, before the Uber arrived and he left me, awash with fear and confusion. His parting words: "Promise me you won't tell a soul," he implored, "not even your best friend. I won't do anything to Charly if you say no. We do this together, or not at all."

I began to shiver and got underneath my blanket, pulling it up to my chin. I had planned to go to the Guggenheim today, before my art class, but now I felt paralyzed. Could I show up in class and pretend to Brian that everything was normal? Surely, he'd know that wasn't the case just by looking at my hands. They hadn't stopped shaking since I'd left Ben.

I had always been the good girl, the polite girl, the one who raised her hand in class and said, "Thank you" when given anything. I'd always worked hard and thought it was good for me, that it made me stronger. How could I possibly consider being a party to murder? To the murder of my sister, the only family I had left in the world. Yet, as I shivered under the blanket, I did consider it. I had no relationship with Charly, no ties other than our shared genes, and now never would. She didn't want one. From what Ben had told me, she was nothing like me—not kind or polite or hardworking. Why did she deserve to be wealthy, and not me? Why did she deserve parents who showered her with affection when I was left with a mother too tired, or too burdened by guilt, to care for me? I thought of the kitchen in their home, the beautiful kitchen that I could spend hours in, cooking up delicious meals. I thought of her art gallery, and of the artists who were part of her everyday world. Why shouldn't that be mine?

I didn't go to the Guggenheim, and I didn't go to art class. I stayed in bed, under the covers, and thought how lovely it would be to live Charly's life.

Three days later, I took the subway into Manhattan. I transferred at East Fifty-Ninth Street to the Number 6 train, got off at East Sixty-Eighth Street, and walked over to Central Park. I was meeting Ben there in front of Bethesda Fountain at 10:00 a.m. It gave me two hours before I needed to report to work at Trattoria Ricciardi. It was a bright day, filled with sunshine, and the temperature in the low seventies made it unseasonably warm for October. At this time of day, the park was lightly populated. Mostly mothers and nannies with babies and toddlers. I got there before Ben and settled on a bench. I'd hardly slept since my last meeting with Ben, tossing and turning each night, trying to convince myself that Charly wasn't deserving of the life she'd been given, then just as quickly acknowledging that it wasn't my place to judge her and carry out the sentence. Then I'd think about Charly, about her callous rejection of me, and ask, "Why not? Why not be rich and be able to have and do all the things I'd missed growing up?" When I'd awoken this morning from the few hours of sleep I'd managed to get, I wasn't any closer to an answer.

"Have you thought about my proposal?" Ben asked me when he arrived.

"I've hardly thought about anything else."

"And?"

"I don't think just looking like Charly means I'll pass for her."

"No, I don't, either. It'll take some work. My parents live in Florida most of the year, but they spend summers at a house they own in High Falls."

"Where's that?"

"About two hours north of here. It's a country village with a sparse population, and no one there knows Charly or me. I never visit because Charly prefers to spend our weekends and vacations during the summer at her father's beach house. My parents come out there when they want to see us."

I wasn't sure how a house in the country would help transform me into Charly.

"They've already left for Florida. They leave a car up there, and I have keys to both the house and the car. You can stay there. I have hours of video of Charly for you to study. Her accent, especially. Your voices are the same, but yours shows that you grew up in Scranton, not New York. Each week, I'll send you reams of information about her friends, her business associates, her likes and dislikes. You'll need to memorize it all."

He stepped back and looked me over.

"I'll give you a picture of her hairstyle, and you can get yours cut and colored to look the same. How much do you weigh?"

"One hundred twenty-two."

"You'll need to lose ten pounds. Join a gym up there."

I'd been shaking my head slightly the whole time he was talking. "This is crazy. It's never going to work."

"Why not?"

"Do you even know someone who'd . . . who'd—"

"Kill her?"

I nodded.

"I might." He opened his briefcase and took out a pen and notepad. He handed both to me, then instructed me to sign Charly's name. When I finished, he looked it over and smiled. "This twin thing is amazing. Your penmanship is exactly like Charly's. No one would question it."

"How long would I stay there?"

"Until Charly's father passes away. The doctors give him three to five months."

I felt myself getting drawn deeper and deeper into Ben's plan. I clutched my sweater tighter around me. Despite the warm temperature, I had started to shiver.

"You'll need to cut off all ties with anyone you know here. Make up some story. You're homesick, or you want to try LA. Tell them anything so they won't be looking for you. And then, no contact."

"Not even e-mail?" I thought that Brian would find it odd if I didn't keep in touch with him. Maybe Lauren, too, now that I'd reconnected with her. I realized how miserable my life had been that no one else would care if I disappeared.

"Maybe a little at first, then kind of fade away. You're too busy to write in your new life; that's what you'll tell them."

"What would I do for money if I'm not working?"

"I'll give you spending money. As much as you need. So . . . are you in?"

Was I? My stomach was churning, and my fingers and toes tingled. I understood that if I said yes, I would be agreeing to commit the worst crime, made even more reprehensible because she was my sister. And I knew that once I agreed, I wouldn't be able to back away from it.

"I don't know. I just don't know."

I tried to block Ben's proposal from my mind. I returned to work, to my art classes, even to the Guggenheim. It helped to be busy. But at night, when I'd lie in bed, unable to sleep, I kept thinking about how different my life would have been if I'd been born second, if I'd been the daughter Rick and Sarah Jensen had adopted. I kept telling myself that a bad break didn't justify murder, that she was my sister, and no matter how cruel she was, she didn't deserve to die. Most of the time, I convinced myself to brush off Ben's proposal. Then I'd picture her townhouse and imagine myself living there. I'd picture her kitchen and imagine myself cooking there. I pictured her art gallery and imagined working with talented artists.

When I'd met Ben at the diner, he'd asked whether I'd thought it unfair that Charly had grown up with so much, and me with so little. The more I dwelled on it, the easier it became to magnify the inequities. As Ben's scathing description of Charly kept swirling through my mind, I began to think of her as unworthy of the riches she'd been given, simply by being born second. I had been offered a path to escape the hardscrabble lives of my mother and grandmother. Why shouldn't I take it?

Ten days after I'd met Ben in the park, after Lou Castro had squeezed my shoulder every morning during breakfast at The Dump, after a table of four and then a table of six had stiffed me on a tip at the restaurant, and after, on the way home from art class, a homeless drunk lurking in the shadow of the subway platform exposed himself as I walked past, I decided I was tired of being the good sister. I was tired of struggling. It was my turn now.

I knew it was evil. I no longer cared. I called Ben Gordon. "I'm in."

CHAPTER 13

I made sure to catch an earlier bus the next day so I'd have time to speak to Gus before customers started arriving at the restaurant. "I'm handing in my notice," I told him when I arrived. "Two weeks."

Gus looked at me with surprise. "What's wrong, Mallory? I thought you liked it here."

"I do. You've been great."

"You going to another restaurant?"

"No. I'm moving to LA. I got a job offer. Art related. I couldn't turn it down."

"Well, if it's good for you, then I'm happy. You're too smart to do this for long." He bent over and gave me a kiss on the cheek. I would miss Gus.

Four days later, before leaving for my art class, I called Adam. He'd called me three times since we'd met for dinner, and each time I'd let it go to voice mail. Now, I had to let him know I was leaving town.

"I'm sorry we didn't get to know each other better," he said after I filled him in on my made-up plans. "If you ever find yourself back in New York, call me."

The last person I needed to cut ties with was Brian. I'd never known a father, and he'd come closest to filling that void.

As soon as I got to the school, I told him.

"You're leaving? But the class has another seven weeks to go!"

"It's a great job offer."

"Doing what?"

I'd practiced my lie in advance. I knew Brian would grill me. "They're going to teach me graphic design. A friend from Scranton works for the company, and she recommended me."

Brian put his hand on his hip. "Well, we're just going to have to come to LA to visit you. Stan goes out there now and then for business, and I'll tag along."

"They have offices throughout the country. My training will be in LA, but I have no idea where they'll send me afterward."

Brian pulled me in to his chest. "I'm going to miss you, Mallory. You're the best damn artist in this class."

He let me go, and I stepped back. I was starting to get misty-eyed, and I didn't want him to see.

"As soon as you know where you'll end up, you'll let me know, right?"

"I will."

"Promise?"

I nodded.

"I mean it, Mallory. If you don't, I'm going to hunt you down."

I reassured Brian, all the time with a lump in my throat. I was going to miss him the most.

The home in High Falls that belonged to Ben's parents was larger than any place I had ever lived. It was off a quiet, heavily wooded road, set back far from the street. A wall of windows overlooked Mohonk Preserve and its acres of trails. Ben had suggested I get a hiker's pass for the preserve, and explore. "It's a good way to walk off extra pounds," he'd said. I'd never considered myself overweight, just curvy in the places it counted. At five foot six, my weight seemed just right. Charly, though, was model slim, wearing size 0 clothes, or sometimes size 2, depending on the cut.

Ben had taken me to the local supermarket, tiny in comparison to the supermarkets I'd shopped at in Scranton, and we'd filled up on food before he'd left me and driven back to the city.

Once he was gone, I set about exploring. In addition to the eat-in kitchen, which was at least twenty feet long, there was an equally large living room with a wood-burning fireplace, a master bedroom with its own bathroom, and two smaller bedrooms. The furnishings were simple but appeared sturdy—a deep rose-colored couch in the living room, with two gingham-slipcovered chairs on either side of the fireplace, a round wooden pedestal table with four wood chairs in the kitchen. The king-size bed in the master bedroom had a mustard-colored upholstered headboard and was covered with a patchwork quilt in colors of brown, beige, and gold. There was no TV reception—the cable had been turned off—but Ben had brought up a box load of DVDs, including home videos of Charly, for the DVD player. There was no Internet connection, or Wi-Fi, but I could use my iPad to access anything I needed.

The house was on ten acres of land, mostly wooded. There was a rocking-chair porch in the front of the house, and a screened-in porch with views of the mountains in back. It felt like paradise to me, a place I'd be happy living in forever. I grabbed my sketchbook, plopped myself down on the back porch, and began sketching the mountains. Before I knew it, hours had passed. The pale-yellow sun had deepened to an orange glow, then slowly disappeared. I went back inside, put a frozen dinner in the oven, then popped a DVD into the player. It contained a video of Charly's twenty-fifth birthday party. It would be my first time studying the woman I was to become.

The next day, I took the car out of the garage and began exploring the neighborhood. Nestled between the supermarket and a drugstore was a liquor store. I stopped in and stocked up on wine. On the one main road that ran through the heart of the hamlet were three restaurants and several artisans' shops. I pulled into one—a pottery store/workshop—and looked over the pieces. They were beautiful, so much more artistic than the standard pottery seen in the big-box retail stores.

"Are you looking for a gift for someone, or for yourself?" a voice behind me said.

I turned and saw a middle-aged woman with short brown hair and a warm smile. "Are you the artist?"

She nodded. "My name is Katy Patel."

"Your work is lovely."

She took me through the store and pointed out some pieces that were her favorites. I picked up a vase and looked at the price tag on the bottom—$1,200. My first reaction was disappointment that I'd never be able to afford one of her pieces, and then it hit me that soon I would. In the not-too-distant future, I'd never have to look at the price of something I desired. I liked the way that felt.

CHAPTER 14

It had become easier for Ben to see Lisa after work now that Rick was no longer coming into the office, especially with Charly heading over to her father's apartment after she'd closed up the gallery. In fact, most nights lately, Ben left work early and spent the evening with Lisa. Tonight was no exception.

"I could get used to this," Lisa said, after they'd already made love and she lay cuddled up next to him.

"Me, too," murmured Ben.

Lisa was silent for a minute, then sat up in the bed and looked over at him. "I mean it. I'd like this to be normal, not some secret rendezvous that needs to be hushed up."

Now, Ben sat up, too. "You know it's you that I love."

She looked at him with eyes that seemed filled with sadness. "I'm not sure that's enough."

"What are you saying?"

"You're married. You have a life. At some point, Charly will want a child. I want those things, too. And as long as I'm with you, in this lovers' limbo, I won't have that."

"I'm going to leave her. We'll be together. It's just . . . I can't do this now. Not with her father dying."

"And after he dies? Won't she be in mourning then, and need your comfort?"

"He has three months left—five at the most. Then, give me six months. After that, I promise I'll divorce Charly."

"Right. You'll walk away from her money. You've made it clear that's not in the cards."

Ben pulled her into his arms. "Six months after Rick dies. I promise. That's all I'm asking you to wait."

Ben arrived home a little after 9:00 p.m. He knew Charly wouldn't return until 10:00 p.m., but he didn't like to cut it close. With his plan already in motion, it was vitally important that nothing disrupt it. He couldn't have Charly getting suspicious by his absence. At moments like this, he thought he should step back from Lisa for the next few months, really play it safe, but that was just his nerves talking. He had everything under control, so why deprive himself of some pleasure?

At 10:05 p.m., Charly walked in. Her eyes were puffy, and she walked as though she were carrying a heavy backpack. As soon as she saw Ben, she stepped into his arms and began sobbing. He stroked her hair and let her cry herself out. When the sobs subsided, he asked, "Is there something new?"

She nodded. "He was turned down for the experimental treatment."

"I'm sorry, sweetheart."

"I wouldn't cry in front of him. I needed to show him I'm strong. But as soon as I left, I broke down."

As Ben held his wife tight in his arms, his only thought was, *I wonder if Mallory can lose enough weight in time.*

Graham was already warming up when Ben arrived the next morning for their weekly racquetball game, and they dove into the competition right away. This time, Graham swept all three games, although Ben only lost the last by one point. After they'd showered and changed, they stopped by the café for a quick lunch.

"Weren't you close with Jeff Mullin in high school?" Ben asked when they were seated.

"Yeah. We grew up on the same block. Our sisters are still friends. Sad case."

"That's what I heard. Came back from Afghanistan all messed up, right?"

Graham nodded. "Hooked on heroin. He was arrested a few times—petty stuff, mostly, then robbed a few homes, you know, to support his habit. When he got out of jail, his folks finally forced him into a rehab center. He got out six months ago and is working at a warehouse. His parents wanted him to move home, but he took a room in some flophouse in Brooklyn. Supposedly, he's still into drugs and still looking for easy money to get them. He'll end up back in jail before long."

Ben held back a smile. He was pretty sure he'd found the guy he needed.

CHAPTER 15

At Ben's suggestion, I went to the local gym, a small building with treadmills and bikes and elliptical machines, along with several weight machines and free weights. I signed up for personal training sessions twice a week and was assigned to Jackie. I wasn't a gym rat. I never had the money to belong to one, or the inclination. Neither was I athletic. My life had been filled with school and work, with no time for anything else.

That done, I found my way to the Mohonk Preserve visitor center, off Route 55, where I filled out a hiker's membership form and received an ID card, then purchased trail maps. I'd never hiked before and was a bit leery of it. I spoke to the helpful volunteer at the visitor center, and she suggested I start with a walk on the Duck Pond trail. "It's mostly level, and pretty short," she'd said, before showing me directions to get there on the map.

I drove to the trailhead, where there was a small parking area, and went through the gate opposite. The dirt path was easy to follow. After about twenty minutes, it veered off to the right and went steeply uphill. I struggled upward for just a short distance before it leveled out again. I enjoyed being alone in the woods. As I walked, I felt the crunch of fallen leaves underfoot. Before long, I reached Duck Pond. I walked to the edge and spotted a large tortoise swimming near the surface. I wished I'd brought my sketch pad with me—the clear pond, surrounded by hills, autumn-colored leaves on the trees painting a stark picture against the deep-blue sky, would have been lovely to draw. I resolved to come back another day.

I found a rock to sit on and slipped off my backpack, then pulled out a thermos with hot chocolate and a bag of trail mix—assorted nuts, chocolates, and dried cranberries. I supposed I should have brought something more conducive to losing weight—maybe coffee and baby carrots—but I hadn't, and I hungrily tore into what I had.

Except for the two hours a week I would train with Jackie, I was alone day and night for the first time in my life. No mother to take care of, no customers to wait on, no classmates to shoot the breeze with. I was completely isolated, charged with one task only—become Charlotte Jensen Gordon. I didn't think it would be difficult. I was used to playing the part people expected of me.

I had watched a few of the videos Ben had left me. He was right—Charly's accent was different from mine. Not by a lot, but enough so that someone who knew her well would wonder about it. I had purchased a recorder and planned to practice speaking into it until our voices were indistinguishable. I didn't think I'd have trouble with that. I was more concerned about losing enough weight. I'd always weighed the same, and I didn't eat that much to begin with. One of the perks of growing up poor. But I supposed I could eat better—fewer carbs and more vegetables. And definitely cut out the sweets. Maybe the wine, also, although only if I absolutely had to.

Being alone left me a lot of time to think about what I was doing. I had given it considerable thought before I'd told Ben I was in. In my reasoning, Charly was a monster who didn't deserve what she had. If Mom had kept Charly instead of me, then I could have been adopted by the Jensens. I could have gone to private schools and an Ivy League college. I could be the one inheriting their wealth.

Watching Charly on the videos, though, changed her from a concept to a real person. She was flesh and blood. She was my sister.

When I wasn't thinking about Charly, I thought about the money. What I would do with it. I knew I would need to get away from New York, away from the possibility of running into anyone who might know either one of us. I loved the idea of living overseas, maybe France, studying art in Paris. Or Italy. Or Spain. With the kind of money I would have, the world would be open to me. I'd never let myself dream, growing up. Now I could dream big.

My phone rang just as I walked into the Gordons' house—my house for now. It was Ben.

"It might happen faster than we thought," he said.

"What do you mean?"

"Rick was turned down for the experimental drug treatment. His doctor said it could take anywhere from two to four months. Can you be ready in two months?"

I thought about it. I'd never tried losing weight before. I didn't know how easy or hard I'd find it. Still, much as I loved this house, loved being in the country, I could see how living in isolation from other people more than two months could drive me batty. "I'll be ready."

"Good. I'm just about finished with a list of everybody Charly knows, all her friends going back to elementary school. And her relatives, of course. With a description of each, and how she feels about them. Little anecdotes about them. Pictures, too. I'll e-mail that to you tomorrow."

"I think it would be useful if I had her passwords on social media. I could learn a lot from seeing what she posts."

"I don't know her passwords. But mine is GypsyMax29, and you can access what she posts from my accounts, since we're Facebook friends. Twitter and Instagram, too. Password's the same."

When I hung up, I immediately headed to the pantry closet, removed the box of chocolate chip cookies and a bag of potato chips, then dumped them in the garbage. I opened the freezer and did the same with the half gallon of black raspberry ice cream I'd bought. When I finished, I hopped in the car and headed back to the supermarket. I needed to pick up veggies and sugar-free Jell-O. It was time to get serious about losing weight.

Two days later, I was startled by the ringing of the front doorbell. I opened it to find a bearded man dressed in a fleece jacket and Timberland boots. He was at least six feet tall, with wavy brown hair that fell midway down his neck.

"Hi, uh, is Judith home? Or Sidney?"

It took me a moment to remember that those were the names of Ben's parents. "No. They're in Florida for the winter. I'm a friend of their son, Ben Gordon. He's letting me stay here for a few months."

"I thought that's where they were. I passed by a few times and saw the lights on in the house. I wondered if they'd come back."

More likely, he wondered if there was an intruder in the house. "Well, thanks for checking in." I hoped my voice gave him the message that I wasn't interested in chitchat, but he didn't move from his spot.

"Is there something else I can help you with?"

"I plow the driveway for Judith and Sidney when it snows. And, well, if you're going to be here over the winter, I provide fireplace logs for my customers. I'd be glad to add you to my list."

I looked over at the stone fireplace in the living room and thought how nice it would be to curl up with a book in front of a roaring flame. "That would be great, but you'd have to show me how to start it up."

"No problem." He flashed a wide smile, and for the first time, I realized how handsome he was. *Stop it, Mallory,* the voice in my head warned. Even before I'd embarked on this charade, I'd sworn off romantic entanglements. This certainly wasn't the time to start.

"So, uh, I'll drop off a half a cord for you tomorrow, say, around eleven? That should hold you for a couple of months. If you're home then, I'll show you how to get it started."

"Thanks. I'll be here. How much will that be?" For the first time in my life, it didn't matter how much something would cost. Ben had given me a credit card and deposited $5,000 into my bank account. If I ran out, he'd assured me he would replenish it. But I doubted this man took plastic. I wasn't even sure he took checks. I had to make sure I had enough cash on hand for him.

"I'll just bill the Gordons."

"No," I said, a little too quickly. "I'm paying my own way."

"Then, a hundred bucks should do it. So, eleven tomorrow. See you then."

He turned away from the door, took a step, then turned back. "By the way, I'm Jake. What's your name?"

"Mallory."

"Pleased to meet you, Mallory." He waved his hand, then left, leaving me wondering if I'd made a mistake using my real name.

CHAPTER 16

At precisely 11:00 a.m. the next morning, I heard a truck rumble up my driveway. I looked out the living room window, saw it was Jake, and opened the front door.

"Are you always this punctual?" I called out to him as he exited his Chevy Tahoe.

"I try to be," he shouted back. He headed to the back of his truck, then loaded firewood into a caddy and wheeled it to the side of the house. Five minutes later, he came to the front door, holding a number of logs in his arms.

I opened the door, and he stepped inside. "The Gordons have a rack for the wood on the side of the house," he said. "I stacked the rest there. It's covered with a tarp." He walked over to the fireplace and placed the logs inside. "Ready for your lesson?"

"Sure."

From his back pocket, he pulled out a box of extralong matches. "Got any old newspapers?"

I shook my head. Did anyone read a newspaper anymore? I got my news from the Internet, just as I suspected most of my contemporaries did nowadays.

"Old magazines?"

Again, I shook my head.

He sighed. "I'll be right back." He ran out to his truck, then came back in with a stack of newspapers in his hands. "Okay, the first and most important thing is to make sure the flue is open."

"The what?"

He waved for me to get closer, then leaned his head inside the fireplace. "See this lever here? Push it back, and it opens a vent for the smoke to go up the chimney. Pull it toward you, and the vent closes. When a fire is going, the vent needs to be open. When the embers are out, close the vent." He tore the newspaper into strips, laid them over the wood logs, then lit the paper with one of the long matches. When the flame caught one of the logs, he stood up. "There. Simple as that. Think you can do it?"

I said I could, then went to get my wallet. I withdrew five twenties to hand to him.

"How about instead of paying me for the firewood, you let me take you to lunch?" he said.

"That doesn't seem like a fair bargain for you."

He smiled his killer smile. "Actually, I think I make out pretty good with that deal."

Ben had warned me to keep to myself as much as possible. But after five days of being mostly by myself, the thought of spending an hour with another human being was too tempting to turn down. "Sure. It's a deal."

Before we left, he showed me how to put out the fire, for those nights I was ready to turn in before the fire had died down. Once it was out, we got into his truck and drove into town, then pulled into the parking lot of the Eggs Nest. It was brightly decorated with funky pictures of people and buildings in Pop Art style. The waitress led us to our table and handed us our menus.

"What's good?" I asked as I looked over the offerings.

"Everything. This place has been an institution for decades."

We gave the waitress our orders, then sat back in our chairs. I studied the man sitting opposite me. With so much hair covering his face, it was hard to tell just how handsome he was, although his eyes were almost as blue as mine, and his straight nose fit perfectly on his face—not too long or wide. His lips were full, and when he smiled, his whole face lit up. "What do you do when there's no snow to clear or firewood to chop?" I asked him.

"This stuff is just filler for the winter months. I'm a landscape architect. I studied it at Cornell."

I'd never gone to college myself, but I knew Cornell was one of the Ivy League schools.

"And you came here to work? I'd think there'd be more of a call for your services in Westchester County. From what I've seen, the landscaping on homes around here seems more natural, less planned."

"Don't be fooled. It takes a lot of work to make a garden look natural. Besides, my territory extends down to Rockland and across the river to Northern Westchester and Putnam County. But my base of operations is here in High Falls, because this is where I grew up. And it's too beautiful to leave."

I nodded in agreement. It was too beautiful to leave, surrounded by mountains, dotted by farmland and cozy hamlets that seemed to be a mecca for artists.

"So, what brings you here?" Jake asked.

It was a question I'd expected, and one I'd prepared for. "I'm writing the next great American novel, or, hopefully, at least a readable one. Back in Queens, I shared an apartment with three other women. It was hard to concentrate with all their noise. So, Ben suggested I stay here for a few months."

He seemed to buy the line, and why not? As I said before, I'm a good actress. The rest of the lunch was comfortable, and when Jake dropped me back off at the house, he asked if we could do it again next week. I figured once a week wasn't going to be a problem. "Yes."

The next day, I had my first training session with Jackie. I told her I'd never worked out before, so she started me off with light weights. Even so, I struggled through the bicep curls and tricep lifts, the leg presses and squats. The hour seemed to go on forever. When it was almost over, she had me hop up on a table and lie down, and she then put me through various contortions stretching my muscles. I thought that was almost as painful as the weights.

By the time I walked into the house, I was limping. I was about to jump in the shower when Ben called. "How's it going?"

"I ache all over."

"That's good."

"Maybe for you. Not for me."

"No, it means you're getting a good workout. You need that. Charly goes to the gym three times a week."

"You're telling me my sister is a masochist?"

Ben laughed. "No, just a rich Manhattan girl, where there's no such thing as too thin. She runs four times a week, also." He paused for a moment. "I just realized . . . you need to start jogging. It's important not to change Charly's routine, at least at first."

I inwardly groaned. Becoming Charly was going to be harder than I'd anticipated.

After a few days of my muscles torturing me following my first personal training session, I'd actually come to look forward to working out with Jackie. I'd successfully started a fire in the fireplace twice and had gone back to Duck Pond with my sketchbook and spent an hour drawing. I was starting to feel like this town really was my home.

As we'd agreed, Jake showed up a week later to take me to lunch. "I have something special in mind for today," he said when I got in his truck. We drove past the restaurants in the village, past some homes, onto a road that was flanked by woods. After fifteen minutes, we pulled into a circular parking area and got out of the truck. Jake grabbed a basket from the back, and we walked over to a paved path. "This is the Ashokan Reservoir," Jake told me. "It provides the water for New York City."

It was breathtaking. The large expanse of water was surrounded by mountains, the peaks dotted with snow.

"It's my favorite spot in the area," Jake said.

We walked a few minutes, then stepped off the path onto the grass. Jake opened the basket and pulled out a blanket, which he spread on the ground. "I thought we'd have a picnic today."

I couldn't have been more pleased. He brought out a bottle of wine, then laid out sandwiches, cut-up fruit, cheese, and a bag of potato chips. As we ate, he pointed out the names of each of the mountains. "That's Indian Head, which sort of looks like the profile of an Indian, don't you think?"

He was right. It did.

"Next is Twin, because of its two peaks, then Plateau and Sugarloaf. They're part of the Devil's Path."

"How do you know that?" I asked him.

"I've climbed each of them, many times."

"Would you take me?"

"Whenever you want."

I thought of myself on top of one of those mountains, strong and fierce and able to take on the world, and a feeling of exhilaration shot through me. In the next instant, I thought about the task I'd taken on with Ben, what I'd agreed to do. I'd come to love this area. I was beginning to feel affection for Jake. But I knew I'd have to give up both. Once

I became Charly, once Ben and I divorced, I would have to disappear. That's what I'd agreed to. That's what I'd thought I wanted.

When I returned from lunch, I popped another DVD into the machine and began watching more videos of Charly. Whenever she spoke, I'd press "Pause," and practice saying the same thing into a recorder. Then I'd play it back, and see if I could tell the difference. I was getting better and better at mimicking her accent each day. After an hour of practicing her voice, I watched the videos through for the umpteenth time. Something had bothered me each time I'd viewed them, and I'd been having a hard time putting my finger on it.

After I'd watched each of them again, I logged on to her Facebook page. She had a slew of friends who posted regularly, but she only did so once in a while. I went back through her history to our shared birthday, and read the birthday wishes posted by her friends. That's when it hit me. I picked up my phone and called Ben.

"I get such a different picture of Charly from the videos and Facebook postings than the one you've painted," I said when he got on the line.

"Hold on a second."

I heard a door close, and then he was back.

"Yeah, well, people always put on a show when the camera is on them."

"That doesn't explain Facebook. Her friends genuinely seem to like her. And when she posts herself, she comes across as really warm."

"Again, the face she shows the public."

I wasn't buying it. Not completely. "Ben, I get that your marriage is bad. I get that divorcing her leaves you with nothing. But is her treatment of you the only reason you want out?"

I was met with silence.

"You still there?"

"We have an agreement, you and I."

"I'm not backing out. I just need to know the whole picture."

"You're right. There is more. Everything I said about her is true. Her public face is all goodness and light, but behind closed doors, she's a horror. What I haven't told you is that I've met someone else."

"You've been having an affair?"

"Yes. But for all I know, Charly might be, also. There have been a number of hang-ups over the past few months when I answer the phone."

I hesitated. In going along with Ben's plan, I'd convinced myself that Charly was the villain, not Ben. Now, I wasn't certain there wasn't something malevolent in him as well. Still, I'd agreed to facilitate a murder, so I was no poster child for decency. "If we're in this together, I need to know everything."

"We *are* still in this together, right?"

"We have a deal. I never break my word."

CHAPTER 17

Ben's hands were shaking when he hung up the phone. He hadn't wanted Mallory to know about Lisa. Not yet. It might give her leverage. Still, she'd taken his money; she'd moved into his parents' house. If she ever went to the police, she'd have to admit her complicity. And, although he could have lied to her, he'd known she'd find out once she'd taken Charly's place and moved into his home. *Better she knows now,* he thought, *than feel later she'd been tricked.*

The ringing of his phone startled him out of his reverie. He looked at the number, saw it was Charly, and picked it up. "Everything okay?"

"How come you haven't come with me to visit my father?" Her voice was steely cold.

"Because I assumed you wanted time alone with him."

"Well, he wants to see you. Pick me up at the gallery at seven, and we'll go there together."

"Sure."

Without even saying goodbye, she hung up the phone. *What the hell was that about?* Rick had never warmed to Ben. He'd tried to steer Charly away from him, and when she'd dug in her heels, he had reluctantly accepted the inevitable. So, why did he want to see him now? It couldn't be good. Was it possible he'd found out about Lisa? About Mallory? Ben shook his head. He'd been careful with both. Maybe the old man wanted to finally make peace with him, now that his time was close. That, too, seemed unlikely. He'd find out what it was about soon enough, he figured. He put his head down and returned to work.

At precisely 7:00 p.m., he met Charly at the gallery. She gave him a peck on the cheek. "I'm sorry I was so short with you this afternoon. The stress is getting to me."

"Completely understandable." He slipped his arms around his wife and pulled her in for a hug.

Rick's condo was in a luxury apartment building overlooking Central Park West, on West Seventy-Second Street. As they exited the gallery, Ben saw a taxi coming up the street and raised his arm to wave it down.

"No, don't," Charly said. "I want to walk a few blocks first. I need the fresh air."

It was a milder-than-usual evening, with a full moon overhead. As always, the streets were crowded with pedestrians making their way home from work. When they reached Forty-Second Street, Charly spotted an empty taxi. They got in, and ten minutes later, it pulled up to Rick's apartment building.

"Good evening, Mrs. Gordon," the doorman said when he saw Charly, then reached for the door to open it. Inside, the concierge greeted Charly by name as well and nodded to Ben. They rode the elevator up to the top floor. Rick's apartment was a duplex, with six bedrooms and a view east over Central Park and south to where the Twin Towers once stood. Before Charly had a chance to use her key, Charly's grandfather opened the door. She gave him a hug, and I shook his hand.

"Any change?" Charly asked him.

He shook his head.

Charly took Ben's hand and led him into her father's bedroom. Although Ben knew how serious Rick's condition was, he was shocked to see how ghastly his father-in-law looked. He was down at least thirty pounds since he'd stopped coming into the office, his cheeks now looked concave, and his eyes were rheumy.

Charly went to Rick's bedside and kissed his forehead. "How are you feeling today?"

"The same." Rick looked at Ben. "Thank you for coming."

Charly pulled a chair close to the bed and motioned for Ben to do the same. When they were both seated, Rick said, "I wanted to talk to you both about the firm."

Ben sat still. He expected the worst from the bastard.

"Charlotte, sweetie, except for some specific charitable bequests, everything goes to you, including the business. Well, most of it. I'm leaving Ted ten percent. He deserves it."

"Daddy, don't talk about this now."

He fixed a hard stare on Ben, then turned back to Charly. "I need to. I need a promise from you. Ben can have a job there as long as he's still married to you, but I want Ted Manning to run it. When Ted's ready to step down, he should pick his successor, not you. Can you promise me that?"

Ben looked over at his wife. She was biting her bottom lip and squeezing her hands together.

"Charlotte?"

"I promise, Daddy."

Rick turned again to Ben. "I wanted you to come tonight to hear this. When I'm gone, I don't want you pressuring Charlotte to turn the firm over to you. Ted's been with me almost twenty years. He deserves it."

"You're right, Rick," Ben said, a serious look on his face and a somber tone to his voice. "Ted should take over the firm. No one knows the business better than he does." *Until Mallory takes Charly's place. Then it's mine. All mine.*

Two nights later, Ben walked into a grungy establishment in the Bed-Stuy section of Brooklyn and immediately spotted Jeff Mullin at the bar. He walked over to him and slapped him on the back. "How you doing, buddy? It's been a while."

Mullin turned to him, and Ben got his first good look. He was easily twenty pounds lighter than he'd been in high school, and he'd been slim back then. His eyes were sunken, with dark circles underneath, and his hair looked like it hadn't been washed in weeks.

"Yeah, almost ten years," Mullin said.

Ben ordered a beer, plus another for Mullin, then said, "Let's go grab a booth." They found an empty one near the back and slid onto the cushioned benches.

Almost immediately Mullin asked, "Why have you been looking for me?"

Ben shrugged. "People talk. I heard things have been hard for you. We were friends once. I just wanted to see if I could do anything for you."

Ben saw Mullin looking over his tailored suit and gold cuff links, and thought he'd been smart to leave the Rolex at home.

"Sure. If you have an extra ten grand at home, I'd be happy to take it off your hands."

Ben looked around the establishment. Across the room, two men sat at the bar, as did a woman at the end, each looking scruffier than the next. Three booths were occupied, one by a single man and the other two with couples. The booths on either side of Ben were empty. He leaned in to Mullin, and with his voice barely above a whisper, said, "How about fifty grand?"

Mullin laughed. "What do you want me to do? Kill someone?"

Ben stared at him without saying a word.

Mullin's eyes grew wider. "Damn! That *is* what you want."

Ben picked up his beer and took a swallow. "Let's say, hypothetically, that someone *did* need that. What would you say?"

"I'd say you got the wrong guy for it." Mullin looked away from Ben, then began running his hands down his pants legs. After a while, he said, "I did my killing in Afghanistan. I'm finished with that."

"Okay, then, our business is done." He pulled a twenty from his wallet and threw it down on the table. "Good seeing you again, Jeff."

As he started to rise, Mullin reached over the table and grabbed Ben's arm. "Hold on. I said *I* wouldn't do it. Doesn't mean I don't know someone who would. For the right price, I could introduce you."

"How do I know I can trust you not to run to the police?"

"Man, the last person I'm going to talk to is a cop."

"Even if you get busted for something? Using this info to trade for a deal?"

Mullin looked around the bar. "I don't squeal on buddies. You still a buddy?"

"We *were* back in high school, when I wrote those English papers for you. And when we both got drunk and broke the principal's office window, I got caught and never named you."

"There you go," Mullin said. "That makes you a buddy. What do you want to tell me?"

"I want to find someone to kill my wife."

Mullin let out a low whistle. "How much?"

"Fifty thousand for you. Two hundred thousand for the killer."

Mullin took a few quick breaths, then downed some more beer. "I got the guy for you."

"Is he trustworthy?"

"I'd trust him with my life."

CHAPTER 18

November 6, 2016

From: bswann129
To: malloryart24
Re: LA
Hi, Love,
Miss you loads. Class not the same without you.
Have great news. Stan has a business trip to LA
next week, and he promised to take me along.
We're getting in on Nov. 8, leaving on the tenth.
Can we see you for dinner?
Brian

November 6, 2016
From: malloryart24
To: bswann129
Re: LA
Hi, Brian,
I'm so bummed out. My company is sending me to
Phoenix for two weeks, and I won't be in LA. I miss
you, too. Tell Stan he owes me a dinner whenever
I get back to NY.

November 18, 2016
From: bswann129
To: malloryart24
Re: Thanksgiving
Stan says come for Thanksgiving, and he'll cook up a feast. He'll even pay for your flight, and you can stay in our guest bedroom.

November 18, 2016
From: malloryart24
To: bswann129
Re: Thanksgiving
I wish I could. They have me on a deadline for a big-ticket project. I'll be working late on Wednesday night before Thanksgiving and back in the office early Friday morning.

Ben made his way over to Holy Apostles Soup Kitchen, on West Twenty-Eighth Street and Ninth Avenue, to help serve Thanksgiving dinner. Usually, Charly joined him, something they'd done together every year since they'd married, but tonight she was spending it with her father and grandfather. It wasn't just Thanksgiving that he volunteered. He tried to do it one night a month, but sometimes work interfered. Or a preference to spend the evening with Lisa. Thanksgiving, though, had become sacrosanct, now out of habit rather than desire. He'd worked at some food shelter, alongside his parents, every Thanksgiving since he was ten years old. His parents had instilled in him from a very young age the importance of giving back. For a long time, it made him feel good about himself when he did. No longer. Now, he continued so he could artfully drop it into conversation with a client, or even a prospective client. To show what a good person he was, so considerate of those less fortunate, so trustworthy. He generously contributed to various charities for the same reason—not just the ones whose events Charly attended for the sake of making connections. No, he gave regularly to his alma mater, and to the New York City Police Athletic League—he thought sports was important for every kid. Sometimes he donated to the Fresh Air Fund. He had gone to summer camp himself and thought that would be good for every kid. It was easier to give money than his time, but clients often congratulated him on his selflessness and then referred their friends to him. Even if his motive for volunteering had changed from altruistic to pecuniary, he still thought of himself as a good person for keeping it up.

He didn't think less of himself for wanting to be rid of his wife. Of course, divorce was one way to do it. But Charly had trapped him into this decision. She had pushed him to give up law school; she had insisted on a prenuptial agreement; she had forced him to accept her father's job offer; she had showered upon him the spoils of wealth. Anyone in his position would know he couldn't just walk away from that.

After he finished serving the homeless men and women who came to Holy Apostles for a meal, he sometimes sat down and talked to a few of them. Some were war veterans, too overcome with PTSD to hold down a job; some he could tell right away had a screw loose in their heads. Some were addicts, living from day to day. But some had lived normal lives, holding down a job, supporting a family, and then *poof*— it all had disappeared. Maybe because they lost their job and couldn't find another. Maybe because a serious illness had wiped away all their savings, and when they'd recovered, they had nothing left. Each man and woman had a different story, a different reason for being there. At first, he commiserated with them, feeling genuine anguish listening to their tales. Now, all he could think about was how quickly he could leave.

Whatever brought these men and women to Holy Apostles, the one thing Ben knew was that nobody who had extraordinary wealth—no matter what obstacles landed in his path—ever ended up on a soup-kitchen line.

CHAPTER 19

November 29, 2016

From: bswann129
To: malloryart24
Re: LA
Another business trip to LA. YEAH!!! This time you have to be there. I just miss you to pieces. Arriving 12/5. Leaving on 12/8, staying at Four Seasons. I insist you meet us for dinner on 12/6 or 12/7. You choose.

I couldn't keep putting Brian off. Stan traveled throughout the world meeting clients, and it stood to reason that Los Angeles would be one of his regular stops. Eventually, I'd either have to cut off all contact with Brian, a possibility I loathed, or meet him in LA. This was one of those times that having a credit card with no limit would come in handy. I called Ben to let him know—after all, he was getting the bills, and I didn't want him to think I was skipping out on our agreement—and then reserved a flight and a hotel room for December 6 through the 9. I had to make sure I left LA after Brian and Stan. I couldn't risk running into them at the airport.

I stepped out of the terminal in Los Angeles and was greeted by balmy weather. I didn't need the down jacket on my arm; my light sweater was enough. I grabbed a taxi and gave the driver the name of the Omni hotel on South Olive Street. I could have stayed at the Ritz-Carlton. Ben wouldn't have cared, but I still wasn't comfortable with the notion that I didn't have to watch my spending. Maybe, when it wasn't Ben's credit card I was using, when the money was my own, in *my* bank account . . . maybe then I could start to ignore price tags. But I wasn't there yet.

I chose my hotel because of its location. I didn't want to be near the Four Seasons, where Brian and Stan were staying. I didn't want to take the risk of running into them and having to explain why I wasn't at work.

With just a taxi-ride view of Los Angeles, I could see how different it was from Manhattan, and, of course, worlds apart from Scranton. It was so much more spread out. Manhattan was compact, humanity squeezed together on a small island. Los Angeles seemed to have no edges.

I settled into the hotel, then went outside to take a walk. The streets had a different feel from Manhattan, too—less crowded, less frenzied. I walked for almost two hours, stopping in little boutiques along the way, trying on expensive clothes, looking at pricey jewelry. I could have bought anything I wanted, but I knew I would only be able to wear something at dinner tomorrow night that had been part of my original wardrobe. Otherwise, Brian or Stan might start asking me questions I didn't want to answer.

I got back to my hotel and ordered room service. I felt beat from the flight, the long walk, and the fact that my body was responding to the three-hour time difference. I struggled to stay awake until 10:00 p.m., then fell into a deep sleep. When I awoke the next morning, the sun was just beginning to rise. I dressed in running gear, then headed to the hotel's gym for an hour run. When I finished, I showered and dressed, then did the most touristy thing I could think of—I went to Universal Studios. I'm not big on amusement park rides, especially the scary ones, but I splurged on the VIP Experience to get an insider peek at the workings of a movie studio.

I arrived shortly after 10:00 a.m. and was assigned to a guide. For the rest of the day, I felt pampered as we toured the back lot of the studio, marched to the front of the lines for rides, and had the best seats for the shows. By the time I returned to the hotel, I was exhausted, but I had less than an hour before I had to meet Brian and Stan for dinner. I lay down for fifteen minutes, then took a quick shower and got dressed.

I was meeting them at Culina, an Italian restaurant in the Four Seasons hotel. When I got there, they were already seated, and both jumped up as soon as they saw me. Brian was the first to grab me in a bear hug. When he pulled away, Stan did the same.

"Sweetie, aren't they feeding you here? You've lost weight," Stan said when we were finally seated.

"It's LA. Everybody here is on a diet. I'm just trying to fit in."

"Well, you look fabulous," Brian said.

I had to admit, it was great seeing them both again. I knew I was supposed to cut all my ties once I'd moved into Ben's parents' house, but Brian had been in my first art class when I'd moved to New York, and every one after that. I just couldn't turn my back on him.

By the end of our five-course meal, each course accompanied by a glass of wine, I was feeling pleasantly tipsy. Brian insisted on waiting with me for a taxi and walked with me to the front of the hotel. He told the doorman I needed a cab and slipped some bills into his hand. Moments later, one pulled up, and a man emerged from the back seat.

"Charly, what are you doing here?"

My first reaction was panic, but I quickly scanned my memory for the pictures Ben had sent me, and the ones I'd seen on Charly's social media pages, of her friends and family. He was her second cousin, Phil, living in Boston. If I were alone, I'd respond with a big smile and ask about his wife, Sally, and his parents, Ginger and Barry. But I wasn't alone. Brian was standing by my side with a confused look on his face.

"I think I must have a common face. People keep confusing me with others, but this is the first time I've been mistaken for a man."

"No, no, Charly's a woman. Short for Charlotte."

"My name is Mallory."

It helped that it was dark outside, with just some lights from the hotel behind me. He simply nodded and apologized, then entered the hotel. I kissed Brian goodbye, and I got in the back seat of the taxi.

Part of me had hoped that, by keeping in e-mail contact with Brian, when this whole mess was finished—Charly dead, me taking her place, divorcing Ben, and divvying up the money—then I could return to being Mallory Holcolm and resume my friendship with Brian. Now, I understood. Keeping in touch with him was too much of a risk. Ben was right. I had to stay in my cocoon.

CHAPTER 20

Ben barely saw Charly anymore. He'd wake up next to her, they'd mumble "Good morning," then each would quickly dress and leave for work. They didn't even have breakfast together. Each morning Charly would beg off, saying she wasn't hungry. Ben wondered if the stress of her father's illness had taken away her appetite. He wouldn't care, except that the more weight she lost, the more Mallory had to lose. He'd taken to leaving the house early to pick up freshly baked cinnamon rolls, Charly's favorite, from the corner shop, then dropping them back at the house before heading into the office. When he returned at night, they'd be gone, but he had no idea whether Charly actually ate them or brought them into the gallery for her assistant.

Ted Manning had taken over running the business in Rick's absence, and he pretty much ignored Ben. If Ben had been playing games on his computer all day, or checking out porn sites, Ted wouldn't know or seemingly care. Ben figured Rick had explained that his son-in-law had a guaranteed job there, at least while he and Charly were married.

A little earlier than usual, Ben left the office for his weekly racquetball game with Graham. He got to the sports club before Graham and began hitting some warm-up shots. By the time Graham arrived, he'd already worked up a sweat. They got right into a game, Ben taking the first one easily.

"You're more relaxed than I've seen you in years," Graham said as they took their first break.

"It's a lot less stressful with Rick out of the office."

"Any more news about him?"

"It's going to happen soon. Probably no more than a month."

"Charly must be freaking out."

Ben took the towel in his hand and wiped it across his forehead. "She is, but we hardly see each other now. She heads off to her father as soon as the gallery closes, then heads to bed as soon as she comes home."

"Maybe when her father is out of the picture, you two can try to reconnect. You used to be crazy about each other."

Ben shook his head. "Not going to happen. After she's finished grieving—six months, at the most—I'm leaving her for Lisa. I've made up my mind."

"That's big. You're really going to walk away from her money?"

"I'm going to do whatever I need to in order to be with Lisa."

Graham slapped him on the back. "Man, I'm proud of you. I can't tell you how long I've wanted to hear you say that. You don't need money when you have love."

Ben smiled as he thought, *Yes, but it's so much nicer to have both.*

Ten days later, Ben headed to Brooklyn again, to the same bar where he'd met Jeff Mullin weeks before. This time, Jeff was there with another man, already seated in a booth in the back. After Ben joined them, Jeff introduced Danny Clark. He looked to be a few inches shorter than Jeff, maybe five eight, and was dressed in army fatigues, his muscles bursting through the tight T-shirt. His hair was worn in a buzz cut, and he was clean-shaven.

"Jeff told you what I'm looking for?" Ben asked.

Clark nodded.

"You ever done anything like this before?"

"You mean outside of the army?"

"Yeah."

"It doesn't bother me, if that's what you're asking."

"You'd have to make the body disappear. No one could ever find it."

"That's doable."

Ben sat back and eyed both men. "How can I be sure you won't talk to the police?"

Clark looked over at Mullin. "Jeff saved my life, and took shrapnel to do it. Left him in constant pain that only narcs seem to help. I inform on you, you tell them about Jeff's role, and there's no way in hell I'm letting him go in the clinker."

Ben nodded, then reached into the inside pocket of his sports jacket and withdrew two envelopes. "Here's ten grand for each of you. Jeff, you get the rest when the job is done. Danny, I'll give you half of the remainder, ninety-five thousand, just before I'm ready for you to do it. The rest when it's over. That work for you?"

They both murmured, "Yes."

"One caveat," Clark said. "We don't meet after it's done. I don't want to be seen with you. I'll let you know after it's over how to get me my money."

"Sure."

"You know," Clark continued, "the husband is always a suspect. How can I be sure you won't squeal on us?"

Ben smiled. "Not this time. No one will even know my wife is gone. No one will miss her. It's foolproof."

Clark reached over and took both envelopes, then handed one to Mullin. "Don't kid yourself. Nothing in life is foolproof."

CHAPTER 21

Today would have been my mother's forty-fifth birthday. When I was very young, I used to draw a picture for her as a birthday present. She'd hug me and tell me how much she liked it, and I always felt loved in those moments. There weren't many times when I did, and as I got older, my anger toward her grew. If she wasn't going to love me, then I wouldn't love her. Tit for tat. Except, I wanted her to love me, to tell me she was proud of my art, of my good grades, of my hard work. I couldn't see past my disappointment.

My mother always bought me a present for my birthday, even if it was something small. She would bake a cake for me, and when she'd returned from her cleaning jobs and we'd finished dinner, she would present the cake with the number of candles for my age, plus two. I remember, on my eighth birthday, smugly telling her that there should be only one extra candle—eight, plus one to grow on. She smiled, but her eyes looked sad when she said, "You're so special that you deserve two extra candles." Now I understood that the second candle was for my sister.

I wonder how my life would have been different if I'd grown up with Charlotte. If my mother had kept us both, the little money my mother had for gifts, even for food and clothes, would have been split between us. But I don't think I'd have been as lonely if I'd grown up with a sister, no matter how little money we had. When you're a child and poor, it doesn't matter if you have a little less—it's all that you're used to.

If, instead, she'd given us both away, would the Jensens have adopted me as well? Would I have grown up spoiled and selfish, like my sister? I'd had a lot of time to fill in my country hideaway, no job to report to, no classes to take. I'd spent hours looking up studies on identical twins, and it seemed clear that personality traits were genetically determined, and since twins shared the same genes, they had similar personalities. Yet, Ben's description of Charly was so at odds with how I saw myself. The studies also said that when identical twins were raised separately, their different life experiences could have an impact on brain development, resulting in different personalities.

I hesitated. The glowing picture I had of myself was borne out of necessity. I had to be hardworking to survive. There were no extras in my life to hoard selfishly. If I acted out, my mother withheld affection more than she usually did. So, who was I really? Did my genes make me the compliant child, always wanting to please? Or was I meant to be cold, calculating, and self-centered, like Ben had described Charly? Whose personality had been changed by her environment? Mine or Charly's?

I knew the answer. It had taken me less than two weeks to agree to murder a sister I'd never met. Until Ben had presented his plan, I'd accepted my life—the poverty, the struggling, the lack of maternal affection. Now, I wanted what Charly had. I wanted her wealth. I wanted the townhouse and the gallery. I wanted her life. I was as greedy and coldhearted as my twin.

I woke up to a foot of snow on the ground. I'd been living in High Falls for seven weeks now, and other than a few sprinkles, this was the first snow they'd had. Everything outside was covered in white, unspoiled by cars or footprints. I was due to have lunch with Jake today but knew that would be canceled. He'd be busy plowing driveways. At least I'd see him when he came to do mine.

I poured myself a cup of coffee, bundled up in a warm jacket, slipped into boots, then took it out on the porch to sip. It was too beautiful to stay inside. The house was surrounded by snow-covered trees, and it looked like a scene from an Andrew Wyeth painting. Just as I thought that, two deer popped out of the trees and skipped across the snow to woods on the other side of the lawn, completing the picture of Americana.

I finished my coffee and was about to step inside when I heard the rumble of Jake's truck, slowly plowing snow as it crept up the driveway. When it reached the top, I waved at him. He opened his window and shouted, "Hi."

"Have time for a ten-minute break and a hot cup of coffee?" I shouted back.

He nodded, then shut off the motor and stepped outside. He was bundled up in a heavy lumberjack jacket, snow pants, and high boots, with a wool cap pulled down over his ears and heavy gloves on his hands.

"It's not that cold outside," I said when he got closer.

"It is when you've been out doing this since five a.m."

"Come on in and warm up."

He stomped up the porch steps and, when he reached the top, shook snow off his boots. I held the door open for him, and we stepped inside. He bent down to take off his boots while I just slipped off mine. I padded into the kitchen, poured coffee into a mug for Jake, then refilled my own. By now, I already knew he drank his black.

When he came into the kitchen, I handed him his cup, and we sat down at the table.

"You must be exhausted," I said.

"Not yet. I'll be doing this until it gets dark. Then I'll collapse."

I sat watching Jake as he drank his coffee. I'd thought him good-looking the first time I'd met him, but as I got to know him, he seemed even more handsome. More than that, he was kind, the type of person who'd go out of his way to help someone without expecting anything in return. If I only allowed myself one friend in my country hideaway, I was glad it was him.

"So . . . ," he began, then took a sip of coffee.

I raised my eyebrow, waiting for him to continue.

"Do you have someplace to go for Christmas dinner?"

The holiday was one week away. If my life hadn't changed with the stare of a customer at Trattoria Ricciardi those many weeks ago, I'd probably be waiting tables. It was open both Christmas Eve and Christmas Day, and customers were overly generous both nights. When the evening was over, I'd crawl into bed and cry myself to sleep. It was the only time I missed my mother. As neglectful as she'd been, she was the entirety of my family.

"Just here," I answered. "I'll probably make a casserole, then watch *It's a Wonderful Life* on DVD."

"Come to my family dinner instead. We'd love to have you."

Warning bells immediately started in my head. I'd rationalized having *one* friend to keep me from going stir-crazy, as well as my trainer, Jackie. It could be dangerous getting too entrenched in the community. What if, when Ben's parents returned, people told them about my stay in their home? I assumed Ben would tell his parents beforehand that he'd lent the house to me, but if someone described me to them, they might realize I looked like Charly. Ben would have a hard time explaining that.

Still, I'd spent Thanksgiving alone. I didn't mind giving up a holiday if it was to work, but somehow, staying in by myself had just made me feel pathetic. I smiled at Jake. "I'd love to."

It was a starkly clear winter's day, with a deep-blue sky and puffy clouds overhead. I was going to climb my first mountain today—Ashokan High Point—with Jake by my side. It was the Catskill peak that could be seen from his parents' property, Jake told me. Before today, I'd gone to Rock and Snow in nearby New Paltz and purchased Gore-Tex hiking boots, and crampons and snowshoes, then practiced walking in them outside the house. Jake had already warned me it would be strenuous.

It was almost 10:00 a.m. when Jake picked me up in his truck. I'd prepared sandwiches and stuffed them, along with a thermos of coffee and two apples, into my backpack. We drove forty minutes to the trailhead, a small cut in the woods that would have been easy to miss had Jake not been with me. We started out by crossing a stream on a bridge made of wooden slats, then began the uphill trek. The snow was solidly packed, so I didn't need the snowshoes. I was able to manage avoiding the occasional patches of ice, so I left the crampons in the pack as well.

Jake was right—despite my newly fit body, I was breathing heavily an hour into the hike. We reached a clearing and took a break.

"You're doing great," Jake said.

I loved his optimism, even if it was fake. I took out the thermos and poured us both some coffee and breathed in the rich aroma before sipping it down. It felt good—not just the coffee but being with Jake, climbing a mountain, and seeing how far I could push my body. I felt ready to become Charly . . . to be the confident, fit, beautiful woman who was used to getting what she wanted. Was I going to get what I wanted? I thought, *Yes*.

After ten minutes, we started up again, and an hour later, we reached the peak. The leaves were off the trees, and I could see mountains all around me—beautiful, jagged, majestic mountains. I wanted to climb every one of them. I wanted to be Charlotte Jensen Gordon and know that everything was in my reach. I knew that I could.

On Christmas Day, Jake picked me up at exactly 5:00 p.m. I had begun to realize that punctuality was part of his personality. I had made a bread stuffing with sausage and dried cherries, as well as a pecan pie, and gathered those up before grabbing my coat and heading out the door with him. The weather had remained cold since the snowfall, and the tree branches were still covered with clumps of white powder.

"I keep meaning to ask you," Jake said when I got in the car. "Do you like to ski? I thought maybe you'd like to go with me. Hunter or Bellayre are both nearby."

Once again, a reminder of my austere childhood. "Nope. Never gone."

"Well, think about it. Especially if it's a snowy winter. Even though they have snowmaking machines, it's much better with the real stuff."

It took only fifteen minutes to arrive at the home of Jake's parents. We turned off the public road onto a dirt drive that, although plowed, still had a thin veneer of snow, then drove uphill for half a mile. We reached their house, standing all alone in a copse of trees. A double strand of white lights framed the two-story house, and a large fir tree on the side of the porch was lit up with multicolored lights. Two other cars were parked around the circular driveway. We walked up the front porch to the double doors, a holly wreath on each. Jake knocked once and, without waiting, opened the door and walked in. The home was filled with the smell of a turkey cooking in the oven. Straight ahead, through a wall of windows, I could see the twinkling lights of Mohonk Mountain House in the distance, with just a tree-filled valley between the hotel and the house.

Jake led me into the kitchen first, where three women were busy finishing up the food preparations. I placed my contribution on the counter.

"Mom, this is Mallory," Jake said to the oldest of the women, who wore a frilly apron over her ample stomach.

"Thank you for inviting me, Mrs. Bowman."

"Please, call me Jenna. And I'm happy you could come."

Jake introduced me to his sisters, then brought me into the living room, where his father and two brothers-in-law, along with his grandparents, were seated around the stone fireplace. Four children sat huddled in a corner with a stack of LEGO bricks. Once again, Jake made introductions. His father, like his mother, insisted I use his first name, Joel, and his grandmother said, "Call us Gammy and Pop Pop. That's what everyone does."

Jake led me to the corner where a Christmas tree stood, tastefully decorated. Scattered around it were open boxes and torn wrapping paper, except for one box, still wrapped. Jake handed it to me. "This is from my mom." I opened it and found a hand-knitted wool scarf in colors of red and green and fought back tears. Her thoughtfulness overwhelmed me.

Jake settled in a chair next to his father, and I went back to the kitchen to thank his mother. "It's beautiful, and just what I need now that winter's arrived in full force."

"I'm glad you like it."

"Can I do anything here to help?"

"Nonsense, you're our guest," Jenna said.

I remained there, anyway. They were easy to chat with, taking turns filling me in on places I should visit while I was living in the area. When it came time for everyone to take seats around the table, I already felt like I'd known them for years.

"Jake tells me you're writing a novel," Joel said.

"Trying to."

"What's it about?"

A good liar is always prepared. "It's a murder mystery. About a man who wants to kill his business partner. He's in debt to him for two million dollars and sees that as his only way out."

"I like mysteries," Joel said. "How does he get caught?"

I smiled. "Now, if I tell you, you won't buy the book. Besides, maybe he doesn't get caught."

"Ah, now I'm intrigued. In every mystery I've read, the bad guy is always punished in the end. Of course, that's not real life. I suppose there are plenty of people who've gotten away with murder."

I hoped that was true.

I fell in love with Jake's family. His father made me laugh throughout the meal, and his mother treated me like a daughter. His sisters, Julia and Sherry, both teachers, entranced me with stories of their students. And their children: four-year-old Jillian, five-year-old twins, Hailey and Zach, and the oldest, seven-year-old Jessica, already assuming the role of boss, made me think once again that I'd like to be a mother. I watched the twins' obvious affection for each other and felt a stab of wistfulness at what I had missed with my own twin.

Jake's grandmother kept asking me questions about my life, not as a grilling but because she genuinely seemed interested. Everyone gushed over the dishes I'd brought, and after dinner, we broke into two teams and played charades. I was hopeless at it but laughed and laughed. When the game was over, Jake's brothers-in-law, Steven and Mark, brought out their guitars, and we all sang Christmas songs.

Christmas with my own mother always had been a solitary experience. Sometimes she had enough money for a tree and gifts to put under it; other times all I'd gotten was a trinket from the drugstore. Rarely had dinner been anything different from every other night of the year. The home of Jake's parents was filled with warmth, not just from the fireplace but from every person present.

When Jake pulled into my driveway, I wasn't ready to let go of the magic of the evening. "Want to come in for a bit?"

He turned off the ignition and followed me into the house. Without even asking, he got a fire started in the fireplace.

"Coffee?" I asked.

"Nope." He patted the seat on the sofa next to him, and I sat down. "I'm glad you came tonight. I'm glad you met my family."

I smiled. "They were lovely. Every one of them."

Jake scraped his hand through his hair, then cleared his throat. "I was wondering if next week, instead of lunch, maybe we could go to dinner."

Here it was—the pitch to move our relationship forward. I was surprised it had taken him this long. Every part of me wanted to say, "Yes," to lean over and kiss his full lips, to take his hand and lead him into the bedroom. I knew that I couldn't. "I like you. I really do. But I don't want to get entangled with anyone while I'm working on my novel. And when it's finished . . . I'll be moving on from here."

"New York City's not so far away."

I put my hand on his. "Can we just put it on hold for the time being? Stick to lunches?"

He nodded, but I knew he was disappointed. So was I. Of all the men I'd met since leaving Scranton, he was the one I could see making a life with. I could picture myself as part of his family. But I was leaving this life behind and, in a few months, maybe less, inhabiting someone else's.

Jake stayed for another hour and then got up to leave. When he was gone, I realized that it wasn't money that I'd missed growing up. It was family.

CHAPTER 22

I'd settled in to a weekly routine. Each morning I'd have two hard-boiled eggs and coffee for breakfast and then start some form of exercise. Twice a week, I trained with Jackie, followed by a half-hour jog on the treadmill; two other days, I ran for an hour on the treadmill; and twice a week, I hiked in Mohonk Preserve. That didn't change when we began getting snow every few days—usually a dusting but sometimes six to eight inches. I'd put on my hiking boots, long waterproof pants, and enough layers on top to keep me warm in the coldest weather. Sometimes I'd go back to Duck Pond; other times I'd do the walk around the circle known as Undercliff/Overcliff and watch the rock climbers as they did their ascent. Once or twice, I parked my car at Spring Farm and hiked up to Mohonk Mountain House, a stately hotel that brought to mind what the grand mansions in olden Europe must have looked like. I gave myself one day to just laze around. Every afternoon, I'd have a light lunch, then I'd rewatch the tapes of Charly, study the notes Ben gave me, and follow her Facebook page. And, of course, I still had lunch with Jake once a week.

Today would be different. Ben had texted me a picture he'd taken of Charly just the other day and instructed me that it was time to get my hair cut and colored to match hers. Tomorrow, he'd drive up and check me out for the first time since he'd dropped me off at this house. I'd made an appointment with a hair salon in New Paltz and arrived there promptly at 10:00 a.m. Once I checked in, I was led to Donna's chair.

"Cut and color today?" Donna asked after I sat down.

"That's right."

She ran her fingers through my hair. "So, what are you looking for, just a little lightening?"

I took out my cell phone and showed her the picture of Charly. "This is the color I used to have. And the hairstyle. I've let my hair go, and I want to get back to this. Exactly this."

She studied the picture. "Sure. No problem."

I'd passed my first test. Donna had given no hint that the woman she saw in the picture wasn't me.

"I'll be right back, hon. I'm just going to mix up the chemicals," she said, before leaving me to stare at the mirror in front of me. I'd never been to a hair salon before. My mother used to cut my hair. Now, I cut it myself. It was why I wore it long—just a straight cut across the bottom every few months, and I was done. It had never been styled, as Charly's hair clearly was, and certainly never colored.

I looked around the salon. There were eight chairs behind the receptionist's desk, four on each side of the room. Farther back were three chairs in front of sinks on one side, and on the other, two chairs for pedicures and two for manicures. Every chair but one was filled, with women ranging from late teens to one silver-haired senior citizen. Only one man occupied a chair.

"I'm back," Donna said in a cheery voice.

"You're busy here," I noted.

"You should see us on Saturdays. Then, you have to book a month in advance."

I knew this would set me back a couple of hundred dollars. After the cut and color, I was scheduled for a pedicure and manicure. It might not be an exact match to Charly's, but it would be easy enough to say I'd decided to change the color.

Donna chatted nonstop as she meticulously applied the dye to my hair. When she'd finished and left me alone for it to process, I took out my iPad and did what I always did when I needed a break from exercise or studying—I looked at travel websites, at locations throughout the world. I thought I'd like to go on an African safari and visit the Sistine Chapel in Rome. Now that I'd gotten fitter, I wanted to hike in the Swiss Alps, then relax in a luxury hut in Bora Bora. I wanted to visit every museum in Paris and the Van Gogh Museum in Amsterdam. I wanted to go on an Alaskan cruise, learn the tango in Buenos Aires, and eat tapas in Barcelona. I wanted to walk on the Great Wall of China and ride an elephant in Laos.

Before I knew it, Donna was back. She brought me over to one of the sinks to wash out the dye, then back to the chair at her station. I looked in the mirror and smiled. The color was perfect. She cut my hair and then began to blow it dry. I averted my eyes from the mirror. I didn't want to look until it was finished.

"So, what do you think?" Donna said when she turned off the hair dryer.

I looked up and saw Charly in the mirror. "It's perfect. Just perfect."

The next morning, Ben drove up in his Lexus 450 SUV. A much more practical car, I thought, than the Porsche Carrera he'd driven me up in almost three months ago. I waited by the door as he bounded up the steps, then opened it just before his knock. I laughed when I saw the look of shock on his face.

"You like?" I asked.

"It's . . . It's . . . I can't believe it. I can't tell you apart. How much weight did you lose?"

"Sixteen pounds," I said proudly.

He stepped inside, and we went into the kitchen. I had prepared lunch—a salad with just red wine vinegar and no oil for me—and an assortment of cold cuts with rolls for Ben. "What do you want to drink with lunch?" I asked him. "Soda, coffee, water?"

"Do you have Coke?"

"Just diet Coke."

"I'll have water, then."

I set everything down on the table, then sat. As we ate, he peppered me with questions.

"What's the name of Charly's grandfather?"

"Herman Jensen."

"My parents' names?"

"Judith and Sidney."

"My grandmother?"

"Linda."

"Where do they all live?"

"Herman, who Charly calls Poppy, lives in Miami Beach and also has a summer home in East Hampton. Your parents spend eight months a year in Boca Raton, where your grandmother lives year-round. The rest of the time, they're here, at this house."

"What are the names of Charly's parents, and where do they own property?"

"Rick and Sarah Jensen. Sarah died when Charly was ten, in a car accident. Rick owns a penthouse condo on West Seventy-Second Street and Central Park West. The doorman there is named Carlos, and the concierge is Smithy—probably not his full name, but that's what he's called by everyone. Her father also has a seven-bedroom home on the water in Southampton, which you and Charly go to on weekends between Memorial Day and Labor Day."

I looked over at Ben and saw he was smiling.

"You sound exactly like her," he said. "No Pennsylvania twang anymore."

We spent the next two hours going over every detail, Ben asking me questions about Charly's life, and me answering every one. When he finished, he said, "The doctor says his kidneys are failing. Rick has a week, maybe ten days left. That's all."

"Have you found someone to do it? To Charly?"

Ben nodded.

"What's his name?"

"You don't need to know that."

"I want to meet him."

"It's better for you that you don't."

"Look, I'm on the line here, too. If something goes wrong and he fingers you, you can turn on me to sweeten your deal. I need to make sure I can trust him."

"It's enough that *I* trust him."

I folded my arms and began tapping my foot, without saying a word. Finally, Ben said, "I'm going to meet him in two nights to give him a payment. You can come with me."

I smiled. "Thank you."

He grabbed his jacket and started toward the door. "I'll text you where and when."

As he pulled out of the driveway, it hit me that this was real. In two days, I would come face-to-face with the man hired to murder Charlotte Jensen Gordon, my sister.

Two nights later, I drove into Brooklyn, to an address Ben had texted me. We were to meet the hit man at 9:00 p.m. sharp. I wasn't familiar with this borough, so I gave myself extra time. I arrived ten minutes early and parked in front of what looked like an abandoned building. There were no lights visible from outside, and at least a quarter of the windows were broken. I remained in the car with the doors locked. At two minutes to nine, there was a tap on my window. I turned and saw Ben, motioning me to get out. I turned off the motor and left the safety of the car.

"Nice neighborhood," I said, assuming he picked up the sarcasm.

"I didn't choose it. Come on. He said he'd be in the back of the building."

It was very dark, and I wondered what I'd gotten myself into by asking to meet him. I flipped through the apps on my phone for the flashlight, and the light helped dispel some of my unease. I skirted the broken glass and debris in the alleyway as I made my way, alongside Ben, to the rear. When we reached it, no one was there. The mid-January temperature hovered just below freezing, and a gust of cold air seemed to go right through me. I pulled the collar of my jacket tighter around my neck.

"He'll be here any minute," Ben said, although his voice didn't sound very certain.

A moment later, a figure emerged from the shadows of the building, and Ben whispered, "That's him." He was short and bulky, with pitch-black hair. My first thought was that I was glad I wasn't alone with him. When he reached us, I saw he had a scar that ran from the side of his eye down to the bottom of his cheek.

As soon as he spotted me, he asked, "Who are you?"

"I'm part of this. That's who."

He looked over at Ben, who nodded.

"You have the money?" he asked Ben.

"I have some questions first," I said.

"What do you want to know?"

"Have you ever done this before?"

"Why? You want references?"

I frowned at him. "No. I want to make sure we're not dealing with an amateur."

"You want my body count? I stopped counting after a hundred."

Ben leaned over toward me. "He was in the army."

The hit man smiled. "Be precise. I was a sniper in the army, trained to kill unsuspecting targets."

"That's a lot different than killing a civilian woman. How do I know you won't back out? That you won't be persuaded by Ben's wife to let her live in exchange for more money than Ben's giving you? That you won't go running to the police, now that you have half the payment?"

"I like you. You're sharp. Sharper than your cohort here. So, here's your answer. I stopped caring about human life back in Afghanistan. Mine, yours, or any other fucking person on this earth. Ben wants to pay me money to get rid of his wife, I have no moral compunctions against that. I do have moral compunctions against stiffing a buyer of my services, so I don't change allegiance. As for the police, I've already answered that question for Ben. He was satisfied."

"How are you going to do it?"

"That's irrelevant for you. It'll be done, and no clues will be left behind. That's all you need to know."

"How will we know you've carried it out?"

The hit man looked over at Ben.

"Actually, I'd like to know that, too," Ben said.

He laughed. "What, you won't take my word for it?"

"The word of a hit man?" I said. "Maybe if this was a murder that would end up splashed all over the newspapers, yeah, that would do. But here, you've promised to make sure no one ever finds the body. So, how do we know she's really dead?"

He thought for a while. "I'll leave a disposable cell phone at your house, with pictures of her on it. Take a look, then throw away the phone."

"She could be pretending to be dead."

He laughed again. "Not in the pictures I'll send." He turned to me. "Satisfied?"

I nodded. "Completely."

He held out his hand, and Ben placed an envelope in it.

"Pleasure doing business with you both," he said, then disappeared into the darkness.

CHAPTER 23

Ben knew this past week had been brutal for Charly. Rick was under hospice care, and Charly had told Ben he was barely conscious most of the time. When Charly arrived home that night from her father's apartment, he expected her to retreat into the bedroom as she always did. Instead, she sat down next to him. She put her head on his shoulder. "I miss you."

What the hell? Ben thought. He picked up her hand and stroked it.

"I miss us. I miss intimacy." She turned to Ben and kissed his lips softly, then harder. She placed her hand on his crotch and began stroking his genitals. He didn't want to, but he couldn't help responding. Any guy would, he knew. When she felt him get hard, she stood up and motioned for him to follow her into the bedroom, then began slowly undressing. He followed suit, only more quickly, then jumped into bed, pulling her to him when she'd taken off the last items of clothing. It had been months since they'd made love, and they tore at each other hungrily. When it was finished, Ben rolled over, confused.

"Thank you," Charly said. "I needed that." She got out of bed and headed to the bathroom, saying, "I'm going to take a shower now."

Ben got out of bed, too. Charly had dumped her clothes on a chair, and he went to hang them up for her. He picked up her skirt and blouse and saw a manila envelope underneath. He couldn't help himself. The shower was still on; Charly wouldn't know. He pulled out the document inside and saw it was a copy of Rick's trust. Quickly, he glanced through it. There were a few charitable bequests, but except for 10 percent of the business going to Manning, everything else went to Charly. Just as he expected. He didn't mind Manning getting 10 percent. It only gave him a seat at the table, not much of a voice to go with it. When he reached the end, he noted the name of the attorney who'd witnessed the trust. He looked again at the envelope and saw the name of the law firm he was with. He grabbed his phone and jotted down both names.

Perfect, he thought. He now knew just where to send Mallory to settle Rick's estate.

The next night, Ben was surprised by a phone call from Jeff Mullin.

"I need a favor," he said.

What the hell is he doing calling me at home? It was just lucky that Charly was late getting back from her father's place. "What do you need?"

"Another advance. Maybe five thousand dollars?"

"I just gave you ten thousand last month. You blew through that already?"

"I, uh, some things came up. Some expenses." He lowered his voice. "I really need it, man. Help me out."

"What's going to happen when the fifty grand is gone? You going to keep calling me?"

"No, man, nothing like that. We have a deal. I, uh, just need some of that early."

Reluctantly, Ben agreed. He couldn't risk Mullin complaining to Clark. Not when Rick was so close to dying. He could practically feel Rick's money running through his hands. After, when it was all over, he'd worry about Mullin. And, if Mullin got too needy, if he demanded more when his cut was gone, Ben would take care of him himself. Nobody would miss a worn-out heroin addict.

"Tomorrow night. Same place, same time."

It finally happened. The once-mighty Rick Jensen passed away. Ben wished he could feel more sympathy for the guy, but it just wasn't there. Still, he needed to keep up the pretense with Charly, so he put on a good act. He accompanied her to the funeral home and helped her pick out a casket and make the necessary arrangements. He went through their photo albums to pick out pictures of Rick and the family to display at the funeral home. He went to Rick's apartment to pick out a suit for him to be buried in. And every time Charly burst into tears and seemed inconsolable, he pulled her into his arms and hugged her tightly.

They would have a viewing at the funeral home for two days, between 2:00 p.m. and 5:00 p.m., and again between 7:00 p.m. and 9:00 p.m. There were simply too many employees and friends in the financial industry who wanted to pay their respects, as well as family and longtime friends, to limit it to one day. Charly's grandfather had flown up a few days before Rick passed, and Ben's parents and grandmother had come up from Boca Raton as well.

It was good for Charly to have her grandfather with her. She'd always been close to the old man. Herman wasn't as overtly negative toward Ben as Rick had been, but Ben didn't actually feel any warmth from him. Still, Herman helped keep Charly distracted from the pain she felt.

Three days after Rick's death, they held the first viewing at Frederick Canton Funeral Chapel on West Eighty-Second Street. Rick had deteriorated so much over the past three months that Charly had chosen to keep the casket closed. Her family was small—her father had no siblings. She had an aunt and uncle on her mother's side and two cousins, one of whom lived in London and sent his condolences.

The room at the funeral home overflowed with flowers, sent by Rick's many friends, the men and women who worked with him, and by his numerous clients. A twenty-by-twenty-four-inch picture of Rick was sitting on an easel, and framed pictures of him with his wife and Charly were placed on a table. By 3:00 p.m. it was standing room only, and the visiting guests spilled into the corridor. All of them, upon seeing Charly, told her what a wonderful man her father was and how he'd be missed. If Ben was within earshot, he had to choke back the bile in his throat.

The evening viewing and the next day's viewings were just as crowded. On the third day, the funeral was held at Park Avenue United Methodist Church, and the pews were filled. Ben, Ted Manning, and two other executives from Jensen Capital Management were pallbearers. Charly sat in the front row with her grandfather, his arm tightly around her shoulders. After the minister's service, at least a dozen people gave eulogies. The ground at the cemetery was too frozen to bury Rick, so after the church service, about fifty of those closest to him and Charly were invited back to Rick's apartment, where food and drinks awaited.

The next day, Charly's grandfather left to return to Florida, and Ben drove him to the airport. On his way back into Manhattan, he sent a text from his burner phone to Danny Clark. Three nights from tonight, Ben told him. I have Knicks tickets, and she'll be alone in the house.

Consider it done, Clark texted back.

Ben slipped the phone back in his pocket, a smile on his face.

Three days later, on a Friday afternoon, Ben called Charly at the gallery. "Graham just called and invited me to a Knicks game—courtside seats courtesy of a business client. Would you mind terribly if I went?"

"No. Go ahead. I could use some time alone."

He knew she'd understand. Although Jensen Capital Management had a luxury box at Madison Square Garden, sitting in the box didn't come with the sweat and sounds of being on the floor. Only once before had he scored a seat there.

Ben did go to the Knicks game with Graham, although it was Ben who'd gotten the courtside tickets through a client. That put him in the view of the cameras from time to time, even though he wouldn't need to account for his whereabouts to the police. Still, on the off chance Charly turned on the game—which was highly unlikely, since she hated basketball—she might catch a glimpse of him there.

He loved all sports, but especially basketball and especially the Knicks, even though they ended up disappointing him every season. Normally, he'd be engrossed in the game, screaming at the good plays and booing the bad calls. Tonight, he barely saw the players. He kept thinking about what was happening at his home. Along with the last payment, Ben had given a key to Clark, with instructions for him to enter from the rear door. Charly was likely to be in bed early, and their bedroom faced the front. She wouldn't hear the back door open, and if Clark was quiet enough, she wouldn't hear him creep up the stairs. With luck, she'd even be asleep. He hadn't asked too many questions about how Clark would kill her; he just knew she'd be slain in the house, then carried away in a trash bag. He hoped it wouldn't be painful for her. He wasn't a monster. He didn't want her to suffer.

The game dragged on, going into overtime before it ended in a Knicks loss. When he exited the Garden, he quickly flagged down a cab and headed uptown to his home. The master-bedroom window on the second floor was dark. Did that mean it had gone as planned? Or did Clark take Ben's money, then bail on him?

Ben turned his key in the lock and, once inside, headed right to his bedroom. He turned on the light and saw . . . nothing. Charly wasn't in the bed, although the covers were unmade. He looked around the room and saw no sign of a struggle. He checked Charly's jewelry drawer. She always took off her four-carat, square-shaped diamond engagement ring before getting into bed, sleeping with just her diamond wedding band. It was there, in its blue Tiffany box. He backtracked down to the first floor and scrutinized the rooms. Nothing was out of place. *Good,* he thought. It had to have gone smoothly.

Just one piece was left. He needed to see pictures of Charly's dead body.

CHAPTER 24

It's done. Ben told me last night that he'd returned home, and Charly was gone. The only thing left is to wait for the pictures—pictures of her dead body. Any day now, my role will begin.

Jake picked me up for our weekly lunch date at 9:30 a.m. He'd refused to explain why we were leaving so early, insisting he wanted to surprise me. I got in his truck, and we drove south for twenty minutes and then across the Mid-Hudson bridge. The Hudson River looked stark, the leaves gone from the bordering trees, the air colorless. When we got to the other side, Jake turned north, onto Route 9, and drove for another fifteen minutes before pulling into a driveway, past a stanchion that said VANDERBILT MANSION NATIONAL HISTORIC SITE.

"What's this?" I asked.

"It's an extraordinary example of American Beaux-Arts design. It's something to see just by itself, but there's an exhibit going on now of paintings by the artist Angela Fraleigh. I don't know if you've heard of her?"

I hadn't, but there were so many talented artists that I was still learning about.

"Well, this exhibit consists of portraits of female heads, seen from behind. From what I understand, there's not a lot written about the women who lived at Vanderbilt, and these paintings are supposed to reflect their elusiveness. I always see you drawing people, and I thought you'd enjoy it."

We pulled into the parking lot, and Jake purchased tickets for us.

"I usually come here in the spring and summer to look at the gardens. They're exquisite," Jake said.

It seemed that was a word that could be used over and over at this site. Everything was exquisite. The mansion, built between 1896 and 1899 by wealthy industrialist Frederick Vanderbilt on six hundred acres of riverfront property, had fifty-four rooms. He and his wife, Louise, had used it as a vacation home. The paintings, by Ms. Fraleigh, were exquisite in their simplicity—pared down to four elements: background, hair, skin, and clothing. There was no reference to class and no way to discern whether the women were wealthy or servants. Even without the gardens in bloom, the grounds—especially the view of the Catskill Mountains across the Hudson River—were breathtaking.

As I walked through the lavishly furnished rooms of the mansion and strolled the manicured grounds, all purchased by a man with extraordinary wealth, I kept thinking to myself, *I wonder if he was happy?*

We left the mansion a little after one, then drove up the road a little farther to the Culinary Institute of America.

"Here's my second surprise," Jake said.

"You're going to give me a cooking lesson?"

He laughed. "No, silly. The student chefs here practice in restaurants open to the public. One's French, one's Italian, and we're eating in the one called American Bounty. It's a farm-to-table restaurant, using locally grown ingredients." We walked inside, he gave the maître d' his name, and we were led to our table. We spent the next hour and a half over a leisurely lunch, chatting easily, laughing often.

When Jake dropped me off back home, I felt overcome with a feeling of sadness. In a few days, I would pack my belongings and return to Manhattan. I knew I'd miss this house. I'd come to think of it as my own. Or in my dreamworld, the lovely country cottage where I'd return after my travels abroad. I would hate leaving it, especially so because it meant leaving Jake as well. He'd been so kind to me and had helped make the past few months go by quickly. I would miss him the most.

CHAPTER 25

Ben paced throughout the townhouse all day Saturday. He'd hoped to find the phone under the welcome mat outside his rear entrance by Saturday morning, the afternoon the latest. Now, it was Saturday evening, and still nothing.

Was it possible Mallory's concerns about Clark had been justified? Had he taken Ben's money and then . . . and then . . . he couldn't figure what. Charly was gone, so he must have taken her. Was she negotiating with him for her life? Offering to double, maybe triple, his fee? Or had they both hightailed it to the police, who would show up any moment to arrest him? No, he was being paranoid. Clark needed to make sure her body would never be discovered. He'd probably just driven some distance to ensure it. That must be it. Tomorrow, the pictures would be waiting for him. They had to be.

He fixed himself a double Scotch, downed it in two gulps, then poured another. He turned on the TV and sipped it slowly. Yes, he was just being paranoid.

Sunday morning, there were still no pictures. He was finding it hard to breathe. After pacing back and forth over the living room rug for an hour, he knew he needed to get out of the house. Waiting was making him sick. He called Lisa. "Can I come over?" he asked.

"You're never here on Sundays. Where's Charly?"

"At her father's, going through his papers."

"I was going to meet a friend for lunch today."

"Cancel."

She hesitated then, and with her voice soft, said, "Ben, maybe's it's time we moved on from this. You have a wife. You should be with her. She needs you now."

"NO!" Ben shouted into the phone. "Not now. Don't do this now. *I* need you."

Another hesitation, then a sigh. "Okay. Come over."

It was dark by the time Ben returned home, and the first thing he did was make a beeline to the back door. He lifted up the doormat and froze. Still nothing. If it didn't arrive by the morning, he would need to have Mallory call Sandy, Charly's assistant at the gallery, and beg off coming in. The flu or some such. *How could it not be here? Something had to have gone wrong. Did they go to the police? Am I being watched right now? Or did Charly convince him to turn the tables, to kill me instead?* Ben thought about calling Jeff Mullin; maybe he knew what Clark was up to. He had his hand on his phone when he stopped. *Maybe they're already tapping my phone? Maybe they're waiting to hear me admit my involvement?* He put his phone away. He took out the good Scotch this time—the Glenlivet—and filled the crystal tumbler, then kept refilling it until he passed out on the couch.

Ben awoke when he heard a loud noise out back. His head was throbbing, and the TV was still running. He glanced at his watch—2:00 a.m.

He stumbled to the back door, opened it, and looked around. No one. He glanced down at the welcome mat and saw a bulge underneath and quickly pulled it up. He tore open the manila envelope that had been placed there, and finally, there was the phone, along with his wife's diamond wedding band. Ben hadn't even asked Clark to return the ring. *For a hit man, he has scruples.* Also inside was a small white envelope. He opened it, and a small key dropped into his hand. A note said, *Leave the balance at Box 2119, Mail Connections, 350 W. 41st Street.*

He grabbed everything and returned to the den. His hands trembled as he opened up the photos icon on the phone. The first picture was of Charly, in the bedroom upstairs, her eyes open in a fixed stare, a red mark around her neck. He felt himself relax. It had gone as planned. He swiped to see the next picture, then gagged, and ran to the bathroom and threw up. On the camera was a picture of Charly's decapitated head, and next to it, her dismembered hands, the ring that had just been returned still on her finger.

CHAPTER 26

Ben called me early Monday morning to say he'd gotten the proof that Charly was dead. He told me to close up the house and call a limousine service to drive me into the city. I realized money didn't matter to him, but that seemed like such a waste when a bus in town would take me into Manhattan. Still, I suppose it wouldn't do for Charlotte Gordon to be pulling a suitcase through Port Authority, so I did as Ben asked.

Before I left, I turned off the main water supply and made sure the sheets were clean, the bed was neatly made, and the dishes were put away. The house looked like Ben's parents had left it. Then, I faced my hardest task. I called Jake.

"I'm leaving High Falls," I told him.

"When?"

"Today."

There was silence on the phone for a beat. "Are you going back to the city?"

"No. I'm heading to California. I've been offered a job there." I figured I might as well keep my excuses simple. I'd used that before with Brian and Gus, and it had worked fine.

Another beat of silence. "I thought we were starting something. Something special."

I wanted to reach out through the phone and hug him, tell him he was right, that I did have feelings for him. Instead, I said, my voice soft, "No, Jake. I told you at the start that it was just a friendship."

I spotted the limo driver pulling up to the house and quickly ended the call. All the way into the city, I felt miserable. Jake was the last person I wanted to hurt, yet I knew I had.

Two hours later, I pulled up to Ben's townhouse. The driver brought my suitcase up the front steps, then left when Ben opened the door. He didn't look good at all.

"Are you okay?" I asked once I was inside.

Ben nodded. "It's just . . . the pictures of her. They were disturbing. It's hard to get them out of my head." He took my suitcase and brought it into one of the guest bedrooms on the second floor. "You should have everything you need here. Get settled. I'm heading into the office."

Like the rest of the house, the room was decorated beautifully. On top of the queen-size bed was a coverlet that had a floral top in colors of brown, gold, and black and a gathered skirt in a simpler flowered design, trimmed with black lace. A dozen assorted pillows in the same colors were piled up under the beige, tufted, upholstered headboard. A Persian rug covered most of the wood floor. The room had its own bathroom and a bow window overlooking the backyard.

I unpacked my clothes and decided to explore the kitchen. It was a cook's dream. It had a Wolf range and built-in Sub-Zero refrigerator, two Miele dishwashers, and a center island that was ten feet long, with a sink in the middle. The appliances were all stainless steel, and the cabinets were a warm off-white. There was a full set of All-Clad Copper Core cookware, and on the counter, a Thermomix food processor and a Hobart mixer. I'd worked in enough restaurants over the years to appreciate the quality and expense of this kitchen.

I decided to surprise Ben with a home-cooked meal tonight. I grabbed the house key he'd left me and headed over to a market I'd passed on the drive in. As soon as I walked in, the man at the cash register called out to me. "Mrs. Gordon, I heard about your father. I'm so sorry." I quickly ran through the list of names Ben had given me of people Charly came in contact with. There was a "Joe" in this market. I hoped that was this man. "Thanks, Joe. I appreciate it." He nodded back, so I'd passed my first test. Tomorrow, when I went into the gallery, it would get harder.

I picked up the items I needed, then headed back to the town-house. When Ben walked in at 7:15 p.m., he called out, "What smells so good?"

"Coq au vin," I answered.

He walked into the kitchen and looked around. "You've made dinner?"

"Yep," I answered with a smile.

"Smells delicious, but going forward, check with me first. Once the prenup is canceled, I expect to be going over to my girlfriend's after work most nights."

"No problem. I just couldn't let this gorgeous kitchen go to waste."

Ben smirked. "Well, that's one way you're not like your sister. She rarely stepped foot in the kitchen. We bought takeout every night."

I shook my head. How ridiculous it seemed to spend a fortune on a professional-quality kitchen and never use it. "Dinner's ready. You hungry?"

"Famished," Ben answered.

I'd already set the table. I brought a salad out first, mesclun lettuce with chickpeas and dried cranberries, and my own balsamic vinaigrette dressing. I picked up the bottle of cabernet on the table. "Wine?"

Ben nodded, and I filled his wineglass, then poured mine.

Ben held up his glass. "A toast. To our future wealth." I thought it was pretty crass but clicked his glass, anyway. "Have you thought about what you're going to do when we split?" he asked.

"I always thought if I had money, I'd study painting in Paris. There's a school there, the Paris College of Art, where I could get a US-accredited BA."

"Sounds like a good plan. You should apply. Soon you'll have enough money to do anything you want." He took a few bites of the salad. "This is delicious."

"Wait till you taste the main meal."

When we finished our salads, I brought the coq au vin out to the table, along with a bowl of fettuccine and a loaf of warm French bread. Ben helped himself, and after eating several spoonfuls, said, "I can't believe you made this yourself. You should be a chef."

"I've always enjoyed cooking, but it's a hobby. Painting's my passion."

We chatted easily throughout dinner, finishing the bottle of wine just before I brought out dessert—tiramisu.

When we finished, Ben sat back in his chair and, with a wicked smile on his face, said, "I think I'm going to like being married to this twin."

Today would be the real test. I was going into the gallery. It would be Charly's first time since her father had died. Sandy had worked closely with Charly, and if I could fool her, I could fool anyone. I'd been briefed on her—what she did at the gallery as well as her personal life. She always arrived early and opened up the store. Later, Phil Jacoby would arrive. He was the gallery's art handler and worked only part-time, unless a show was getting ready to open. I wasn't worried about him figuring out the truth.

I dressed in Charly's clothes, which fit me perfectly, and got there just before 10:00 a.m. As soon as I entered, Sandy came up to me and wrapped her arms around my shoulders. "How are you doing? You know, you could have stayed out longer. I can run things here."

I gave her a quick hug back and thanked her. She looked me over. "You look better already. Less gaunt."

"It was stressful," I said, a catch in my voice, "leading up to the end. Now that it's over, it's almost a relief. He was suffering so much." I managed to squeeze a few tears from my eyes.

"I took the long weekend to just veg out. I laid in bed for three days and watched old movies. TCM had a marathon of Hugh Grant movies. I saw every one."

"Well, you deserved that rest."

It was clear that Sandy had no reservations about me. I was Charly Gordon.

CHAPTER 27

Ben felt like a six-ton elephant had been plunked down on his chest for months and now had finally lumbered away. He could breathe again. The finish line was in sight, and he was sprinting toward it.

It had been disconcerting yesterday to watch Mallory get out of the taxi and walk up the steps to his townhouse. He'd known identical twins who had subtle differences, especially once they became adults, that enabled people to tell them apart, but Mallory truly was an exact replica of her sister.

As he walked past Rick's corner office this morning, he stopped in his tracks. Sitting behind Rick's desk was Ted Manning. Someone from their maintenance staff had removed Rick's wall hangings and was in the middle of replacing them with ones that had been in Manning's office.

Ben stopped in the doorway. "What the hell?"

Manning looked up from the computer. "I'm sorry. This is probably disturbing to you. I waited until after the funeral, but we have to move on now."

"Don't you think you should have talked it over with me first? I might have had different plans for this space."

"With all due respect, Ben, you're not an owner of the firm. Your wife is. And she understands and is agreeable to me taking over the running of it."

"With all due respect, Ted," he practically spit out his name, "Charly is in no position now to be making those decisions. She's still grieving."

"The market doesn't stop because she's in mourning. And right now, she's the one who owns this firm. And I'm the only one with the expertise to keep it going. So, you're just going to have to deal with me running it. Unless, of course, you'd like to take your talents somewhere else."

"Fuck off, Ted. This isn't finished."

Ben fumed as he finished the walk to his office. That corner space belonged to him, not Manning. He snapped at his assistant to bring him coffee, then tried to calm himself. Manning was right. Ben didn't know enough to run the business. He needed to keep Manning happy. The corner office wasn't that important. In a few weeks, Ben would make it clear who the boss was. *Let Manning think he's in control for now,* he thought. *Mallory will soon set him straight.*

It had taken Ben three days to get together the cash needed for both Clark and Mullin, but he now had it tucked safely away in his briefcase. He hadn't wanted to make a large withdrawal, one that would be reported to the IRS, so he'd needed to move some accounts around and then withdraw just under $10,000 from each. He left work and headed over to Mail Connections. It wasn't just mailboxes—the place shipped letters and packages all over the world. The mailboxes were in the back, far from the counter where the staff worked and free from prying eyes. Ben withdrew an envelope containing $95,000 and placed it in Box 2119. He locked up the box, pocketed the key, then headed over to the same bar in Brooklyn where he'd first reconnected with Jeff Mullin.

A half hour later, he walked into the bar and spotted Mullin at a booth near the back. He slid in opposite him.

"You got something for me?"

Ben nodded, then took the second envelope with $35,000 inside out of his briefcase and handed it over to his old friend. Mullin grabbed it and stuffed it inside his pants pocket. "This calls for a celebration, don't ya think?" Mullin said. He called over the waitress and ordered two beers.

"I did good for you, right?"

"You did," Ben said.

It was too bad about Mullin. They'd been friends once, and it made Ben sad to see his life destroyed. Maybe this money would help him get it together. Yes, Ben thought, he'd done something positive for his friend. Given him a chance at a fresh start. And, if he didn't take it, if he used it for drugs, then came back to Ben begging for more, he would stop him—permanently.

It had taken longer than Ben had hoped for Rick to finally kick the bucket, but things had gone smoothly ever since. Not one person gave any sign they suspected Mallory wasn't Charly. Whether it was Sandy, her assistant; the doormen and concierges at Rick's apartment, where Mallory had returned to start going through Rick's papers; or the artists she dealt with, they all believed she was Charly. He had to admit, it was a perfect plan. You couldn't suspect the husband of wrongdoing if no wrong had been done. And he had to pat himself on the back for the way he'd manipulated Mallory into thinking Charly had rejected her. She was putty in his hands after that.

CHAPTER 28

A week after I arrived in Manhattan, Ben told me he'd made an appointment for us with two lawyers. The first was this morning with Josh Kantor, Rick's estate attorney. I'd gotten used to dressing in Charly's clothes. When I looked at myself in the mirror, I didn't see Mallory Holcolm any longer. I saw my sister, and it gave me the chills. When I was ready, we headed downtown to the office of Kantor, Bello, and Weissman. Josh had attended Rick's funeral and had already given his condolences to Charly.

"How are you holding up?" he asked.

I'd worried a bit about meeting him. He'd known Charly since her mother had died. After the first few minutes of chitchat, I relaxed. He'd readily accepted I was the woman he'd known for sixteen years.

"What do I need to do to get started on settling my father's estate?" I asked him now.

"I'll handle all of that for you. Of course, you know you're already on the deed of your father's condo, so that passes to you automatically, and there's no tax due until you sell it. The house out in the Hamptons, though, he bought while your mother was still alive. It's probably valued at about ten million. Rick had just over fifty million in cash. He's earmarked thirty million of that for various charitable bequests. His stocks and bonds, right now, are valued at one point two billion. The good news is that you don't pay tax on that until the stock is sold, and then it's with a stepped-up basis."

"What does that mean?" I asked.

"Well, as you know, the reason your father's hedge fund is so successful is because he had a nose for picking winners. So, for instance, he has Google stock that he purchased at the initial public offering for eighty-five dollars a share. Each share has become two, because the stock split, and is worth almost sixteen hundred dollars. If you sell it a year from now, you only pay tax on the amount over sixteen hundred dollars, not eighty-five. That's what a stepped-up basis means. It's as if you bought the stock on the day your father died, and so you only pay tax on profits after that.

"Now, we get to Jensen Capital. Your father knew the end was near and asked me to have a valuation done of the business. It comes in at one point four billion."

I suppose I shouldn't have been surprised. After all, Ben had told me Rick was worth $2 billion, but I guess I'd always thought he was exaggerating. The number had seemed too staggering to be real.

"Your father has given ten percent of the business to his associate, Ted Manning, in gratitude for his service. The rest of his partnership share, sixty percent, goes to you."

Ben quickly chimed in. "What about the other thirty percent?"

"You already own thirty percent as a limited partner," Kantor said as he looked at me. "Your father gave you that after your mother died, when he set up the business as an FLP, a family limited partnership. As a limited partner, you don't have voting rights or the right to sell, and so the gift tax he had to pay at the time was based on a discounted value. And, of course, the business was worth much less back then, so the gift tax was considerably less than would be owed now for that thirty percent."

"What does this all mean?" Ben asked. "What's the bottom line?"

I stared at Ben. This was supposed to be *my* inheritance. Didn't he realize how inappropriately eager he sounded?

"Well, the federal inheritance tax rate is forty percent, and New York state inheritance tax is another sixteen percent."

I could see Ben doing a quick calculation in his head, and then his eyes bugged out.

"You mean taxes will be almost five hundred million?" he asked.

I wished I could will Ben to quiet his reaction. Half a billion still left more than $2 billion—more money than either of us could spend in a lifetime, I figured.

"The good news is that Rick prepared for that kind of hit almost ten years ago. Jensen Capital was really taking off, and he didn't want you," he nodded in my direction, "stuck with a huge tax bill. He created an irrevocable life insurance trust—an ILIT—and named me as the trustee. I then purchased life insurance in the amount of two hundred fifty million dollars as trustee of the ILIT. Now, I submit a claim on the insurance, and when it's paid, it's not considered part of your father's trust, and it's not taxable. That money will then be used to pay half of the estate tax that's due."

"That's brilliant," I said. I looked over at Ben. He still had a sour look on his face. *What a greedy bastard,* I thought.

I thanked Kantor and stood up to leave, but Ben stopped at the doorway to ask one more question. "How long will all of this take?"

"I'll have to get a new tax ID for the trust, and file a tax return for it, but you can get access to the cash immediately. Changing the ownership of the stocks and bonds will take a little longer. Figure about two months to wrap everything up."

Ben squeezed my hand as we left the office. "You did good, kid."

I suppose I had.

The next morning, we headed to Steve Goldfarb's midtown office on Park Avenue. He was the attorney who'd drawn up the prenuptial agreements Ben and Charly had signed before they were married. He worked in a midsize firm, specializing in matrimonial and family law. We were ushered into his office as soon as we arrived.

"I heard about your father, Charly. My deepest condolences," he said, a somber look on his face.

"Thank you."

"So, how can I help you today?"

"You may remember, the only reason I agreed to a prenuptial agreement was to satisfy my father. He was so insistent. Now that he's gone, I want to revoke it."

Goldfarb cleared his throat, then began tapping his fingers on the desk. "You know, your father was looking out for your welfare. I advise everyone who has substantial assets to have a prenuptial agreement."

I took Ben's hand in mine. "I love Ben very much. I've shared my life with him for the past six years. Now, I want to share my wealth." I looked over at Ben and smiled, then turned back to Goldfarb. "This is my Valentine's Day gift to Ben." I could see Goldfarb becoming more agitated as I spoke. A sheen of sweat appeared on his forehead, and he was rubbing the back of his neck.

"If I remember correctly, your prenup was very generous to Ben. If you divorced, he would get a million dollars for each year of marriage. Unless the divorce was the result of an affair."

I smiled. "But I'm worth so much more than that. Especially once Dad's estate is settled. I trust Ben completely, and I want to do this to show my trust." All this time, Ben sat quietly next to me, his back straight in the chair.

Goldfarb slowly shook his head. "I strongly advise against it. But if you insist, I'll draw up a revocation. I'll have my assistant call you when it's ready."

"I'd like you to do it now. We can wait."

"I have another appointment soon. I promise, I'll have it in a day or two."

I remained in my seat. "I suspect you can have a paralegal prepare it in less than a half hour. How about we go get a cup of coffee and then return in an hour?"

The attorney sighed deeply, then nodded. "One hour. I'll see you then."

An hour later, we were back. Once again, we were brought into Goldfarb's office right away. A young woman was already seated by his desk, and Goldfarb instructed his assistant to remain. "Charlotte, Ben, this is Amy. She's prepared the revocation." He handed copies to Ben and me to read over, and when we finished, offered us pens. We signed each of the three copies, then Amy, Goldfarb, and his assistant signed as witnesses.

We left the office, and before heading our separate ways, Ben hugged me. "We did it," he whispered in my ear. "We're both going to be filthy rich. We can have the lives we want."

I pulled away, then smiled weakly. "But look at the cost," I said, then turned and walked away. I had performed as promised. My job was done.

CHAPTER 29

The next day, Ben got to the gym early and decided to grab a latte at the café while he waited for Graham. After it was handed to him, he glanced around and saw that every table was taken. Sitting alone at one was a stunning brunette, still clothed in her spandex tights, with a sports bra covering her ample breasts. He walked over. "Mind if I sit here?"

She smiled and looked even more beautiful. "Not at all. I've seen you around. I guess we work out at the same time."

She'd noticed me! He felt his heart begin to race. Charly had been pretty, but this woman was in another league altogether. Model pretty. Maybe even an actress. He surreptitiously glanced at her left hand. *No rings.* He'd wanted to be free of Charly so that he could marry Lisa. Now he began to think he shouldn't rush into that. He'd often marveled at men, wealthy but otherwise unappealing, who'd attracted women who should have been out of their reach. Soon he would be that man. With $1 billion, he could have any woman he wanted. He'd keep stringing Lisa along until the money was in his bank account. Then he'd hold out for someone like the woman sitting opposite him.

He smiled back at her. "I'm Ben. What's your name?"

Back at work after the gym, Ben had just gotten off the phone with a client when Manning popped into his office.

"I heard from Rick's estate lawyer. He told me Rick's given me ten percent of the company."

"Yeah, I know."

"I spoke to Charly and let her know how much I appreciated it. I also asked her how involved she wanted to be herself, going forward. She told me you were going to represent her interests."

"That's right."

"Look, I know we haven't always gotten along. I admit, I saw you as a freeloader, taking advantage of being the boss's son-in-law. But I also saw you really stepped up your effort when Rick took sick. We both want this company to do well. How about we bury the hatchet?"

Ben wanted to tell him he was an insufferable prig, that he'd rather bury him than bury the hatchet. Instead, he smiled and held out his hand. "Absolutely, Ted. Clean slate."

After Manning left, Ben turned back to his client list, but he couldn't concentrate. Ever since the meeting with Goldfarb, he'd kept thinking about his payday, his reward for putting up with Charly as long as he had. He'd been irritated, at first, when he'd learned Rick was giving Manning 10 percent of the business. Now, he realized that could work for him. With a piece of the pie, Manning was more likely to stay on even after he watched Ben take control of the business. Somehow, though, he couldn't square Mallory getting as much as he did. He'd suffered for years. She'd just come on board four months ago.

The business was supposed to be his share of the marital assets when he and Charly split. Maybe he should take some of the cash and stocks, too. After all, it would be imprudent to have everything tied up in just one place. What if the business tanked? He could convince Mallory of anything, he figured. She'd grown up with nothing, so even half of what he'd promised would be a windfall to her. Well, really, that amount of money would be extraordinary to anyone.

Although he'd have no claim to the townhouse in a divorce, since it was a gift from Rick in Charly's name only, Mallory would have no use for it. She needed to stay away from New York, preferably far away. Otherwise, she'd risk running into people who knew Charly. She'd said she wanted to travel, to perhaps study art in Paris. That's where she should go. He should keep the townhouse. He'd need a place to live in New York while he ran Jensen Capital. And the beach house, too. The summer crowd knew Charly and Rick. Too chancy for Mallory to stay there and maybe run into someone she was supposed to know. Mallory should be grateful for any of the money. Two hundred million. That seemed like the right amount for her. She wouldn't know what to do with more. If she balked, he could tell her she'd get nothing. After all, what could she do? Go to the police? Hardly.

He'd explain to Mallory that he wanted to start a charitable foundation, give money away to deserving groups. Maybe more programs to feed the hungry. He believed in charity, in doing good deeds. She couldn't object to that. And he really would start a foundation. It would be another thing he could point to that would make others want to do business with him. Of course, he wouldn't put the whole $300 million that he was holding back from her into the foundation. She didn't need to know that. Ten million seemed like a good sum. That could feed a lot of men and women. Children, too. Especially children. In fact, by giving so much money, he could cut out his volunteer work and still look good to clients.

Maybe Mallory didn't need to stay on for the estate to be settled. After a month, she could say she was traveling, relieving some of the stress from the past few months. Or scouting out new talent. He'd call her back whenever something needed to be signed. Or just FedEx documents to her. That would be good. One month together, and then just he and Lisa—or someone new—would have it all to themselves.

One hundred million. A nice round number. That's what he'd give Mallory. Really, she didn't deserve more.

Two days later, Ben had just stepped outside his office to grab a cup of coffee when his secretary stopped him.

"Your wife is on line two."

If you only knew, Ben thought as he stepped back inside and picked up the phone. Mallory had seamlessly moved into his life as Charly Gordon. No one suspected she was anyone else. No one had any thought that Charly was dead, her body disposed of someplace far away. "What's up?" he asked.

"Danny Clark stopped by. He said he needs to see you."

"What the hell! I made the final installment, left it in a postal box at Mail Connections, just as he instructed me. What's the guy trying to do now? Shake me down for more?"

"I have no idea, but he's coming back, at eight o'clock. He said you'd better be home."

"Dammit, not tonight," he muttered to himself.

"So, are you coming home?"

"I wasn't planning to."

"Look, you're the one who hired him, not me. Whatever he wants, you need to straighten it out."

"Shit!"

"You'll come home?"

"I'll be there," he answered reluctantly.

He hung up, then sat back in his seat. This wasn't good news. Maybe when Clark saw their house, their furnishings, he figured he'd settled too easily for the amount Ben offered. Maybe he thought Ben might be a perpetual payday. It didn't matter. If Clark wanted more money, even if he claimed it was just once more, Ben knew it wouldn't stop. He had to put an end to it right away. He'd been willing to kill Mullin, if it came to that, and Mullin had once been a friend. He'd have no remorse getting rid of Clark. He'd already done what Ben needed. Now he was excess baggage.

He picked up the phone again and called Lisa. He'd planned a big evening with her tonight, their first time going out to a restaurant together. Not just any restaurant, but the Gotham Bar and Grill, in Greenwich Village.

Before he even said a word, Lisa answered the phone, saying, "I hope you're not calling to cancel."

"Sorry, babe. Something came up at work, and I'm stuck here well into the night." He heard a deep sigh on the other end. "I'll make it up to you tomorrow night."

"You better."

"That's a promise." He intended to keep Lisa happy, at least until someone better came along.

As soon as he walked into the townhouse that night, Ben could smell something savory coming from the kitchen. "What's cooking?" he asked Mallory as he stepped inside. She looked like a fifties housewife with her hair pulled back and an apron around her waist.

"Lamb stew," she answered.

He glanced at his watch, saw it was ten to seven. "Will we be finished before Clark gets here?"

"It's almost ready."

He grabbed a beer from the refrigerator, then headed into the den and plopped down on his favorite chair. He picked up the remote to turn on the TV, then slipped off his shoes and loosened his tie. It was too early for a Knicks game, but MSG Network was showing a rerun of an old game back in the late sixties between the Knicks and their fiercest rivals, the Boston Celtics, when the home team could actually win games.

Fifteen minutes later, Mallory popped her head into the den and asked if Ben wanted another beer. "Sure."

Two minutes later, she was back, handed him the bottle, then sat down in the seat opposite him. He gave her a fleeting look, then turned back to the game. When Mallory didn't move, he paused the game. "What?"

"I've been wondering. What made you think I would go along with your plan to kill Charly? I mean, when you first met me. You didn't really know me then."

"Sure I did. You're Charly's identical twin. She was greedy as hell, so you had to be, too."

"But that could have been because of the way she was raised, not from genetics."

"Well, you did go along, so what's the point of the questions?"

"I was just curious. You were taking a big risk. I could have gone to the police. Or to Charly."

"Your word against mine. I was already rich. You had nothing. I was pretty sure they'd believe me over you."

"Well, speaking of nothing, how about fronting me some more money while we're waiting for the payoff?"

Ben picked up the remote and turned off the TV. He cleared his throat. "I'm glad you brought that up. I've been thinking . . ."

He saw Mallory's eyes narrow.

"I think the split needs to be something different from what we discussed."

"Why?"

"Well, the business should really be out of the equation. Maybe it makes money, maybe it doesn't. Either way, you wouldn't have any expertise to bring to it, so you couldn't run it. And I just don't think there's a market for selling a hedge fund."

Mallory's eyes bored into Ben. "Okay, so I'll take the real estate in exchange for the business, and we'll split the cash. That gives each of us over five hundred million."

"You're not going to stay in New York after we're divorced. You won't need the real estate. I'm going to keep the townhouse and the beach house. We'll sell Rick's apartment."

"And split that?"

"I think you should get one hundred million as your share. Total."

"What!" Mallory stood up and began pacing around the room. "That's not our deal!"

"I want to start a charitable foundation, and donate the bulk of the money to it. When you think about it, a hundred million is an extraordinary amount of money. You'll still be able to do anything you want for the rest of your life."

"Maybe I want to start a charitable foundation myself." Mallory whipped her head around and stared at the dark TV. After a few moments, she turned back and, with her lips drawn in a tight grimace, said, "We split the money, fifty-fifty."

Ben shook his head. "Sorry, Mallory, that's not going to happen."

"You still need me. There are documents I have to sign."

"And you'll sign them if you want to see any money at all."

She stormed out of the room in a fury. Ben had expected that response, but it didn't change anything. In the end, she'd have to accept what he offered. He turned the game back on, satisfied that he'd played it just right with Mallory.

A few minutes later, Ben heard his name but didn't look up. Mallory called it again, louder. He held up his hand to shush her, without turning his head. "A minute. Key play here." The Celtics were ahead, but the Knicks had a chance to take the lead. It didn't matter that the game had been played almost fifty years ago; it was still exciting to watch.

Now, she said his name sharply. He paused the TV and swiveled around. His eyes widened, and his mouth dropped open, while his heart felt like it would explode in his chest. He rubbed his eyes and prayed that it was just an apparition he was seeing.

"Hello, Ben," Charly said, a smiling Mallory by her side.

PART TWO

CHARLOTTE

PART TWO

CHAPTER 30

October 2016

My husband is having an affair. I don't think Ben knows that I'm onto him. I wanted to scream, to let out the fury inside me, but of course, I couldn't. Not while in the gallery.

Our relationship has been strained for a while, yet every time I tried to talk to Ben about it, he retreated. Finally, I hired a private investigator. I know—how clichéd. But there it was. I didn't trust Ben and paid someone to follow him. I needed to understand what had happened to us. Her name's Lisa. A social worker. I'll bet he's told her terrible things about me, that I'm spoiled and cold and don't care about him, only about my business and . . . and, maybe some of that was true. Not that I didn't care about him. I did, a great deal. Even loved him, I thought, before receiving the envelope that lay on my desk. But my business has taken a lot of time and effort to get established. There's a great deal of competition in the art world. My mother's connections helped a little, but it was a long time ago that she was on the board of the Metropolitan Museum of Art. She died almost sixteen years ago. Still, Dad has a lot of friends with money to burn, and he's steered many of them to my gallery.

I looked at the pictures that accompanied the report and wondered what he thought was so special about her. Plain brown hair that hung straight to her shoulders, an upturned nose, eyebrows that needed tweezing. Pretty, in an ordinary sort of way. Her clothes looked like they'd come from someone's castaways. They just didn't seem to suit her body—her much-larger-than-mine body. Every time I retained water, Ben asked me if I'd gained a few pounds, yet this woman who was kissing my husband had at least fifteen pounds on me.

I couldn't stop staring at the pictures. Should I confront him? Tell him I know? What if he wanted to end our marriage? *Do I want to end our marriage?* I thought about that and realized I couldn't handle Ben cheating on me. Marriage counseling was an option, I supposed, assuming he agreed to immediately stop seeing Lisa. But is that what I wanted? He'd betrayed me, after all I'd done for him. No. I didn't want him back. He was tarnished goods now.

I was supposed to be working on the gallery's books, but instead I was wound up with thoughts about Ben and that woman—Lisa. My reverie was interrupted when Sandy, my assistant, called out to me that my father was on the phone. I put the investigator's report and his pictures back in the envelope and placed them in my bottom desk drawer, then picked up the phone.

"Hi, Dad."

"Sweetie, I have some bad news."

My father never had bad news. He put a positive spin on everything. Everything except Ben. "What is it?"

"There's no easy way to say this, so I'm just going to come out with it. I have liver cancer."

Suddenly, nothing about Ben mattered anymore. Tears welled up in my eyes, and I couldn't find any words.

"It's terminal."

I began to sob. "No, don't say that. There has to be something. A liver transplant. I can be tested. Maybe I'm a match."

"It's too late for that. It's spread too far."

My sobbing intensified. Sandy peeked her head into the back room and, upon seeing me, came over and put her arms around me.

"It's okay, Charlotte. I've accepted it. I've suspected for a while something was seriously wrong. That's why I had testing done."

"B-b-but you never told me."

"I didn't want to worry you unnecessarily."

"I can't lose you, too."

"You were always going to lose me. It's just come earlier than we expected."

"Where are you now?"

"At home."

"I'm coming over. Right now."

"I'd like that."

I was shaking when I hung up. My hands kept shaking all the way to my father's apartment. I let myself in with my own key, then called out to him.

"I'm in the den," he called back.

I hadn't seen my father in a few weeks—rare for us, but he'd begged off the last two Sundays—and I was shocked by how he looked. His skin was sallow, and he'd already lost some weight. I walked up to him, and he wrapped his arms around me.

"Oh, Daddy," I said, and then began crying again.

He held me tight to his chest and stroked my hair, like he used to when I was a little girl and had injured myself. We were already close before my mother died, but after her death, we'd become inseparable. The only time I ever went against him was in marrying Ben, and now I knew he'd been right about that.

When I'd recovered some composure, I pulled away. "Tell me everything the doctor said."

He motioned for me to sit down, and I took a chair opposite his desk. "I've pretty much told you everything. The cancer is advanced; it's already metastasized."

"What about surgery?"

"It's not an option."

"Then chemo, or radiation?"

He shook his head. "I could try it, but it's not likely to help survival, and it's not pleasant to go through."

I felt myself get angry and tried to tamp it down. My whole body felt like one knot of tension. "There must be something. What about a trial? Aren't there any?"

"My doctor has prescribed medication to help with my nausea and bloating. And he's trying to get me into a trial at Sloan Kettering."

I felt my first sense of hopefulness. There were new medications coming onto the market all the time. There *had* to be one being tested for liver cancer. "Haven't you donated to Sloan Kettering?"

"I know what you're thinking, sweetie. But this is the one thing that my money can't buy. Whether I'm selected for the trial or not won't depend on how much I've donated. It will be based purely on my medical records. I should know by the end of next week, but my doctor wasn't hopeful."

My tears started again. Confronting Ben would have to wait. I couldn't lose both Ben and my father at the same time. I just couldn't.

By the time I walked into my house, I was drained. It was a mild night, and I'd walked through the park, bypassing the taxi that Carlos, the doorman at Dad's condo, had offered to hail. I needed to clear my head before I saw Ben, but the walk hadn't done that.

My townhouse had been a gift from Dad when I got married. He didn't call it a wedding present, since he put it in my name only, a fact that continually irritated Ben. Our official wedding gift was a honeymoon in France. A week in Paris at the Four Seasons Hotel George V, and a week on the French Riviera at the Château Eza. It was the first

time Ben had ever been surrounded by such opulence. We were deliri-
ously happy then. We'd stroll along the Champs-Élysées and stop at
outdoor cafés for coffee or wine and hold hands while we watched other
lovers walk by. During the day, we spent hours at the museums—the
Louvre, of course, which couldn't possibly be appreciated in one day,
so we went back the next; the Musée d'Orsay, its origins as a train station almost as interesting as the masters hung within: Delacroix and
Renoir, Monet, Manet, Cezanne, and Van Gogh, and so many others;
the Centre Pompidou, surely the most interesting building housing
art, with its primary colors and exposed pipes and air ducts; the Musée
Picasso, which, during our visit, had a Giacometti exhibition alongside Picasso's masterpieces. It felt dizzying to be surrounded by such
a cornucopia of paintings. If Ben had shared my love of art, I would
have moved to Paris in a heartbeat. I loved New York City—I loved
its crowds and messiness and hodgepodge of cultures—but Paris filled
my soul.

At night, we walked along the Seine and talked about our life
together, about the careers we'd begin, the family we'd start, the home
we would make. Everything seemed possible then.

After Paris, we flew to Nice for a week lounging on the sun-soaked
beaches of the French Riviera. Our suite at Château Eza, on the Côte
d'Azur, overlooked the Mediterranean Sea. When we weren't on the
beach, or shopping at the quaint boutiques, we'd lounge in our room's
outside Jacuzzi and sip champagne. The two weeks seemed like a dream,
one from which I didn't want to awaken. If I'd asked Ben to stay in
France, I know he would have. Back then, he'd do anything for me.
Even give up law school.

There it was. The elephant in the room we never spoke of. I'd
ruined his life by pushing him into a career he hadn't wanted, with a
boss who disliked him. And he was right. If I'd been more patient, if I'd
been willing to wait another three years to get married so that he could
become a lawyer, would he still have been drawn to another woman's

arms? I didn't know the answer. I only knew he wasn't happy, and I had a role in that. That knowledge didn't stop me from hating him for what he'd done.

I called out to him from the foyer.

"In here," he shouted from the den.

I hung up my jacket, then walked over there. The television was tuned to a basketball game, now on mute. He stood up and pulled me to him. "I'm sorry, honey. How's he doing?"

"It's bad."

"Can I do anything for you? Did you eat?"

"I'm just tired. I'm going to bed now." I could deal with only one crisis at a time. Ben's infidelity would have to wait.

CHAPTER 31

Dad insisted that I go about my business every day, even though I would have preferred to be by his side. I reluctantly agreed that I would continue at the gallery but go directly to his apartment once I closed up, to spend each evening with him. I'm certain Ben won't mind. In fact, I suspect he'll be relieved. It will give him more time with his paramour. I've steeled myself to the fact that he is seeing someone else but cling to the hope that it's about sex, not love. When this crisis with Dad is over—hopefully because he's recovered, but if he doesn't, after his funeral—I'll confront Ben with my knowledge of Lisa. Until then, I've decided to simply push my image of them together to the deepest recesses of my mind. Willful blindness.

I arrived at the gallery a little before 10:00 a.m., and as usual, Sandy had readied everything for our opening. Although we attracted some share of walk-in traffic, most of our customers were steady ones and made appointments. I had two scheduled for today, the first at 10:30 a.m. Mrs. Sonia Belvedere and her husband had recently purchased a country home in Rhinebeck, New York, an elegant retreat on thirty acres bordering the Hudson River. She was one of my dad's clients, and I'd worked with her before. Now, she was looking for artwork to adorn her new weekend home.

A few minutes before she was scheduled to arrive, the phone rang, and I recognized my grandfather's number. I picked it up on the first ring. "Hi, Poppy."

"Is it true?" he asked without so much as a hello.

"You spoke to dad?"

"Just got off the phone with him. Tell me he was being overly dramatic."

"Have you ever known him to be? He's the family optimist."

"Damn!"

"It's possible he'll get into a drug trial."

"Good. When will he know?"

"I'm not sure. Maybe in a week?"

"Well, I'm flying up. I need to be with him."

That was my grandfather—someone who could always be counted on. Even though he now lived in Florida, I always knew he would be back if I needed him. "I'm glad. Dad will be happy, too."

I heard a knock and looked up to see Sandy standing in the doorway, mouthing that my appointment had arrived. "Let me know when you book a flight, and I'll pick you up at the airport."

"Nonsense. I'll take a cab. And I'm coming up today, so I'll see you tonight."

"Love you, Poppy."

"Ditto, Pips." That had been his nickname for me since I was a toddler. Short for *pipsqueak*, I'd been told. I hung up and pulled out a folder marked *Sonia Belvedere*, then walked into the showroom. I felt better already.

I arrived at my father's apartment a little after 7:00 p.m. and immediately got a bear hug from my grandfather. Although he was approaching seventy, he was still a big man, skimming six feet tall, with a barrel chest and a full head of mostly gray hair.

"You should have given me a heads-up," he said when he finally pulled away from me. "Your father looks like shit."

"He's lost a lot of weight in just a short time. He's having trouble keeping food down."

"He's got to eat."

I saw the worried look on his face and reached out to hold his hand. "How long can you stay?"

"I thought I'd try to make it to Thanksgiving, but I can stay longer if you need me. It's just, you know, the cold really does a job on my bursitis."

"I didn't even expect you to stay that long. You've got to take care of yourself. I don't want to lose you, too."

"Hey," he said, a sharp tone to his voice. "Don't talk about losing your father. This isn't over yet."

I nodded, then headed into my father's bedroom, Poppy right behind me. Dad was sitting up in bed, a tray of uneaten food on his nightstand. I walked over and gave him a kiss. "How are you feeling?"

"Not too bad." He smiled weakly. "I managed to get some work done today."

I could see the dullness in his eyes, the feebleness of his posture, the slackness of his jaw. "Liar. You're feeling worse, aren't you?"

He hesitated a moment. "It hasn't been a good day."

"When will you find out if you're in the trial?"

"Dr. Haber called this afternoon. They turned me down."

I couldn't help it. The tears started rolling down my cheeks, even though I wanted desperately to hold it together for Dad.

"Come here, sweetie," Dad said, as he patted a spot on the bed.

I sat down, and he took my hand in his. "You are my beautiful daughter, and I don't want to leave you." He looked over at Poppy, standing at the foot of the bed. "I don't want to leave you, either, Dad. I will fight this as hard as I can, and I will do everything Dr. Haber tells me to do. But . . . I also want to accept with grace what I have no control over. And it would give me great comfort if I knew that you both were able to do that as well."

I wiped away my tears with the back of my hand, then leaned down on the bed and lay my head on Dad's chest. I wished that I could grant my father his wish, that I could accept the inevitable, not rail against it. I just had too much fury roiling inside me. Anger that my mother had died when I was so young. Anger that I might lose my father too soon. Anger that Ben, the one person I needed to lean on as I went through this, was cheating on me.

Despite my grandfather's presence, I felt alone. There was no best friend that I could talk to about Ben. He had been my best friend since we'd met, our second year of college. Sure, there were women—men, too—I was friendly with, but none with whom I'd share intimate secrets. I'd grown up an only child, so my parents had filled my afternoons with ballet and horse-riding lessons, with gymnastics and soccer, with museum visits and theater performances. I'd spend a few years at an activity and then grow bored and be on to something else. I spent two years studying fencing and two more convinced I was meant to be a figure skater. The one constant over the years was art. I'd always loved drawing. It was a busy childhood, but one that didn't lead to any close friendships.

School was the place I should have found my one true best friend, but I never did. I tended to be shy and didn't reach out to others. I wasn't excluded. I was pretty and came from money and wasn't awkward, so I was invited to after-school playdates and parties when I got older, but I was the hanger-on, not the main attraction.

From the age of five, I knew I was adopted. "Chosen," my parents told me. The word was supposed to make me feel special, to take the sting away from the knowledge that, in order to be chosen, I had to first be given away. My parents loved me fiercely; I never doubted that. Yet, I grew up with the painful awareness that first, before I was loved, I was rejected. I suspect that's why I'd always held back from forming close attachments with schoolmates. Part of me feared I'd be turned away again if someone got to know the true me—the unlovable me. The first time I ever truly opened myself up was with Ben. And that fear, the one that had dogged me since I was five, was now realized. My husband was rejecting me.

CHAPTER 32

A day away from the office, and I'm thrilled. I need the fresh air to clear my head of the nightmare scenarios that keep swirling around. I'm headed out to Greenport, along with Phil, who was driving the company van, to visit one of my artists. Phil did all the physical work at the gallery—hanging paintings, moving them around in the racks kept in the back, retouching paint on the walls when needed. He was only twenty but had a good eye for art, and often accompanied me on visits to my artists.

I'd first spotted Conrad Jefferson at a Manhattan art show eleven months ago that showcased emerging talent. At the time, he'd been represented by a small uptown art gallery but had yet to make a sale. Conrad was different from the usual artist. Most were young, usually under thirty, hungry for recognition from art connoisseurs. Conrad had spent a career as a plaintiff's personal-injury attorney, regularly clearing between $200,000 and $300,000 each year. When, at forty-two, he hit his first big payday, pocketing almost $1 million after taxes, he bought a lovely old farmhouse on the north fork of eastern Long Island, with views of the bay. He hadn't wanted the fussy wealth of the Hamptons for his children. When the weather was fine, he took his family from their Great Neck home out to Greenport for long weekends.

At fifty-four, he took on a class-action lawsuit and ended up collecting a $9 million fee. With his children already grown and living on their own, he decided it was time to retire and pursue his passion—painting. He added a studio onto the Greenport house, sold his family home, and moved with his wife to this former little fishing village.

When'd I first met Conrad, I told him he had a lot of raw talent, but he wasn't yet where he could be. I told him I'd consider taking him on in a year if his work evolved. It had, and I'd signed him up for my gallery. He was now ready to be included in a group show I was planning, showcasing new talent. Phil and I were here to choose which paintings to include.

Phil pulled into Conrad's driveway, and we walked up to the front door. When my knock was answered, my mouth dropped open. The man in the doorway held out his hand. "Hi, I'm—"

"Ezra Jefferson!" I couldn't believe the hottest new contemporary artist in the last five years was standing in front of me. "Are you related to Conrad?"

Just then, Conrad entered the foyer. "Charly. Phil. Glad you're here. I see you've met my son." Son? Of course, I'd fleetingly wondered if they were related, but since Conrad never mentioned Ezra, and Jefferson was a common surname, I'd just assumed they weren't. They certainly didn't look alike. Although they were both around six feet tall, Conrad was built more broadly, with a soft body. His face was round with thin lips and narrow eyes. Ezra was all sinewy muscle, with large, soulful eyes and full lips. The one feature they shared was softly curled honey-blond hair.

I shook Conrad's hand. "Why didn't you ever tell me Ezra was your son?"

He grinned sheepishly. "You know how kids of famous parents always want to make it on their own? Well, it's the reverse with us. My first gallery took me on because of Ezra and then let me languish. I wanted someone who believed in me."

Conrad led me into his studio, Phil and Ezra following close behind. As we looked over his paintings and debated which ones to take for the exhibit, I kept thinking what a coup it would be to land

Ezra Jefferson for my gallery. It wouldn't be easy. I knew he was represented by one of the top galleries in Manhattan. Still, I'd stolen away other artists before. And I welcomed the challenge. It might take my mind off my father . . . and Ben.

Two days later, I met Ezra for lunch at the Red Cat, on Tenth Avenue. After we gave the waiter our orders, I asked, "How long have you been with the Simon Sloane gallery?"

"Six years. I've never been anywhere else."

"Are you happy there?"

"They've been good to me."

"How good? What's your split with them?"

"The usual. Fifty-fifty."

"I could do better than that."

He laughed. "You're trying to poach me. I'd hoped maybe you were interested in me on a more personal level."

I held out my left hand. "Married." Then added, "For now."

Ezra was easy to talk to. I didn't expect him to abandon his gallery on the first lunch. It always took wooing. And I had to admit, I looked forward to seeing him for as long as it took.

I'm ecstatic! Dad got into a trial program. He kept telling me that it doesn't mean the trial will work, that it could make it worse, but at least now, there's something to hold on to. I needed this. I've been working myself ragged each day getting ready for tonight's opening of the new exhibition, and then spending each night by Dad's bedside. My grandfather has been a godsend. Even though Tatiana, Dad's longtime live-in housekeeper, is there to prepare his meals and help him out, she's not family. Poppy talks to me three or four times each day, keeping me apprised of what's going on, until I'm finally with them.

"Fifteen-minute warning," Sandy said as she popped into my office.

"Thanks." Tonight's guests would start arriving soon. I went into the bathroom and changed into a black Zac Posen sheath dress, with short sleeves and cutouts in both the front and back. Next, I slipped on a pair of black suede Louis Vuitton low boots, embellished with silver-and-pink baubles. I love shoes. I have ever since I was a child. My closet at home contained at least eighty pairs of every type of footwear. Ben often made fun of me, but I didn't care. It was my one concession to being wealthy. I mean, I admit I spent lavish amounts of money on clothes. Being fashionably dressed was important in the art world. So, I had my Céline bags and designer dresses, but the only thing I bought excessively was shoes.

Tonight, I was displaying the work of three artists: Conrad Jefferson; Emily Wilson, a young phenom from LA; and Baruti Nkosi, a South African artist I'd discovered in London. Each was a contemporary painter with a unique style. Nkosi wasn't able to attend, but the other two artists were expected to arrive at any moment.

I'd just finished refreshing my makeup when my two artists arrived, followed soon after by the first of my invited clients. I expected there would be many walk-ins to the show, but it was my clients who would receive the focus of my attention. The gallery had become successful in less than three years because I'd tapped every connection my father and I had, and I'd developed a roster of wealthy art collectors who relied on my advice. I'd sent invitations to almost one hundred people and hoped that at least one-third of them would show up. The one person I knew wouldn't be here was Ben. He'd come to my first two shows, then begged off after that, complaining that he just didn't fit in. At first, I was hurt, but now, Ben was the last person I wanted here.

An hour after the doors opened, I'd already exceeded my expectations. Sandy had made sure the wine was flowing, more than sixty patrons filled the space, and "sold" red dots had been placed on more than half of the paintings. I was feeling giddy with success. I'd been circulating among the guests all evening, but now I made my way over to Ezra, who had arrived earlier with his father.

"Pleased?" I asked Conrad.

"Very."

I turned to Ezra. "I could do this for you, too."

He smiled, a radiant smile that made his deep brown eyes shine, and dimples appear in his cheeks. "I know you could. But I'm happy where I am."

"Sometimes change is good."

"I need more convincing. Maybe over dinner?"

I hesitated only a moment. It would mean staying away from my father's bedside another evening. I knew he wouldn't mind, but that wasn't what held me back. I couldn't deny the heat I felt standing next to Ezra. Part of me wanted to act on that attraction, to get back at Ben for betraying me. Part of me knew that would be wrong.

"Whenever you want," I answered. "Just name the night."

CHAPTER 33

I'm finding it hard to control my anger toward Ben. Once the private investigator I'd hired had handed me the evidence of Ben's affair, I'd told him I'd no longer require his services. I had no need for proof that he continued to see Lisa. It was obvious, each night when I returned from my father's apartment, that he'd been with her. He pretended that he'd been home all night, watching television, but I saw the self-satisfied look on his face. I wanted to scream at him, to slap his face as hard as I could, to throttle him as I asked how he could have done this to us. I wanted to take the Glock 19 that I kept in my desk at the gallery and shoot that smile off his face, then gloat as I stood over his dying body. Instead, I came into our townhouse each night, feigned exhaustion, then headed to our bedroom. If I wasn't already asleep when Ben turned in for the night, I pretended to be.

The only thing that's gotten me through these weeks has been Ezra. I've met him four times for dinner. So far, it's just been playful flirting, although I know he'd be amenable to more.

Tonight is Thanksgiving. Ben and I always spent it volunteering at a soup kitchen. This year, I asked Ben to join me at my father's apartment instead, where Tatiana was preparing a traditional dinner. He demurred. Said he'd be more useful serving the homeless. Frankly, I was relieved.

I arrived at Dad's apartment with two pies I'd baked myself, one apple and one pecan, and a bowl of turkey stuffing, also made by me with a recipe I'd created. I didn't cook often—my gallery took most of my energy—but I enjoyed it when I could. Something about the aroma of food while it was cooking was terribly comforting.

I let myself in with my key and headed to the kitchen, where Tatiana was busy preparing our meal. I gave her my contributions, then joined Dad and Poppy in the living room. I gave them each a hug, then sat down on the couch next to Dad.

"How are you feeling today?" I was happy to see him out of the bedroom. Lately, he'd been so fatigued from the day that he'd retreated to his bed by the time I arrived from work. He was dressed in slacks and a long-sleeve shirt, open at the collar, but his face was still drained of color.

"A little better," he answered.

I didn't believe him. His hand was resting on his stomach, and every few seconds, he winced. He'd been on the new trial drug for several weeks now, but I hadn't noticed any improvement.

"Do you think you can eat tonight?"

"Sure. Especially your stuffing. Been looking forward to it all day."

"Where's that fool husband of yours?" Poppy asked. I never knew whether my grandfather disliked Ben only because Dad did, or whether he'd formed his own opinion of him. I explained that Ben was feeding homeless people tonight, then quickly changed the subject. Dad had little interest in art, and Poppy had even less, but we all enjoyed college football, so we talked about the day's games. Before I knew it, Tatiana rang the bell for dinner. She joined us at the table, and we began as we always had when I was a child, by stating what we were thankful for.

Poppy began. "I'm thankful that I don't have to go outside in this god-awful cold weather."

I laughed. We New Yorkers were grateful that we hadn't had real winter yet—the temperatures were still in the upper forties, dipping down to the midthirties at night.

"I'm thankful that I have a beautiful, loving daughter and a father who still knows how to comfort me," Dad said.

I started to speak, then the words choked in my mouth. It was obvious what I was most thankful for—that my father was still alive, still with me. I stopped and took a breath. "I'm thankful for my family, that I have a family. Nothing is more important." I'd learned long ago that it wasn't biology that made a family. It was unconditional love, and I'd always had that from my parents and grandparents. I'd hoped that I'd start my own family, with Ben and lots of children, but now I knew that would never happen. Any love I once had for him was gone. He was as dead to me as my mother.

My grandfather returned to Florida the Sunday following Thanksgiving, and I returned to my usual routine of daytimes at the gallery and evenings with Dad. A week later, I got the news: Dad's trial wasn't working. Instead of reducing the tumor, it had spread even more. His doctors were taking him off the drug. "Probably two months left, the most three. That's all," his doctor had told me.

As soon as I hung up the phone, I went to my office in the back of the gallery and bawled. Sandy had seen my face when I was on the phone and knew to leave me alone. I cried deep, heaving sobs, my head buried in my hands. After five minutes, the tears began to dwindle.

I would soon be an orphan. I had my grandfather, and I had one aunt and uncle and two cousins, but they weren't enough. No one took the place of a parent. I had mourned for a whole year after my mother died, coming straight home from school, cutting out all friends and activities, hibernating in my room, until finally, on the one-year anniversary of her death, my father said, "That's enough," and forced me back into living. But during that entire year, I knew I still had my father. I knew that I had someone who loved me more than anything else in the world.

A few years after my mother died, when I was twelve, I thought about searching for my birth mother. Dad had said he'd help me, if that's what I really wanted, then cautioned me that sometimes the fantasy was better to hold on to than finding out the reality was much different from I'd hoped. I thought about it for days, then weeks. Finally, after three months of weighing it, I decided against searching her out. If I found her, and she rejected me, it would hurt too much. It would feel like losing my mother all over again.

Now, facing the loss of my father, I thought about it again. *Maybe. Maybe after Dad's gone. Not right away. Down the road. Maybe I'll find her, and she'll be happy to see me. Maybe then I won't be alone.*

I've done it. I had dinner with Ezra last night, and afterward, still feeling the buzz from three glasses of wine, we went back to his loft and made love. So now, I'm an adulterer, too. Except I felt I deserved this. If Ben hadn't been unfaithful, I never would have considered cheating on him. I returned home from Ezra's bed, and as usual, Ben was plopped in front of the TV, feigning the boredom of someone who'd been in the same spot all night. He asked his usual, "How's Rick?" question. I answered my usual, "The same," and then I headed to our bedroom alone, as usual.

Now, back at the gallery, I picked up the phone to call my attorney. When Steve Goldfarb got on the line, I asked, "Can you pull up a copy of my prenuptial agreement?"

"Sure. Hold on a sec." Thirty seconds later, he said, "Got it. Now, what's going on? You and Ben having problems?"

"To say the least."

"Listen, Charlotte, you're under a lot of stress with what your father's going through. That has to affect your other relationships. Step back from whatever you're thinking, and wait until things settle down."

"Our conversation is covered by attorney-client privilege, right?"

"Of course."

"Good. I don't want my father or grandfather to know about Ben. He's having an affair. Has been for months, maybe longer. Since before Dad's diagnosis."

I heard an intake of breath on the other end. "I'm sorry, Charlotte. You have too much on your plate to have to worry about this, too. But my advice stands. Wait until things settle with your father, and then try to work things out with Ben. Maybe marriage counseling."

"I'm not doing anything now. Dad's not going to survive; his doctors were clear on that. When he passes away, I want Ben out. I just need to make sure what our prenup says."

"Ben gets one million dollars for each year of your marriage, up to a maximum of ten million. But if you have proof of his affair, he gets nothing."

"What if I have an affair?"

"Are you?"

"Just hypothetical."

"Then you don't get any of Ben's assets."

Ha! Ben had no assets. Just the piddling amount he'd been able to save from his earnings. I smiled. I wanted Ben to walk away without anything: no money, no job, no future. I wanted Ben to hurt.

CHAPTER 34

The weeks leading up to Christmas were always busy for me. Once the holiday was over, I always took the rest of the week off. Usually, Ben and I took that week to soak up the sun on some Caribbean island, but this year, I wouldn't leave Dad. By now, we were barely talking, anyway. Today was my first day back at the gallery after New Year's, and I had a lot of paperwork to catch up on—most pressingly, getting the tax records in order for the gallery's estimated tax payment, due in less than two weeks. Just before noon, Sandy told me a prospective client was on the line. "Can you take it? I need to get through these figures."

"She's insisting on speaking to you."

Reluctantly, I picked up the phone. "This is Charlotte Gordon. How can I help you?"

"Charly, it's Mallory. Mallory Holcolm."

"How can I help you?"

"It's . . . it's . . . your . . . Wait—didn't Ben tell you about me?"

My back immediately tensed. Ben's lover was named Lisa, but maybe he had more than one. Maybe he was seeing several women.

"No," I answered coolly. "My husband has never mentioned your name."

There was a hesitation on the line, and then she said, "It's urgent that I meet with you."

I opened up my scheduling book. "I could see you tomorrow afternoon. How does three o'clock work?"

"No. I know this is going to sound strange, but I have to see you today. Now. But not at the gallery."

"Ms. Holcolm, I'm sorry, I can't get away today at all, but I'm very interested in working with you on your art needs. If it must be today, then my assistant is very talented, and she'd be happy to come to your place."

"Charly, please."

Suddenly, her voice sounded different, familiar, as though before she'd been playing with an accent. "Have we met before?"

"I'm at the West Bank Cafe, on West Forty-Second. I have a table in the back, on the left side. You can walk here in fifteen minutes. I have on a black suede hat with a wide brim and sunglasses. Whatever you do, don't tell Ben."

I could feel myself start to get angry. "Look, I don't care for all this cloak-and-dagger. If you have something to say to me, then just say it."

"I'm not trying to alarm you," the woman said. "But your life truly depends on meeting me. I'll see you in fifteen minutes." And then the line went dead.

What was that nonsense about my life? It *was* nonsense, of that I was certain. Out of curiosity, though, I did a computer search of the name Mallory Holcolm and came up with nothing. *Just some crackpot.* I picked up my pencil and got back to work, but after five minutes, I realized I couldn't concentrate. *What the hell,* I thought as I grabbed my coat. If nothing else, it would be a funny story to tell Dad tonight.

It was freezing outside. When I'd left for work this morning, I hadn't expected to be traipsing outside in my high-heeled shoes and barely warm wool coat. I'd taken a taxi to the gallery, as I usually did in the winter, and planned to take one to Dad's when I closed up. Instead, I was pushing past the throngs of pedestrians, holding the collar of my coat up to my neck in an effort to block the wind. I would have taken a cab to the restaurant, but finding one along Tenth Avenue wasn't easy this time of day, and by the time I spotted one with a vacancy, I was only two blocks away from my destination.

When I stepped inside the café, the young woman behind the register said, "Just one?"

"No. I'm meeting someone already here."

She nodded for me to go on in, and I headed toward the rear. I spotted a woman in a black hat sitting in the corner and walked over. "I'm here," I said as I sat down.

She looked at me silently, reached up, and took off her hat, then the sunglasses that covered half her face. I took one look at her and burst out crying. She leaned over and touched my hand.

"It's okay. I know how you feel."

"You're my sister," I said through my sobs, not as a question. It was obvious.

"I'm your twin. Your identical twin. You didn't know anything about me, did you?"

"No." I cried even harder. She stood up and came over to me, then hugged me tightly. When I finally calmed down, I asked, "How? How did you find me?"

Mallory sat back down in her chair. "Your college friend, Matt Findly. He came into the restaurant I worked in and thought I was you. He told me about your gallery."

"Did you go there?"

"Not inside. But I glimpsed you through the window. I saw how much you looked like me."

"But why didn't you come inside? Why are we meeting here?"

"That was a few months ago. Something happened in between. Something I'm ashamed to tell you."

"What?"

Mallory dropped her head to her chest and shook her head. "I can't tell you in here. When we leave." She looked back up at me. "Are you hungry? Do you want to order lunch? I'm famished."

I couldn't believe she was thinking about food. I felt like a cataclysmic bomb had exploded right in front of me, completely changing the landscape of my world. I sat there mute and watched as Mallory motioned for a waiter. When he came over, she said, "I'll have the Cobb salad, hold the onions."

I began to laugh. She looked at me quizzically. "That's exactly what I'm having. I hold the onions, too."

"Anything to drink?" the waiter asked. As if on cue, we both said at the exact same moment, "Iced tea, with a slice of lemon."

I sat back in my seat. "I guess it's true what they say about twins. Genetics rule." I hesitated. "But I never had a feeling that someone was missing, that part of me was gone."

"I never did, either."

I couldn't keep myself from staring at her—at my sister. Of course, there were superficial differences: her hair was longer, without any real shape to it, and darker. That's because I lightened mine, and she obviously didn't. Her nails were short and unpolished, and I weighed a few pounds less, but not by much. I was clothed in a designer dress, and she wore jeans and a sweater. I suspected my adoption had been to parents wealthier than hers.

"There's so much I want to know about you," I said. "What are your parents like?"

"I didn't have a father."

I'd wondered why my parents hadn't adopted us both. They'd certainly had enough money to raise two children comfortably. Maybe this was the answer. "I suppose you were adopted first, and because she was single, your mother could only afford to take one of us."

"I'm not adopted. Our mother gave you away and kept me."

My mouth dropped open, and I began rubbing my arm, unthinkingly repeating the motion my adopted mother made when she tried to calm me. Mallory knew my birth mother, the woman I'd thought about so many times over the years, always pushing away the possibility of searching for her. This woman sitting across from me—my sister—held the answers to my questions. My heart raced, and I began to feel lightheaded. "Tell me," I said. "Tell me about her."

"She raised me alone. Our father died in the Gulf War when she was pregnant with us. She was just seventeen at the time, and her own mother insisted she give the baby up for adoption. When Mom refused—"

"Wait. What's her name?"

"Sasha. Sasha Holcolm. Mom wouldn't hear of it, so her mother threw her out. She thought that would bring her to her senses, but it didn't. She moved away and got a job. She didn't know she was having twins until she gave birth. She knew it would be difficult raising a child on her own, at her age, with no skills. Raising two would be impossible."

I kept taking deep breaths, trying to collect myself. All around us, people sat at tables, eating their food, glancing down at their smartphones, oblivious to the earthquake that was occurring at my table. Because that's what it felt like—a wide opening in the ground, shaking my body. Yet, I knew that when the rumbling stopped, I could look inside the dark hole and uncover the mystery of my life.

"We were always poor," Mallory continued. "Mom cleaned houses six days a week. She didn't have very much time for me."

I reached over and took my sister's hand. "I'm sorry. It was very different for me."

"I know."

I pulled my hand back. "How?"

"I know everything about you, but I don't want to talk about that here. When we go outside."

It was maddening, her dangling this mystery, the one that started with her phone call to the gallery. "Then let's get the check and go," I said, even though our salads were only half-finished.

"Not yet. I'm still eating."

I sighed deeply. Mallory clearly had a schedule, and I was just going to have to go along with it. "So, who's older? You or me?"

"I am, by two minutes."

"I suppose that's why you're being so bossy," I said, smiling.

"It's why our mother chose me to keep. Because I was first."

"Does our mother know you've found me?"

She shook her head. "Mom died three years ago."

I began to cry again. I didn't know why. I'd never met my birth mother, had never tried to find her. Yet, for a moment, she had become real. And just as quickly, she was gone.

Mallory reached into her purse and handed me a tissue. "She would have liked to find you, I think. There were times she looked at me with a strange expression on her face, and I suspect she was wondering about you then. I think she always regretted giving you up."

I wiped the tears from my cheeks. "Do you have a picture of her?"

Mallory nodded, then once again opened her purse and pulled out an envelope and placed it in front of me. "I have a few pictures of her on my cell phone, but by the time I got one, she was already very sick and didn't look like herself."

I picked up the envelope and pulled out two pictures. The first was of a young woman, holding a baby in her arms. She had chestnut-brown hair, delicate features, and a bright smile. I thought she was beautiful. "This is her, holding you?" I asked.

Mallory nodded.

In the second picture, she looked ten years older, although the child by her side—Mallory, looking just as I did at that age—was holding a birthday cake with a large number-five candle in the center. Her eyes had puffy circles underneath, and her smile had dimmed. I was glad Mallory hadn't brought any later pictures. "I don't think we look like her, do you?"

Once again, Mallory pulled an envelope from her purse. This time, she took out a picture and handed it to me. There was my birth mother, looking longingly up at a soldier, dressed in his army uniform. He had blond hair and the same large, blue eyes we did. "Our father?"

"I think we look like him, don't you?"

I had to agree. "Are your—our—grandparents alive?" I asked.

"Our maternal grandfather walked out on our grandmother when Mom was only one. And Mom never saw her own mother after she was thrown out. I was told recently that she's dead."

"And our father's parents?"

She shrugged. "I don't know anything about them. Not even their names."

We finished our salads, and as we waited for the check, I said, "I don't know anything about you. Where do you live? What do you do? Do you enjoy art?" I could have kept asking questions, but I stopped to give her a chance to speak.

"I've loved drawing since I could first hold a crayon in my hand."

"Me, too."

"I was studying at the Manhattan Institute of Art and supported myself by waitressing."

"Was? What about now?"

"When we're outside."

I leaned back in my chair. "I loved drawing, too, and I thought I was very good at it. But by the time I left for college, my mother encouraged me to major in something more practical. She didn't think I was good enough to make it into a museum, and in our family, you didn't do something unless you could excel at it. So, I run the gallery and try to discover talent better than me."

Mallory smiled. "I guess that's one thing Mom gave me—confidence. She always praised my drawings, and encouraged me to follow my dream."

The waiter came over with our check, and I grabbed it to pay for us both, but Mallory threw down two twenties. "My treat."

I wasn't going to argue. I just wanted to get outside and hear the rest of her story. We left the restaurant and began walking.

CHAPTER 35

Mallory didn't say anything as we walked, so after a few minutes, I broke the silence. Although we were surrounded by people, we were invisible to them as they scurried past us. "You said you know everything about me. What, exactly?"

She turned to look at me. "I know you have five hundred thirty-eight friends and family on Facebook. I know you have more than five thousand Twitter followers and a little less on Instagram."

"Anyone could know that."

"I know your closest friend is Janine Wilson, and you met at college."

"Matt must have told you that."

"I know your best friend from first grade through high school was Heidi Preston, but you grew apart when she went to college at Stanford, although you still send each other birthday cards every year. Out of nostalgia, she asked you to be a bridesmaid at her wedding two years ago. You had to decline because you were attending an important art show in Munich."

I didn't understand how she knew this, and I felt myself take a step away from her.

"I know your favorite cousin is Eddie Engle, even though his sister, Justine, is closer in age to you. I know that your favorite movie is *When Harry Met Sally* . . . and that you're afraid to watch horror movies. I know your favorite teacher was Mrs. Reading in the third grade, and you had a crush on Billy Ceszek in the seventh grade. I know your favorite vegetable is spinach, preferably sautéed, and your favorite ice cream flavor is black raspberry." She stopped to take a breath. "Both are my favorites, too, by the way. And I know you put ketchup on French toast." She smiled. "You're on your own with that one."

I stopped walking. Mallory took a few steps before she realized I wasn't next to her, then backtracked to me. "I don't understand," I said.

"You asked me why I didn't come into the gallery when I saw you through the window. It was because I was afraid. I didn't understand what I was seeing. So, I ran away. It took me a week to work up the courage to go back, and when I did, the gallery was closed. It was the night you'd learned about your father's diagnosis."

"Three months ago."

"Yes." She motioned for me to start walking again, and I did. "I looked up your home address and went there. Ben let me in."

"My husband? Ben knows about you?"

"As soon as he saw me standing in the doorway, he knew we were sisters. He asked me to wait to contact you because your father's illness was causing you so much stress, and I agreed. In the meantime, I tracked down a longtime friend of my mother's and learned the truth about us."

"But three months? Ben asked you to wait this long?"

"No. After a few weeks, Ben said that he'd told you about me. He said you didn't want to see me. You were afraid I was going to hit you up for money."

"That's ridiculous. Of course I'd want to meet you. My God, I never dreamed I had a sister, a real blood sister."

"Ben told me other things about you. Nasty things. Then he asked something of me."

I looked over at her, but she wouldn't meet my eyes. She mouthed some words, so low that I couldn't hear them. I asked her to repeat what she'd said. She leaned into me and whispered in my ear, "Ben has arranged for someone to kill you. He asked me to step in and pretend to be you so no one would know you were missing."

I pulled back sharply and stared at her incredulously. It was still freezing outside, but I no longer felt the cold. Instead, I felt my body flush with a heated fury and, at the same time, felt like a rope around my neck was cutting off my air. "You agreed!" I spit out. She didn't need to answer. I could see from the expression on her face that she had. I spun around and began walking away as quickly as I could in three-inch heels.

Moments later, I felt a pull on my arm. Mallory had run after me.

"Don't be foolish. What are you going to do? Run to the police? Ben will deny everything. He'll probably even deny that you have a sister. 'Must be the stress you're under,' he'll tell them. And he'll find another way to do it. At the beginning, he said he'd only do it if I agreed to step in. But I don't believe him. He's too invested in it. And he wants to be with his girlfriend. You have to be smart now."

I stared at Mallory with a venom I didn't know I could feel. I tried to pull away from her, but she wouldn't let go. "I hate you. You're not my sister. You're a monster. A monster." Finally, I wrenched myself free, but I couldn't run anymore. I sank down to the ground, leaned against the building, and dropped my head into my hands. My whole body felt numb. Mallory crouched down next to me.

"I don't blame you," she said. "What I agreed to was horrid. But I thought you had rejected me, without even meeting me once. Ben had convinced me that *you* were horrid. That you were cruel and demanding and spoiled. That you humiliated him at every opportunity. That you treated your friends the same way. If we did this together, I would get half of your money."

"So, you were doing it for the money. Is that supposed to make me excuse you?"

"We were identical twins. You were given up for adoption and lived a life of luxury. I was kept and had nothing."

"There's no amount of money that would make me agree to kill someone."

Mallory's face twisted into an ugly smirk. "Spoken by someone who never went without. Whose every need was met. Who never went hungry and was always loved. Yes, if that's how I'd grown up, I would find it very easy to say the same thing."

I wanted to lie down in the street and disappear. Just an hour ago, I'd been ecstatic to discover I had a sister. Not just a sister, but my identical twin. Now, that euphoria had been replaced with a sense of loss so profound that it was unbearable. I'd come to terms with the fact that I'd soon lose my father. Now, not only had I been betrayed by the woman who shared my genes, but my own husband wanted me dead.

I wasn't naive. I knew my marriage wouldn't last much beyond my father's funeral. But despite the anger I'd felt toward Ben these past few months, despite the fantasies I'd entertained from time to time of physically harming him, it still seemed unreal to me that Ben would actually hire someone to murder me. Yet, why would Mallory lie about this? "What made you change your mind?"

"Your lips are turning blue," Mallory said. She looked around. "There's a Starbucks across the street. Do you want to go inside and get warm?"

I nodded, and she stood, then held out a hand to help me up. We crossed the road, got on line, and ordered two Caffè Mistos, then grabbed a table in the corner.

After we were settled, Mallory leaned in to me and, speaking softly, said, "Ben had convinced me that you were a beastly person. And I tried not to feel so angry, but I couldn't stop. Angry that you didn't want to meet me. Angry that you had so much and I had so little. Angry that my mother never had time for me and your parents doted on you. But when I began studying you, so that I could fool people, I realized Ben was lying. The things you posted on Facebook, on Twitter, the things your friends posted about you—I could tell you weren't the cold, demanding witch he portrayed. You seemed warm and caring."

"You were following me for months. It took this long for you to realize Ben was lying?"

She cast her eyes downward and slowly shook her head. "It took me this long to realize that family was more important than money."

I didn't know what to think. I felt disgust for this woman sitting across from me. I didn't think I'd ever forgive her for conspiring with Ben. And yet, and yet . . . she was my blood.

I took another sip of my coffee. "We have to go to the police."

"I know."

"They may charge you with conspiracy to commit murder."

"Yes, they might." The people at the table closest to us stood up to leave, and Mallory waited until they'd gone. "I've thought a lot about what to do." She took her wallet from her purse, leafed through some cards until she found what she wanted, then pulled it out. "I know a policeman, well, sort of know him. I think we should call him, then go together to see him."

I nodded. I didn't care which policeman we went to, as long as he put a stop to this.

Thirty minutes later, we were sitting in an interrogation room in the Tenth Precinct of Manhattan, with Detective Kevin Saldinger. Mallory had met him in one of her art classes and thought he might be less likely to arrest her on the spot. The room smelled like a mixture of sweat and Pine-Sol. We had entered the white brick building on West Twentieth Street and been ushered right inside, after Mallory gave the desk officer her name.

"Thanks for seeing us so quickly," Mallory said.

"You made it sound urgent."

"It is."

Mallory told him everything she'd told me. It was almost as painful hearing it the second time as it had been the first. When she finished, Detective Saldinger scratched his head. "Here's the problem I see. I have you"—he pointed to Mallory—"confessing to a crime, with nothing concrete to tie it to your"—he pointed to me—"husband."

"How would I benefit from killing my sister? Ben would inherit everything, not me."

"I don't know. Maybe you have some sort of vendetta against her. Maybe, for some reason, you hate her husband and want to set him up for this."

"You can't just do nothing," I said. "I believe Mallory, and assuming she's telling the truth, I'm afraid to go home. I'm afraid of what Ben might do."

Mallory cut in. "Ben won't hurt you while your father is alive. He's afraid Rick will realize that I'm not you."

"I didn't say we wouldn't do anything," Saldinger said. "It's just . . . we're going to need more. Let's say Mallory is telling the truth. Your husband doesn't know she's turned, and so he's going along with a plan. That plan is to wait until after your father dies."

I didn't feel comforted. It had been difficult enough going home each evening to a man I knew was cheating on me. How could I carry off pretending I didn't know he wanted to kill me? Mallory must have seen the worry in my eyes, because she reached over and took my hand.

"I know you're strong enough to keep going, because I'm strong enough to keep playing along. And we're the same, you and me."

I felt the tears well up. I wanted my father to protect me, to keep me safe, but I couldn't tell him what I'd learned. His condition was too fragile. I needed to bear this knowledge alone. I squeezed my hands together, willing myself to hold back from crying. "What should I do?"

"For now, it's what Mallory should do. You need to string Ben along, pretend that nothing's changed. New York's a one-party consent state, so you can tape your conversations with him. Try to get him to talk about the plan. Do you know if he's already found someone to kill your sister?"

Mallory shook her head.

"That's key information. Try to get him to talk about it. If we get anything that corroborates your story, I'll apply for a warrant."

"What's going to happen to me?" Mallory asked. "Will I be arrested?"

"From what you've told me, you've violated New York Penal Law Section 105.15—conspiracy to commit an A Felony. You've planned a murder with another person, and you've taken overt acts toward that end. Studying your sister in order to become her is part of the plan. You can get up to twenty-five years for that."

The color drained from Mallory's face, and I could see her hands start to shake.

"However," the detective continued, "it helps that you've come forward this early, before a murder took place. If you work with us, help us get not only Ben but the guy he's paid to do this, I suspect the DA would be willing to consider probation. But you're going to end up with a record. That's just a fact."

I was glad. I wanted Mallory to pay *something* for what she'd agreed to do to me. "What should I do now?" I asked Saldinger.

He turned to me. "Just try to remain calm and act normally."

Easy for him to say, I thought as we left the police station.

CHAPTER 36

I wandered back to the gallery in a fog. I didn't know how I would return home tonight and not react to Ben. I didn't know how I'd keep from my father all I'd learned today. He'd always been able to tell when something was bothering me. For once, I hoped that his illness would dull his observation skills.

Sandy handed me a list of phone calls I'd missed while I was out, and I began to return them, forcing myself to speak with a welcoming lilt to my voice. When finished, I returned to the tax records, losing myself in the dull minutiae of the numbers. Just before 6:00 p.m., I finally finished. With my elbows on my desk, I dropped my head into my hands and wondered how I would get through the next few weeks. I wondered how my husband had come to hate me so much.

I was nineteen when I met Ben. I'd been studying in the library when he'd sat down opposite me. For forty minutes, he didn't say a word to me as he worked on his laptop. I kept eyeing him over the textbook I was reading, catching glimpses of his green eyes. His brown hair flopped over his forehead and stopped an inch past his ears, and I thought he looked like Adonis. Finally, after what seemed like an interminable wait, he said, "Want to get out of here and grab a drink?" No "Hello, what's your name?" No "What are you studying?" Just right to the point. I think I started to fall in love with him before we'd even left the library.

We went to a popular campus hangout, and we each showed our doctored IDs to order drinks—a beer for him and a Cosmopolitan for me. Three drinks later, I ended up back in the bedroom of his off-campus apartment, and we made love for the first time. After that, I never dated anyone else. It was always Ben. I never even looked at another man. Not until Ezra, and I wasn't sure if that hadn't started partly as payback for Ben's affair.

As graduation loomed, I thought I couldn't live without Ben. He wanted to go off to law school and wait until he was established in a law firm to get married. I couldn't bear the thought of that. I was ready for my life to start and unwilling to postpone it. "Why don't we get married now, and I'll follow you to law school?" I'd suggested.

"I can't afford to get married now," he'd answered. "I'm taking out student loans as it is to pay for school."

"I'll get a job and support you," I'd countered.

"I'll be studying day and night, and you'll resent working at a scut job and never seeing me," he'd replied.

And then, finally, I'd said it: "If you go to law school, then it means I'm less important to you than a job. I'm breaking up with you." He'd relented, after I'd sweetened the offer with a job at Dad's firm. Nine months after graduation, we were married at the Pierre Hotel at the south end of Central Park, with four hundred guests in attendance.

Ben had seemed happy. I knew that part of him thought about what his life would have been like if he'd gone to law school, but I know that he started out enjoying his work, and especially his six-figure beginning salary. Ben hadn't grown up with money. When we married, he was thrown into a world of expensive cars and clothes and any toys that grown men wanted. Of traveling wherever his whim took him. I know he liked those things. Why did it change? How did our relationship become so toxic that he wanted to kill me? If he'd fallen out of love, why didn't he just ask for a divorce?

I knew the answer. I'd introduced him to the world of wealth, and he didn't want to give it up. Dad had insisted on the prenuptial agreement, and I'd gone along just to please my father, even though I'd thought we'd never divorce. Now, the marriage was shattered beyond repair. I just had to make sure I survived the wreckage.

"You're awfully quiet tonight," Dad said. "Something bothering you?"

I broke out of my trance. I should have been thinking about Ben, about how to deal with living in the same house with him, but instead, I kept thinking about Mallory Holcolm. "No, nothing. Just thinking about the gallery's taxes. I was working on that all day today."

Somehow, it felt more shocking to me that I had a sister, a twin sister, than that my husband wanted me dead. I'd known our marriage was in trouble for almost a year. I'd known he'd been addicted to money much longer than that. So, as disturbing as his plan was, it wasn't a shock.

But a sister! I so wanted to despise her; yet, I wanted to know her, too. I wanted to know more about her life, about our mother, about the ways we were similar and the ways we diverged. I wanted her to be my confidante and me hers. I'd known since a young age I was adopted, and it hadn't bothered me, but now, for the first time, I had a blood relative. I wanted desperately to be close to her; yet, at the same time, my thoughts kept reverting to her alliance with Ben. Still, blood had won out with her. In the end, she'd come to me. She'd walked away from his scheme and into my life. Now, I had to decide whether to let her in.

My father groaned, and I stood up to get his next dose of medicine. When I returned with it and a glass of water, he said, "You know, you don't have to be here every night. Tatiana is perfectly capable of bringing me medicine. Stay home with Ben some nights."

"When you're better, I'll stay home with Ben. In the meantime, I'd rather be with you."

"Nonsense. You've always felt a sense of duty. I'm letting you off the hook. If you insist on seeing me every night, come for a half hour, then go home."

"Daddy, I promise you," I said, telling him the absolute truth, "this is exactly where I want to be."

I walked in the door of my townhouse at my usual time—a little after 10:00 p.m. Ben was where he always was—sitting in the den watching television. Usually, it was some sporting event, but tonight it was a political show. From the time I'd met Ben, he'd told me he wanted to go into elective office. Law school was the path he'd seen for that. Part of the reason I had been able to convince him to work for Dad was because of the connections he'd make with wealthy individuals, people who could later back his candidacy when he was ready. Once he'd settled into his new life, the reality of a politician's salary took hold, and he'd never expressed interest in that career again. Still, once in a while, when there were no sports to watch, he'd turn on a political talk show.

"Hi," he called out to me when he heard the front door open, then shut. I managed a mangled "Hi" back, then hurried into the bedroom. I couldn't face him—not yet. I undressed and stepped into the shower, making it as hot as I could stand. A few minutes later, Ben stepped into the bathroom. "You okay?"

"Sure," I answered. "I just felt grimy."

"Any change with your father?"

"He's the same. Listen, I'm beat. I'm going straight to bed when I finish in here."

"Well, nothing new there," he muttered as he left the room.

"Fuck you, fuck you. Fuck you!" I wanted to scream. Instead, I said nothing.

CHAPTER 37

I didn't hear from Mallory for ten days. During that time, Dad's condition worsened. I'd called in hospice, and we all knew it was just a matter of weeks now. Thoughts of my father had filled my head during this period, enabling me to distance myself from ruminating about my sister and my murderous husband. Seeing Ezra had helped, also. I wanted to tell him about Mallory, about Ben, about their plot against me, but I didn't.

Mallory called me at the gallery. "Are you okay?"

"Just super. I have a sister I didn't know about, a husband who wants to kill me, and a father who's dying. Why wouldn't I be okay?"

There was a beat of silence, and then, "I just got off the phone with Detective Saldinger. I've set it up for Ben to take me to meet the man he hired. To . . . you know."

"To kill me, you mean?"

"Yeah, that. Saldinger and his partner are going to stake out the place. If the hit man leaves after us, he'll grab him at the meet site, before he gets to his car. If not, then he'll follow the guy home. And I'm going to wear a wire."

I wished I could say that my chest lightened, but it was too filled with despair over my father for this news to make a dent. "When's it happening?"

"In two nights."

I couldn't help myself. She was still my sister. Before hanging up, I said, "Be careful."

Three days later, I got a call from Detective Saldinger. "Can you come into the station? I need to go over some things with you."

"I'm working with a customer now. It'll probably be an hour or two."

"Come as soon as you can," he said.

I hadn't heard from Mallory since her meeting with the hired gun last night, and so I had no idea how it had gone. I'd hoped she would have called me right after it had finished, but I couldn't blame her for keeping a distance. I'd certainly been chilly to her when we'd last spoken. I tried to give my customer my full attention—she was one of my regulars and important to the gallery—but I confess that I probably rushed her more than I normally would have. As soon as she left, I grabbed my coat and told Sandy I was leaving.

New York had been going through a cold spell that seemed unending at this point. It had snowed last night, and although the roads had been plowed and the sidewalks shoveled, brown slush was everywhere. I was glad I'd worn boots to work, although once again, I hadn't planned to be walking anywhere today, and the thin heels and slippery walkways made for slow going. By the time I arrived at the police station, I was chilled through and through.

"Cup of coffee?" Saldinger asked once I was settled in the interview room.

"Love one, thanks. Just black."

He left the room, and five minutes later returned with two steaming cups in hand. He placed one before me, then sat down at the table. "Did Mallory tell you where she was last night?"

"She told me a few days ago she would be meeting with the man Ben hired, but I haven't heard from her since. Did you catch him?"

"Afraid not. We had the place staked out, but he never came back to the street. After a few hours, we searched the building, but there was no trace of him. The only thing we know is that he's a former army sniper. We're trying to work with the army to see if they can point us to someone in the New York area who might fit Mallory's description of him." He opened up a folder and pulled out a picture of a man. "Actually, Mallory drew this for us. I don't suppose you recognize him?"

I shook my head. "So, does this mean you'll just arrest Ben?"

The detective gazed at me kindly. I hadn't really looked at him closely when I was here last, but now I saw his strong jawline, his aquiline nose, but most of all, his eyes. They seemed to say that everything would work out.

"We could. But we really want to get everyone who's involved." The detective leaned back in his chair and folded his arms. "Have you spoken much to your sister since you were here last?"

"No, just once, when she told me about the meeting."

"Mallory was wired, and we have a recording of the meeting. It's clear Ben paid someone to kill you and that Mallory was part of the plan. The hit man is supposed to provide Ben with a picture of your dead body when it's done. We have enough to arrest Ben and Mallory right now, but then we don't get the hit man. You're a one-off for Ben. Maybe not so with the guy he hired. If he's someone who does this for a living, we want to lock him away. Maybe Ben will give him up. Maybe not. We'd prefer not to leave it to chance."

I drew in a long breath. "You want me to keep pretending with Ben."

"I know it's asking a lot. I'll understand if you don't want to."

I could end it all right now. Let Detective Saldinger arrest both Ben and Mallory, and I could put to rest any lingering fear over what Ben might do to me.

"I don't know if this will make a difference to you," Saldinger continued, "but if we get the hit man, he might confirm that the murder was your husband's idea, and your sister just went along with it. Then, it increases the chance that the prosecutor makes a favorable deal with her."

"How would this work?"

"Ben will text the hit man with the day he wants it done. We know it won't be until your father's funeral is over. Mallory will make sure he tells her when it's supposed to be. We'll have someone staked out at your place, and as soon as he shows up, we'll grab him."

"And if he won't tell Mallory in advance?"

"Then we'll arrest him as soon as your father is buried."

I felt so confused. I needed someone to help me sort through this mess, but there was no one I could go to.

"Can I think about it?" I asked.

"Take a day. Two at the most."

As I walked back to the gallery, I realized there was only one person I could talk to. As soon as I got there, I went into my office, closed the door, and phoned my grandfather.

"Hi, Poppy."

"Pips? We just spoke this morning. Is there a change?"

"No, Dad's the same. I need advice from you."

"Sure. Ask away."

"When Mom and Dad adopted me, did you know anything about the birth mother?"

"Just the hospital where you were born. It was in Scranton. Are you trying to search for her?"

"No. It's just . . . I have a sister. An identical twin sister."

"What! Did she contact you? Is that how you know?" His voice was filled with excitement.

"She did. Two weeks ago."

"That's wonderful. Tell me about her."

I started to speak and then burst out crying instead. He tried to ask me what was wrong a few times until he finally gave up and let me cry myself out. When I finally regained control of myself, I told him the whole story. He was silent for a bit, then said, "Your sister, what's her name?"

"Mallory."

There was silence for a few beats. "I think you should give your sister a chance. Let the detective lock down her story. She's your family."

CHAPTER 38

After speaking to my grandfather, I felt like a weight had been lifted from my chest. I wasn't in this situation alone now. Although he was far away from me, in his Florida home, I still was comforted by him. I decided to call Mallory. I bombarded her with questions about our mother, about her life. When I asked about our father, Mallory knew almost nothing, other than his death during the Gulf War. "What about his parents?" I asked.

"Mom never talked about them."

"Aren't you curious?"

"I never thought about it. Mom was my whole world. There were no grandparents or aunts and uncles or cousins. It was just us."

"Wouldn't you like there to be more?"

"I learned from a very young age to not wish for things. It just led to disappointment."

"Let's try to find them," I said. "It could be a project we do together."

"I wouldn't even know where to start."

"I do. With your birth certificate. It must say your father's last name. And he probably grew up in Allentown, like our mother. Or at least nearby."

"I have a box of Mom's papers. It might be in there. I vaguely remember that when I applied for my learner's permit, Mom brought my birth certificate with us."

"Did you see our father's name?"

"I didn't even look at it. All I cared about then was being able to drive."

"Good. It'll be our project. I need something to keep my mind off my father—and Ben."

When I arrived at work the next morning, there was a message from Mallory. I quickly called her back.

"I found my birth certificate," she said. "Our father's name is John Harris."

"Ugh. I suspect that's a pretty common name. But if his parents are still in Allentown or nearby, we might be able to track them down."

"If they're alive."

"Right."

I'd wondered last night why I'd fixated on finding my biological grandparents and realized it was because I needed to focus on something positive. Even if they rejected us, they could tell us what our father was like. What kind of person he was. What his passions were. They could help fill in the blanks of who *we* were. Who I am.

I said goodbye to Mallory, then turned to my computer and did a search for anyone in or near Allentown with the last name Harris. I came up with more than two hundred names and phone numbers. I forwarded the list to Mallory and suggested she start at the bottom, making phone calls, and I'd start at the top. It gave me something to do, and for that I was glad. Ever since meeting Mallory, since learning of Ben's plans, I'd had difficulty concentrating. Fortunately, I didn't have any new shows planned for another month. I did have two artists, Marc Horowitz, a painter, and Sergei Kinsky, a sculptor, who'd been accepted for the Whitney Biennial, beginning in March. The museum featured the work of the best emerging contemporary artists every two years, and it was a great career boost to be selected. I expected it would bring new collectors to the gallery seeking to buy their work. I picked up the phone and began dialing.

Two hours later, with no success, I took a break and called Detective Saldinger. "Mallory told me that Ben's plan, after I'm dead, is to go with her to the attorney who drew up our prenuptial agreement and have it voided. When that's done, they'll wait for Dad's estate to be settled, divvy up the proceeds, and then she'll split. At least, that's Ben's timeline, according to Mallory."

"It won't get that far. We'll arrest him as soon as we grab the hit man."

Much as I wanted this to be over as quickly as possible, I also wanted to ensure that Ben would have no possibility of squirming out of a long prison sentence. I had friends who worked as criminal defense attorneys, and I'd seen them spin straw into gold. "Would it be a stronger case, or a longer sentence, if you could prove he was doing this to rob me of billions?"

"Are you serious—billions?"

"My father is very wealthy."

"We have a solid case against your husband right now. However, being able to demonstrate that the reason he didn't just ask for a divorce, that his goal was to get his hands on a massive amount of money, can certainly make our case bulletproof. But, Charly, that's going to stretch this out for you a long time. You'd need to disappear until your father's estate is settled. Probating a will in New York can take six months. Even longer when there are a lot of assets."

"No. All his assets are in a trust. Other than some charitable bequests, I'm pretty sure it goes to me immediately upon his death. I just need to make sure Ben knows that."

"If you're certain you can deal with this taking longer, then that's what we'll do. But anytime it becomes too much for you, call me. We can always go back to the original plan."

"Thank you, Detective Saldinger. I think I'll be okay. Having a sister, being able to talk to her, has made me stronger."

"Just be careful," the detective said, his voice low. "The odds are that your sister is telling the truth. But it's also possible this was her plan all along, and after Ben's out of the picture, she'll bump you off herself, and keep everything. Then go on living as Charlotte Gordon."

My body slumped down in the chair. The warmth I'd begun to feel toward Mallory was now tied up in a Gordian knot. I didn't know what to think. I didn't want to think. I hung up with the detective, and began, once again, making rote phone calls to every Harris in Allentown, Pennsylvania. If I was going to lose my father, then lose my sister, I wanted as much family with me as I could find.

CHAPTER 39

The temperature was below freezing, but that didn't stop me from jogging outside. I belonged to a gym, and often went there when the weather was this cold, but I needed the brisk air to clear my head. I dressed in my running tights, then layered up, ending with a fleece jacket. I grabbed a wool hat, put on my gloves, and headed outside. Although it was cold, I knew once I began to jog, my body would warm up. I headed toward Central Park, then entered it at East Sixtieth Street. There was a five-and-a-half-mile route I followed, always in the company of myriad other joggers, bicyclists, and in-line skaters, all taking advantage of a respite from the city's fumes. By the time I approached the park, I was in a steady rhythm. When I reached that state, my body was on autopilot, and I usually could then work out any problems that worried me. Today it was my sister.

I didn't know what to make of Detective Saldinger's warning. I wanted so much to trust Mallory, to believe she'd come forward to stop Ben, but was I fooling myself? Forty minutes later, when I entered my townhouse at the end of my run, I still didn't know the answer.

I showered and changed for work, and arrived there an hour later. I'd barely taken my coat off when Mallory called.

"I found them," she said. "I found our grandparents."

"What did they say?" I could hear the lack of warmth in my voice. After Detective Saldinger's speculation about my sister's motives, I didn't know what to think. She was my identical twin, I kept telling myself. We shared the same DNA. Then, I reasoned, how could she even consider killing me now that we'd reconnected, now that she knew me? Before, I was just an abstract concept to her. But after spending months studying me, she had to know how much alike we were. Since I couldn't conceive of such a betrayal myself, then certainly she couldn't. Then, I would remind myself that by her own admission, she'd agreed to participate in a murder, in my murder. If she could do that, wasn't she capable of anything? I didn't know the answer. I only knew I had to protect myself.

"They didn't say anything. I panicked."

"What do you mean?

"It was a woman who answered. I asked if she had a son named John who was killed in the Gulf War, and when she said, 'Yes,' I hung up."

I burst out laughing. "Those poor people. What must they be thinking?"

"I thought maybe you could call them, explain who we are?"

"Give me their number."

I wrote it down, then quickly got off the phone. There was another call I needed to make that had more urgency. I dialed the number for my attorney, Steve Goldfarb, and made an appointment to see him that afternoon. Then I called Gertrude Harris, the woman Mallory had hung up on. She answered on the third ring.

"Mrs. Harris?"

"Yes?"

"I spoke to you earlier, and we were disconnected. It was a problem with my phone. I'm sorry."

"How can I help you, dear?"

"You said your son, John, was killed in the Gulf War."

"That's right."

"Do you remember if, back before he enlisted, he was dating a woman named Sasha Holcolm?"

"Do you mean Susan Holcolm?"

Did I? I'd later ask Mallory if our mother had another name, but how many Holcolms dating a John Harris could there be? "Yes, that's who I mean."

"You're looking for the other John Harris. Our sons were friends. Ironic, isn't it, both boys with the same name and both died in that war?" I heard a deep sigh. "Such a tragedy."

"Do you know if the other boy's parents are still in the area?"

"No, they moved a long time ago. I don't even know where. We weren't friends with them. Just our children were friends."

"Do you happen to know their first names?"

She was quiet for a moment. "Maybe Eileen? Or Ellen? I think that may have been the mother. I don't know his father's name."

I pressed my hands to my forehead. This search was heading toward impossible. I thanked Mrs. Harris, then got back to work.

At 3:00 p.m., I arrived at the firm of Winslow and Goldfarb. Their office was in midtown, not far from the gallery, in a sleek high-rise on Park Avenue. I was ushered into Goldfarb's office as soon as I arrived. Before she left the room, his assistant offered me coffee or water, but I declined. I didn't expect to be there long.

"How's your father doing?" Goldfarb asked as soon as I sat down.

I shook my head. "He has hospice care now. It's going to be soon."

"I'm so sorry, Charlotte. How can I help you today?"

"It's about my prenup."

"Are you still thinking about divorce?"

If only it were that simple, I thought. I held out my right hand and pointed to my palm. "See this scar?"

I noted a look of confusion on Goldfarb's face as he picked up my hand and traced the scar with his finger, then nodded.

"This conversation is covered by attorney-client privilege, right?"

"Of course."

"You can't say anything to my father."

"Naturally."

"I have an identical twin sister."

I held back a laugh as Goldfarb's eyes bulged. "Her name is Mallory Holcolm, and she both looks and sounds exactly like me. But I got this scar when I was twelve years old."

"Why don't you want your father to know this?"

I sighed. "It's complicated. But sometime after my father passes away, she and Ben are going to come see you. She's going to pretend to be me, and tell you that she wants to tear up the prenuptial agreement."

"Well, I'm certainly glad you've warned me. I'll make sure from now on to always check the hand."

"I want you to do what she asks. And pretend to be surprised. Maybe even try to talk her out of it."

Goldfarb's eyebrows shot up, and his mouth dropped open.

"You're the only one who can revoke it. It won't be valid otherwise."

"That's the point. I want Ben to believe that it's no longer in effect when in fact it is."

He leaned forward on his desk, his chin cupped in his hand. "You're asking me to participate in a deception."

"It's Ben who'd be trying to trick you. You'll just be preventing him from succeeding."

He nodded. "I'm comfortable looking at it that way. But Charlotte, are you sure you can't tell me what's going on? I'm worried about you."

I thought about explaining everything to Goldfarb, then decided to hold back. It was now a police matter. Better not to involve anyone unnecessarily. "Thank you, Steve. There isn't anything for you to concern yourself with. I'm fine. Really." As I spoke those words, I fervently hoped it was true.

I returned from my father's bedside a little earlier that evening, and instead of slipping under the covers of my bed, doing my best to avoid Ben, I sat down next to him on our couch and told him I missed him, that I missed making love to him. I had to force myself not to gag as I said those words. I wanted this charade to end as soon as possible, and for that, Ben needed to know about my father's trust, and which lawyers he should turn to after he believed Clark had succeeded in killing me.

I led him into our bedroom and slowly undressed before him, then threw my clothes on a chair. We fell onto the bed, and within minutes, Ben was inside me. I felt nothing—less than nothing—but I pretended to be aroused. When it was over, I headed to the shower. I knew Ben hated messiness. I knew he'd hang up my clothes. I knew he'd see the manila folder with my father's trust inside. And I knew he would examine it.

CHAPTER 40

I'd given up on the search for our paternal grandparents. Maybe I'd go back to it later, when I didn't have so much on my plate. But I still yearned to know more about my birth mother. Mallory had confirmed that her birth certificate listed our mother's name as Susan, and she'd told me what she knew of her, but I wanted to know the woman before she'd become worn down by her hard life. I called Mallory. "Wouldn't you like to know what our mother was like before she had you?"

"I never thought about it."

"Well, I would. You said your mother's friend knew her since childhood. Do you think if we paid her a visit, she would talk about her?"

"I'm sure she would."

Two nights later, instead of going to my father, I left the gallery early. Mallory had driven down from High Falls, and we met at a rest stop off the New Jersey Turnpike. "I don't believe it," I said as soon as I saw her. "I knew we looked alike, but this is so weird."

"It's all part of the plan. Ben sent me a close-up photo of you, and I took it to a hairstylist."

She left her car in the parking lot, and we drove together the rest of the way to Philadelphia. Lauren was waiting for us.

As soon as we walked in, she looked at both of us. "I can't tell who is who."

"I'm Charlotte. Or Charly."

She threw her arms around me and hugged me tight. When she pulled back, I could see her eyes were moist. "It would have meant the world to Sasha to see the two of you together."

We moved into the living room, and Mallory and I sat down while Lauren went into the kitchen and came back with a plate of cookies. "She named you Amelia," Lauren told me. "She always wondered about you, whether you had good parents, whether they loved you."

"I did."

"That would have made her happy."

"Tell me about her," I asked. "What she was like as a child, what she enjoyed doing."

"I suppose Mallory told you she had a difficult life," Lauren said.

I nodded.

"Well, in spite of that, she was always feisty. Nothing could stop her. I guess that's why, when her mother gave her an ultimatum about the pregnancy, she left home."

Mallory leaned forward on the couch. "I found my birth certificate, and it listed Mom's name as Susan. Who changed it to Sasha?"

"She did that when she moved to Scranton—not legally, though. It's just what she told people to call her. She told me she'd wanted a fresh start, and a new name was part of that."

"Do you know if she liked art? Did she paint?" I asked.

"No and no. Your dad was the artist. Never did much with it, but he could draw anything."

My father. It reminded me of the roadblock we'd hit in trying to find his parents. I wanted to know more about him, too. "How did they meet?" I asked.

"At a party. Some senior boy bought a keg when his parents were out of town and invited the prettiest girls. Johnny was friends with the boy's older brother, and they hung out at the house, mostly to make fun of the younger kids. But as soon as he saw your mother, he was sunk. I swear, it was like a lightning bolt hit him. He'd had a reputation for fooling around with a bunch of girls, but once he saw your mother, she locked up his heart and placed it next to hers. They were never apart until he enlisted. And the reason he joined up was to have a better life for him and your mother."

"Do you think that's why Mom never married?" Mallory asked.

Lauren nodded. "I think she was afraid if she did, she'd forget your father, and she never wanted to do that."

I lapped it all up, eager to learn everything I could about them. We spent two hours with Lauren, and if we hadn't had a two-hour drive home, I could have spent two more. She brought out pictures of her and Sasha, starting from when they were young children, and even a few that included John. I stared at each one and, for the first time, started to understand who I was.

On the drive back, my phone rang through the Bluetooth. I didn't recognize the number that came up on the screen, but I answered it. "Is this Charly Gordon?"

"Yes."

"This is Gertrude Harris. I spoke to you last week. About John Harris?"

"Yes, but your son wasn't the one I was looking for."

"Yes, well, I was telling my daughter about it, and it turns out she's Facebook friends with your John Harris's sister, Amy. She sent a message to her and got a phone number for Ellen Harris. She lives in LA now. Do you want it?"

"Of course."

Mallory rummaged through her purse and pulled out her phone, then typed in the number.

I thanked Mrs. Harris, then hung up. "Should we call Ellen now? It's three hours earlier in California." I could see from the brightness of her eyes that Mallory was as excited as I felt. She nodded, and I gave a voice command to dial the number. It was answered on the second ring.

"Is this Ellen Harris?"

"Yes."

"And you once lived in Allentown?"

"Yes? Who is this?"

"My name is Charly Gordon. Back in Allentown, did your son date Susan Holcolm?"

I heard a sharp intake of breath. "Do you know where Susan is? We looked and looked for her for so long."

I felt my heart start to beat faster. "She passed away a few years ago."

Ellen said, "Oh," with a voice that seemed filled with sadness.

"But I'm her daughter. And your son was my father."

"Oh my, oh my, is this true? I can't believe it. We looked for you, too."

"You knew my mother was pregnant?"

"John wrote and told us. They were going to get married when he returned on leave, but then he was killed. We were so distraught, I'm sure you can understand. But after his funeral, after a few weeks had gone by, we called Susan. We wanted her to know that we hoped to be part of our grandchild's life. Only she was gone. Disappeared."

"Her mother kicked her out because she wouldn't have an abortion."

"If only she'd come to us. We would have taken her in. We would have cared for her and the baby."

"Babies, actually."

"What do you mean?"

"I have an identical twin sister. She's sitting right next to me."

"Hi, I'm Mallory."

Ellen burst out crying. Through her sobs, she managed to get out, "Two of John's children, two pieces of John, and we never knew."

I waited for her to calm down. "Ellen, I'm in the car now, driving. Is it okay if I call you back later?"

"Oh, yes, I want to hear all about you both. And, I hope, maybe we could meet?"

"I'd like that."

"So would I," Mallory chimed in.

"My father is very ill now," I continued, "and I'm helping care for him, so it will have to be when . . . when it's resolved."

"Of course, of course. I'm just so happy you called. I know John Senior will be, also."

So, my grandfather was alive as well. Over the past few weeks, my family had increased by three. As I disconnected the call, I glanced over at Mallory. Her brows were knitted together, and her eyes glistened. "Are you okay?"

"If Mom hadn't run away, my life would have been so different. She wouldn't have always struggled to provide a home, to buy food. Maybe she would have gone to college. I would have had grandparents." Suddenly, her eyes widened. "We would have been together! Mom wouldn't have given you away." She shook her head, then leaned it against the window.

Mallory was right. If our grandparents had taken in our mother, provided her a home and a place to raise her daughters, I wouldn't have been adopted. I would have grown up with my biological mother and twin sister and two grandparents. I would have been raised in a working-class home without the luxuries and opportunities my adoptive parents had given me. I'd grown up pampered and had been happy. As much as I'd wanted to learn about my history, about my biological roots, I realized I wouldn't have wanted to exchange my life for the alternate one Mallory had presented. I wanted my life of wealth.

I was glad my mother had given me away.

CHAPTER 41

I'd begun to question my decision to hold off Ben's arrest. As my father's condition deteriorated, I knew the time was drawing close for Ben's hit man to strike. I'd lie in bed at night, my murderous husband next to me, and tremble. *What if he purposely gives Mallory the wrong night? What if the hit man eludes the police?* And the scariest thought of all: *What if the detective was right about Mallory, that she wants me dead to take it all?* When I had those worries, I thought it was crazy to allow Ben's plan to go forward. I'd lie awake, afraid to close my eyes. When morning would finally come and I'd see Ben's smug pretense at caring about me, about my father, my resolve would return. I would do what was needed to ensure he was punished for his crime.

A week after the visit to Lauren, I arrived at my father's apartment just before 7:00 p.m. and was met by Janice, his hospice nurse, as soon as I let myself in. "Your father's condition has deteriorated," she told me. "It's just a matter of days now—maybe three or four at the most."

I slumped down onto the couch and buried my head in my hands. I'd known the time was near, but putting a date on it felt like a punch to my stomach. "How can you tell? How can you be sure?"

"I've been doing this a very long time, dear. I know the signs. His breathing has changed, his pulse is rapid, and his blood pressure has dropped. He's also showing confusion when he's awake."

I fought to hold back tears. "Is he awake now?"

"No. He's sleeping. But when he does wake up, and you go in to see him, you'll hear a faint rattling sound in his chest. Don't be alarmed. It's because his muscles have weakened, and it's hard for him to move mucus and phlegm through his lungs. I've given him medicine to make it a little easier. Also, his confusion might make him agitated, and he'll say things that make no sense. It's common at this stage. Try to ignore the things he says, even if it's hateful."

"Dad would never say anything mean to me."

"He's not himself now. He may accuse you of lying or cheating him, but that's a symptom of the disease."

I had to call Poppy. It was time for him to fly north again. I knew he would want to be by Dad's side when the end came. My chest ached with the realization that I would soon be an orphan, yet I knew it had to be even worse for my grandfather. No parent should ever have to bury a child. It completely subverted the natural order of how life should be.

He answered the phone on the first ring. When I told him he needed to come back to New York and explained why, I could hear his breath catch, and then silence. "Are you okay, Poppy?"

"No, Pips, I'm not. But I will be. Are you okay?"

"No. But I will be."

I arrived home a little past 8:00 p.m., much earlier than I had been coming home the past few months. I heard the television on in the den, and then Ben call out, "Who's there?"

A moment later, I walked into the room.

"This is early for you." Ben said. "Something happen?"

"Dad's taken a turn. It's just a matter of days now. I came home to pack a bag. I'm going to stay there until the end. Sandy will run the gallery."

Ben didn't even bother to try to comfort me, take me in his arms, and ask if I'd be all right—but would it really matter if he had? It didn't seem worth the effort for either of us to pretend. Instead, Ben just said, "Sorry," and sat back down in his chair.

I cut through Central Park on the walk back to my father's apartment. Even though it was dark, it was still early in the evening, and the park was filled with people. I don't know what made me turn around, but when I did, I saw a man twenty paces back who looked just like the picture Mallory had drawn of the hit man. I picked up my pace. Five minutes later, I turned again, and he was still there. My heart began to beat more quickly. I thought about running, but I was still dressed in my stiletto heels from work. I knew all the stories of muggings that had taken place in the park, even with lots of people around. Could Ben have called the hired gun so quickly? Told him my father was near the end? No, it was too fast. I'd been home only fifteen minutes. I spotted a bench up ahead with a father and teenage son seated, a lamppost over it, and as soon as I reached it, I sat down next to them. Surely, he wouldn't try something with others this close. I clutched the duffel bag I'd packed back at my townhouse to my chest. A minute later, the man passed me by, and I stared at him. He didn't look like Mallory's picture, after all.

CHAPTER 42

My grandfather arrived at Dad's apartment just after noon the next day. For the next three days, at least one of us was always by Dad's bedside, giving him morphine when he'd wake up in pain, then watching as he'd fall back under its spell. He couldn't swallow any longer, so I'd administer sublingual drops of morphine onto his tongue. It supplemented the transdermal patch of fentanyl on his skin that Janice had placed. It was three days of watching my father die, and when he did, instead of being inured to the inevitable, I broke out in uncontrollable sobs. My grandfather, who looked like he'd aged three years in those three days, took me in his arms and held me tight until I was able to slow my tears.

I called hospice, and Janice arrived an hour later. She made the official pronouncement of death, after which I called the Frederick Canton Funeral Chapel, and they came and took away Dad's body. The funeral home I'd chosen, located on the Upper West Side, was the place the rich and famous were taken when they'd drawn their last breaths. With its own security staff that ensured only those invited to the funeral were granted access, and its lovely chapel, it had gained a reputation as the top funeral home in Manhattan.

Once Dad was gone, I stayed in the apartment with my grandfather. Neither of us wanted to be alone, and even though Ben waited at our townhouse, I would still feel alone there. We both began making phone calls, to family, to friends. Despite Detective Saldinger's caution about Mallory, I felt an urge to call her. She picked up on the first ring.

"He's gone, isn't he?" were her first words.

"Yes."

"I'm sorry, Charly. I know how much pain you're in now."

"Because of how you felt when your mother died?"

"No. It's something else. I felt overcome with sadness about three hours ago. Is that when he passed?"

I was speechless. Since meeting Mallory, we'd both noted similarities in our tastes, in our habits. But this? She was right, though. Three hours ago, I was sobbing in my grandfather's arms. Somehow, it made me feel better to know how connected we were. "So, it's going to start soon. Ben's plan."

"Don't think about that now. Just mourn your father. And call me whenever you need to talk."

The next few days passed in a blur. Poppy helped me pick out a casket. The funeral home had every kind imaginable, with prices that soared into six figures, but Dad wouldn't have wanted that. Instead, we picked out a classic mahogany casket with solid brass trim. From there, we headed to Dad's church and met with Reverend Stokes, Dad's minister at the Park Avenue United Methodist Church. He would conduct the service, and even though he knew Dad well, we filled him in on his life.

Three days after his death, we held the wake. Over two days, more than five hundred people came to pay their respects, and most cornered me to say what a wonderful person he was. By the time the funeral was held, I'd cried myself out. I sat there, in the first pew, Ben on one side and Poppy on the other, as one by one, family and close friends walked to the front to eulogize Dad. I only half listened. All I could think about was that in a few days, the man sitting by my side, my husband, would text a man to say, It's time to kill my wife.

Shortly after 10:00 p.m., I got a call from Mallory.

"It's going to happen Friday night. I just spoke to Detective Saldinger and let him know. Ben will be at a Knicks game. Are you ready?"

I was. I almost looked forward to it. I had one more call to make, to my sculptor showing in the Whitney Biennial. "Sergei? It's happening Friday. Is it finished?"

"Da."

"Good. You know what to do, right?"

"Pictures. I bring them to detective."

"That's right."

"I wish I knew why you need."

"Better that you don't. And thank you again for your help."

I hung up and smiled. Everything was set.

CHAPTER 43

I was jittery all day Friday. I had spoken to Detective Saldinger the evening before, going over the plans once more. "Are you sure you can't have one of your men inside the house with me?" I'd asked.

"This guy's an army sniper. They're used to making themselves invisible. I don't want to take the chance that he's staked out your house from early in the day and spots someone entering and not leaving. But I promise you, we'll be nearby. He won't see us until he tries to go in your back door, and then we'll be right on top of him."

Tonight, my life was going to change. I kept watching the clock, waiting for the time when the basketball game would start. I knew Ben would then be at Madison Square Garden. He'd never miss the beginning of his precious Knicks game. He seemed to care more about them than anything else. Maybe even more than his girlfriend. More important, Detective Saldinger had agreed with me that, even with Mallory stepping in to take my place, Ben would want to establish he was at the game if something went wrong.

Even though I hadn't yet returned to work, I tried to stay out of the house as much as I could during the day. It made me too nervous to just sit around. With every man walking behind me, or next to me, or even in front of me, I wondered if he was the one. The man hired to murder me. So many men I passed looked similar to Mallory's sketch. I spent the morning shopping—always a stress reliever—and the afternoon touring the Met, returning to my townhouse a little after 5:00 p.m.

The game started at 7:30 p.m. I turned on the television, and once I saw the tip-off, I went into my closet and pulled down a duffel bag from the top shelf. I couldn't take what I already owned with me, on the off chance that Ben would notice if some of my things were missing. So, over the past few weeks, I'd purchased a few new clothes as well as cosmetics and toiletries. They were already packed inside the bag.

I took off my engagement ring and placed it inside my jewelry box, then tossed the comforter on the bed, to make it look like it had been thrown off me. There was nothing to do now but wait. It was already dark outside. The man my husband had hired could come at any time, but I thought it likely he'd wait. The sidewalks were still busy with neighbors coming home from work or heading out to dinner.

I sat on my bed and attempted to read a book, but it was hard to concentrate. All day I'd been second-guessing my decision to let this go ahead. What if the hit man evaded the detectives? After all, he'd managed to disappear the night Mallory had met him, leaving the police scratching their heads. More frightening, what if he got past them and entered my home without their knowing? I scooted over to Ben's side of the bed and opened the top drawer of his night table. I took out the handgun nestled under some papers, checked that it was loaded, and then returned to my side of the bed. I felt better with the gun on my lap.

My bedroom faced the front of the house. I'd already checked and had seen that Ben had left a key under our welcome mat at the back door. That's where he'd enter—the hit man. I knew that I shouldn't, that I should stay put, but by the time 9:00 p.m. rolled around, every ten minutes I went into the guest bedroom, which faced the rear yard, and pressed my ear to the window, listening for something—for anything.

I had just entered the guest bedroom again at 9:50 p.m. when I heard the sound of a handle being turned. Seconds later—or maybe it was minutes, the fear that filled me having taken away all sense of time—there were loud voices and what seemed like a scuffle coming from the kitchen. I ran back to my bedroom, grabbed my gun, and pulled the blanket up to my chin. My body shook all over, and beads of sweat dripped down into my eyes.

Moments later, I heard footsteps coming up the stairs and briefly wondered whether I should run into the bathroom. *No,* I reasoned. My bed faced the door. From this perch, I could immediately see whoever came in. I'd have a clear shot if it was the hit man. My heart felt like it was going two hundred beats per minute.

It seemed to take forever for the steps to reach my door. Slowly, it opened. I held the gun in front of me, pointed straight ahead.

"Charly?"

It was Detective Saldinger. I rushed out of bed and threw my arms around him. When I let him go, he said, "We have him. We have the guy." He looked me over. "You okay?"

I nodded. My heart was slowing down, almost back to normal.

"We can end it now. I can wait here and arrest your husband as soon as he returns home."

I thought about that. It was the safe bet. They had the hit man. They would arrest Ben. Mallory, too, I supposed. I could return to a normal life. But it didn't feel finished yet. My rage at Ben was still boiling inside me. I knew he had enough money to hire the best criminal defense attorneys. Maybe they'd say he was suffering from some temporary delusions, some type of mental illness. He'd probably point the finger at Mallory, say she came up with the idea, and fed into this illness. What if he got six months in a psychiatric facility, then walked free? I couldn't bear the thought of that.

"I want to finish our plan. I want to leave."

Saldinger nodded. "You ready to go?"

"Yes." I picked up my duffel bag and walked out of the room and down the stairs. The hit man was seated on my living room couch, his hands cuffed, and two policemen stood over him. Saldinger led me outside to his car, then drove me out to LaGuardia Airport.

I'd been careful to book my ticket for Florida from the gallery's computer. If Ben harbored any suspicions, he would find nothing to shore them up at home. When I arrived at the airport, I said goodbye to Saldinger, then checked in for my 11:15 p.m. flight. My grandfather had left me a key to his house before he'd flown home so that I wouldn't need to wake him when I got there.

By the time I arrived at my gate, I had a half hour before boarding started. I called Mallory.

"I'm at the airport now."

"What happened? I've been on pins and needles waiting for someone to call me."

"They got him. The hit man."

"Thank God. And you're okay?"

"Not a scratch."

"Good. Nervous?"

"No. You're the one who should be. You have to pass for me. And convince Ben you're still going along with him."

"I've been convincing him ever since you and I met. He's so anxious to collect your money, he'll believe anything now."

My money. An obscene amount of money. I'd never given it any thought while growing up. It was simply there, available for me to have whatever I wanted, from parents willing to indulge my every wish. That didn't change once I'd married. Ben had a handsome salary from Dad's business, and just like it had been when I was growing up, I'd never wanted for anything. Granted, my tastes weren't extravagant. At least, not for the circles I traveled in. I owned no furs and no diamonds, aside from my engagement ring, which Ben had paid for; one diamond pendant necklace that my father had bought me when I'd turned twenty-one; and two pairs of diamond earrings. I wore designer clothes, but that was required in my line of work. And I had more shoes than any woman should own—my own personal extravagance.

When this charade was over, I would be enormously wealthy, and Mallory would still have little. "I was thinking. You've saved my life. Literally. When this is over, I want to give you some money."

There was silence on the other end. Finally, Mallory said, her voice soft, "That's not why I came forward. I don't want money. I want a sister."

Detective Saldinger was wrong about Mallory. She wouldn't turn on me. Not now. I was certain of that.

I slept until after 10:00 a.m. and woke to bright sunshine streaming through the slats of the wooden shutters covering my bedroom window. I walked into the kitchen and found my grandfather sitting at the table, reading a newspaper.

"Well, the princess has awakened," he said.

I walked over and kissed his cheek, then poured myself a cup of coffee from the pot.

"There's a box of donuts over there," Poppy said, pointing to a spot next to the refrigerator.

"Ugh. Too much sugar. You shouldn't have them, either."

"When you get to my age, why not? I'm not going to last forever. I might as well enjoy the remaining years."

Suddenly, tears welled up in my eyes. "Don't say that. I need you."

His face dropped. "I'm sorry, Pips. That was insensitive." He smiled. "Besides, I've got strong genes. I'm going to be around for a good long while."

I finished my coffee, then dressed for a run. I'd left behind temperatures in the thirties and welcomed the seventy-two degrees that greeted me. By midday, it would reach the low eighties. I understood why my grandfather didn't want to return to New York. Tomorrow, I would head for the beach. Today, after my run, I needed to shop for clothes. And maybe a piece of jewelry to perk me up. I deserved it.

The next day, I got a call from Detective Saldinger. "Where are you?"

"At my grandfather's, in Florida."

"Okay. Two things. First, the guy your husband hired, his name is Daniel Clark. He was asked to leave the service with a psychiatric discharge. We searched his apartment and found a hundred grand in cash under his mattress. We couldn't get anything out of him, even after we said we knew Ben hired him. Completely mum. We did find a picture in his room of him and another guy in uniform. We checked it out, and the other guy's name is Jeff Mullin, who, as it turns out, went to high school with your husband."

"His name sounds vaguely familiar, although I don't think Ben was in regular touch with him."

"Our best guess is that Ben reached out to Mullin, and Mullin put him in touch with Clark. If that's true, it helps show that your husband was the one controlling the situation. I have some guys out to pick up Mullin now. Hopefully, he'll be more talkative. Otherwise, Mallory's testimony is going to be key."

"What's the second thing?"

"I have to tell you, from the pictures I just saw of what's supposed to be you, I'd be convinced you were really dead."

"You met with Sergei."

"I just came from his studio. Did you ask him to be so gruesome, or was that his idea?"

I laughed. "All mine. I wanted Ben to be really sick about what he'd arranged."

"I'm glad I didn't ask him to just drop the cell phone off at the station. I mean, it was really spooky how lifelike the body parts were. If I just saw the pictures, I'd think you really were dead. Sergei brought me back into his studio and showed me the bodies he'd sculpted. If I walked past any one of them sitting on a park bench, I'd probably sit down and start a conversation. That's how realistic they are."

"He's very talented."

"So, here's what's next. I'm going to leave the phone with the pictures under your back doormat tomorrow night. My guess is that Ben will get Mallory down to the city right away. As soon as she and Ben change the prenuptial agreement, we'll arrest him."

"Don't we need to wait for the estate to be settled?"

"Nope. The DA says revoking the prenup is enough to show motive."

"Can I ask you to hold off a few days?"

"Why?"

"I'd like to come back to New York and confront him with Mallory, get him to confess."

"Absolutely not! It's much too dangerous."

"We can do it in my house. I'll be wired, and you can be right outside."

"Look, we don't need a confession. We have the recording from when Mallory and Ben met up with Clark. And we'll have the changed prenup, which shows the reason he did this. He's going away for a long time."

"I want him to admit it was his idea, not Mallory's. Please. I really need to do this. I need to see his face when he first realizes that it's over for him. That instead of getting away with murder, he's going to spend the rest of his life in prison."

I heard a deep sigh over the phone. "All right. I shouldn't say yes, but you've been through a lot. I'll give you this."

"Thank you, Detective." As I hung up, I could feel my excitement rise. I could already picture Ben's face when he saw the two of us together. First shock, then realization, then panic. I felt great.

CHAPTER 44

"It's done," Mallory told me three days after I'd fled to Florida. "I'm heading to your house in a few minutes."

"Did Ben say anything about the pictures?"

"Just that he got them."

I would have loved to have been a fly on the wall when he'd flipped through the photos on the cell phone and seen my severed head. I knew Ben well. He had no stomach for gore. I hoped he had nightmares from seeing Sergei's handiwork.

I still had to wait for Ben to take Mallory to Goldfarb's office to revoke the prenuptial agreement. A cagier man might take months to do that in order to dispel questions, but I knew Ben. He was probably itchy to get that done. If he didn't act fairly quickly on his own, though, Mallory was prepared to prompt him. Until then, it was comfortable being with Poppy, away from winter. After months of watching my father die, it felt like a needed vacation.

My grandfather lived on the twenty-first floor of a high-rise condo in a three bedroom, four-bath apartment overlooking the ocean in Bal Harbour, at the northern tip of Miami Beach. Everything about the building and the community was ultraluxurious. He'd spent the bulk of his career in Manhattan real estate, constructing high-end buildings, and built up a fortune in the process. He'd hoped Dad would take it over, but it didn't turn out that way. Dad's interest in money was purer—he wanted to deal with it directly. Even though Poppy was disappointed, he gave Dad the seed money he'd needed to start his own hedge fund.

After my grandmother died, Poppy moved his business down to southern Florida. He was now semiretired, letting his longtime chief operating officer handle the day-to-day matters. As a wealthy widower, he had more than enough women clamoring for his attention and was usually out every night with one or another. He was still attractive and only a bit overweight. He was always saying he needed to take off a few pounds, and I was always telling him to go to the gym. He'd just laugh at me. "That's for you young folk," he'd say.

This week he was staying in with me, even though I'd told him it wasn't necessary. "Let's go to Carpaccio for dinner tonight," he said when I came back from the building's lagoon-shaped pool. The ocean had beckoned just a few feet away, but I preferred the lounges by the pool, where I wasn't constantly shaking off sand.

"Great." It was my favorite restaurant in Bal Harbour, one that attracted visitors from all parts of Miami—celebrities and socialites, athletes and artists.

It was a beautiful evening, the temperature hovering around seventy, with just a light breeze, so we chose one of the outdoor tables. The waiter had just served our main dishes—mine was *pescespada acapulco*, fresh swordfish with artichokes, lemon butter, white wine, and diced shrimp—when Poppy asked, "When will this be over for you?"

I'd decided not to tell him of my plan to confront Ben. Better that he not have cause for worry. "As soon as Mallory revokes the prenup. Then Ben will be arrested, and I'll return to New York."

"Don't take this wrong—I'm happy to have you here. It's just . . . everything has been so stressful for you. I'm sure you want it to end, to have a normal life again."

"Thank you, Poppy."

"So, will there be a trial?"

"I suppose so, unless Ben agrees to a plea bargain."

"And they'll put him away for a long time?"

"Very long."

I didn't tell my grandfather that I thought no amount of time was long enough. Even though with Ben's handsome face and buffed body, he would be considered prime meat for the prison population, and even though I knew he would be subjected to daily tortures there, it still wasn't enough for me. I had given him everything, and he'd wanted more. Now, I wanted more.

CHAPTER 45

I had started to get bored silly when Detective Saldinger called. "Your sister has revoked your prenuptial agreement and started the process of settling the estate. It's time to come home."

"Okay, Detective. I'll fly home tomorrow."

I arrived at LaGuardia Airport at 2:30 p.m. the next afternoon and took a cab directly to my father's apartment. I still had a key and had made sure to tell Mallory that she shouldn't arrive before 6:00 p.m. That's when the staff changed over. It wouldn't do to have the doorman wonder how he'd seen two of us enter the building.

It was the first time I'd been there since my father's funeral. After spending night after night for so many months by his side in this apartment, I felt a tug as soon as I stepped inside. The lights were all off and the curtains drawn, so I switched on the foyer light. Ben had let Tatiana go as soon as he'd received pictures of my "death," giving her only two days to clear out her belongings. I never would have done that. She'd lived in this apartment for more than a decade. When Mallory told me, I sent a check to her at her sister's apartment in Queens for one year's salary.

I walked through the rooms of the apartment. The hospice equipment was gone, and everything was in place, as though my father was simply at the office, waiting to return home. It hit me hard, once again, that I was alone. The new people in my life: Mallory, perhaps my father's parents, were just that—new. They didn't share my memories.

I settled down on the living room couch with my iPad and surfed the Net, checking out the hot new artists, deciding which upcoming art exhibitions I wanted to attend, pretending that my life was normal. But I knew it wasn't.

At 6:30 p.m., Mallory arrived, bags of Chinese food in her arms. "We could have had something delivered," I said.

"I know. I wanted to test our twinness again—see if you like the same dishes I do."

I opened the bags and pulled out a quart of egg drop wonton soup, shrimp chow mein, and chicken kung pao. "Perfect," I said.

When we finished eating, Mallory asked, "So, what's the plan?"

"I'm meeting with Detective Saldinger at the precinct tomorrow morning. He's going to set me up with a Bluetooth device that'll let them hear everything Ben says."

"Probably a pen. That's what they gave me when Ben took me to meet Clark."

"I'll come to the townhouse after Ben gets home, and we'll confront him. Detective Saldinger and his men will be outside, listening, and when Ben admits what he's done and sees both of us together, they'll come in and arrest him," I said.

"Some nights he doesn't come home at all."

"I'll call him, pretend I'm you, and give him some reason for him to get back."

Mallory nodded, but not with a great deal of confidence.

"Don't worry. It'll go fine."

"I hope so. I want to get back to my life. That's if I don't get sent to jail along with Ben."

"What? Waiting tables?"

She turned to me, and for the first time, I saw a flash of anger in her eyes. "I liked my life. It was a life I earned."

I reminded myself that, despite our shared genes, my sister was a stranger to me. Briefly, I wondered if I'd been mistaken. If, despite her protestations that she didn't want my money, that had been her aim all along. And even if it wasn't, what was to say she wouldn't want it down the road? She claimed she wanted only a relationship, but wouldn't she also want the things I could do, the things I had? I know I would, and she was identical to me.

"I wish I could talk you out of this," Saldinger told me the next morning. "I get why you want to do it, but what if he goes crazy and tries to hurt you?"

"You'll hear it and run inside."

"That gun that I saw you with. The night we got Clark. Can Ben get at it?"

"It's kept in the bedroom upstairs. He won't have a chance to reach it."

He just shook his head slowly. "If I felt I needed a confession from him, I could have wired up Mallory anytime over the past week. I've told you, it's not necessary."

"I need to see the look on his face when he realizes I'm alive. That's all."

Saldinger sighed, then glanced around the precinct room uneasily. There were at least a dozen desks in the open space, half of them empty, the other half occupied with men and women busy at their computers or with open files. No one was looking our way. "It better not blow back in my face. That's all I can say."

I smiled. "It won't. I promise."

He handed me what looked like an ordinary pen. "This is a transmitter. It'll allow us to hear what's going on, and we'll record it on our end. Just press down the top to turn it on and again to turn it off. It'll work inside your pocket."

I placed the pen in the pocket of my slacks. "Got it."

"What time do you expect him tonight?"

"I'm going to call him from the townhouse, pretend I'm Mallory, and give him some reason to come home. Figure around six-thirty, seven."

"I'll have an unmarked car outside starting at six. Call me once you speak to your husband."

I said goodbye, then left the station. I decided to walk uptown to my townhouse. Manhattan was my home. The crowded streets, the loud noises, the smell of food from the myriad restaurants all gave me a feeling of comfort. Lounging by the pool at Poppy's, or jogging along his stretch of beach, was a nice diversion, but I'd go crazy living there year-round. Manhattan was good to those with money, delivering a plethora of restaurants and culture—theater, ballet, opera, symphony, and, of course, museums galore. It was where I belonged. I couldn't imagine what it would have been like growing up in Allentown, Pennsylvania. I was glad I hadn't.

CHAPTER 46

On my walk uptown, I stopped at one of my favorite boutiques and picked out two pairs of identical black woolen slacks and two of the same black-and-white silk tunics that fell just below my hips.

I let myself into the empty townhouse. Ben was at Jensen Capital, and Mallory was at the gallery. I looked through the rooms to see if anything was amiss. Although I knew Ben was a neat freak, I had no idea whether Mallory was a slob—but everything was in place. I brought the new clothes up to the guest bedroom and hung one set of the slacks and blouse in the closet. I stopped quickly in the master bedroom, picked up some items I needed, then headed back downstairs and called Ben.

"What are you still doing at home?" he asked.

"I'm leaving for the gallery soon. Were you planning on coming home after work?"

"Nope. Heading out to Lisa's."

I seethed anew on hearing her name. "There's a problem here that I need you to handle."

"What?"

"Your friend dropped by the house. The guy you hired for—you know."

"What the hell? I made the final installment, left it in a postal box at Mail Connections, just as he instructed me. What's the guy trying to do now? Shake me down for more?"

"I have no idea, but he's coming back at eight o'clock. He said you'd better be home."

I heard muttering on the other end of the phone. "Ben?"

"I'll be there."

I left the townhouse and walked through Central Park, which was bursting with people on this day that seemed like a promise of an early spring. Carlos, the doorman, nodded to me when I arrived.

Once in the apartment, I started going through Dad's papers. Ben had asked Mallory to do that, and although she'd pretended she had been, I had instructed her to leave that to me. She wouldn't know what I might want to keep. She had, however, purchased boxes for me. I started in Dad's office. Most of the documents in his file cabinet were office-related. I put those together in three boxes, figuring I'd have them delivered to Ted Manning. They were probably duplicates, but he could decide what to do with them.

I pulled out the bottom drawer, and it contained only two folders. The first, marked *Personal Records*, contained the birth certificates and baptismal certificates of my parents, my mother's death certificate, and her Social Security card. The second folder was marked *Charlotte*. Inside was my birth certificate, with my adopted mother's and father's names. Next, my adoption papers. I had been three days old when my adoption took place.

Clipped to those papers was a small envelope. I opened it up and pulled out two handwritten pages.

To my beautiful daughter Amelia,

Today is the hardest day of my life. Today, I signed papers for you to be adopted. As soon as you were born, I knew I had to do this, but I've cried for two days straight. You were a surprise. I didn't know I would give birth to twin girls. I want so much to keep you both, but I'm only seventeen years old, and my mother has disowned me, and your father died fighting for his country.

They told me the man and woman who are adopting you have a lot of money. I'm glad. That means they can take care of you better than I can. I hope they love you, but it will never be as much as I love you.

If you're reading this letter, it means your parents have told you about your sister and me. We live in Scranton, Pennsylvania, now, but I don't know where we'll be when—or if—you get this. I hope one day you find us.

Your loving mother, Sasha (Susan) Holcolm

I sat on the chair, stunned. My parents knew my mother's name, where she lived. They knew I had a twin. They kept me from both of them. They must not have told Poppy, because he'd seemed surprised when I'd told him about Mallory. All these years, I could have had a relationship with my sister. I could have known my mother. Now it was too late.

At a little after 7:00 p.m., I started to make my way to the townhouse. Just before I reached my home, I texted Mallory to make sure Ben had arrived. He had. Detective Saldinger was parked a few houses away from mine. I don't know how he managed to get a spot so close—finding a parking spot on the street in Manhattan was akin to finding the pot of gold at the end of a rainbow. Maybe the pot of gold was easier. I stopped at his car to say hello, and he introduced me to his partner, Frank Sidoriak.

"What'd they do?" I asked. "Assign partners alphabetically?"

He laughed. "Nope. Just happened to work out that way." He quickly turned serious. "You all set? Got the pen?"

"All set."

"Walk ahead, then turn the pen on. I want to make sure it's transmitting okay."

I did as he asked, and he gave me a thumbs-up.

It was time to go inside, to finish what Ben had started.

I made my way to the back door, then texted Mallory to let her know I was there.

Mallory texted back, I'm ready, and I quietly opened the door into the mudroom that led to the kitchen. Mallory was waiting for me, dressed just as I was, in the new clothes I'd bought this morning. We each had our hair pulled back into a ponytail. Anyone looking at us would be hard-pressed to discern a difference.

"Where is he?" I asked.

"Where do you think? There's a Knicks game on."

Of course. That meant he was in the den, glued to the television. I glanced over at my sister and felt a tug of sadness. I wished we hadn't met this way. I wished I'd known her when we were growing up. I wished our lives had been equally blessed with wealth. I wished Detective Saldinger hadn't planted the seed of doubt in me. I didn't buy into his concern that Mallory had designs of her own to replace me. Not now. I just couldn't be sure that wouldn't change down the road, and I feared that uncertainty would make it hard to have a relationship with her, when this ordeal finally ended.

I nodded to her, then walked from the kitchen over to the den. I peeked in, then casually asked upon spotting the empty beer bottle, "Want another?"

Ben looked up from the couch. "That'd be great."

I returned to the kitchen, retrieved a bottle from the refrigerator, then brought it to Ben. I sat in a chair opposite him. He gave me a fleeting look, then turned back to the game. When I didn't move, he paused the game. "What?"

I slipped my hand into my pocket and flipped on the transmitter pen. "I've been wondering. What made you think I would go along with your plan to kill Charly?"

Ben didn't hesitate. Within minutes, he acknowledged that he was the one to come up with the idea. He had gone to Mallory and convinced her to go along. I knew that Detective Salinger, ensconced in his police car outside the townhouse, heard every word Ben said. I was about to leave when I decided to ask Ben for an advance on the inheritance.

He picked up the remote and turned off the TV. I figured this had to be serious—either that, or the game was a blowout. He cleared his throat. "I'm glad you brought that up. I've been thinking . . ."

Always a bad sign, I thought.

"I think the split needs to be something different from we discussed."

I had to restrain myself from laughing. Not only did the bastard plan my murder, he now wanted to cheat his accomplice. "Why?"

I pretended to fume as Ben went through his explanation for keeping almost all my money for himself. When the charade started to bore me, I stormed out of the den and back into the kitchen. It was time for the fireworks. I slipped my hand into my pants pocket and clicked off the transmitter pen. "Did you hear?" I asked my sister.

"Every word."

"Let's go."

Side by side, we walked to the den. Ben had already turned the Knicks game back on and didn't look up when we stood in the doorway. Detective Saldinger wouldn't enter the townhouse from the unlocked back door until he heard Ben react to seeing Mallory and me together. That had been his promise to me—to let me watch Ben's reaction when he realized I was alive.

But that wasn't enough for me.

I called Ben's name, but he didn't look up. I called it again, louder. He held up his hand to shush me, without turning his head.

"A minute. Key play here."

When he finally paused the TV and swiveled toward us, his face turned a deadly pale.

He stared at us both with his eyes wide, his mouth open.

"Hello, Ben," I said.

His head twisted back and forth between us as his eyes rapidly blinked.

"You're . . . you're not dead." His voice came from his trembling lips as a croak.

"Who, me?" I said.

"Or me?" Mallory said.

"But . . . the pictures. You were . . . dismembered."

I laughed. "I work with artists, you fool. They can make anything look real."

He swept his hand across his forehead and wiped away the beads of sweat that had formed. "You went to the police?" he asked both of us, not knowing which one was his wife.

"Did I?" Mallory said.

"Or didn't I?" I chimed in. "You can't really tell us apart, can you?"

He stood up from the couch and started to approach us. "You bitch," he hissed, still turning his head back and forth between us.

I slipped my hand under my tunic and pulled out the gun I'd retrieved from Ben's night table earlier that day. I pointed it straight at my husband. "I'd stop there if I were you."

"Charly, what are you doing?" Mallory shouted at me. I didn't answer. I just kept my eyes on Ben.

"Charly, put that away. I don't know what she told you, but it was all her idea. She paid the hit man. She found him and paid him. She told me if I didn't go along, she'd kill me, too."

"You can't believe that," Mallory said to me.

I didn't. Not that it mattered. I took a step toward Ben, and he backed away from me. I kept approaching, backing him toward the wall, not getting close enough for him to grab the gun.

"Charly," Mallory said, "it's over for him. Let Detective Saldinger handle it now."

"So he can get some fancy lawyer who'll come up with some way-out defense? Remember the Twinkie defense? Got the guy cleared of a murder charge."

"You're not a murderer," Ben said, his voice now low and steady, his eyes locked on mine. He'd reached the wall. I stopped just out of his arm's reach. "You don't want to do this. I'm going to prison. You don't need to, also."

It gave me pleasure to see the fear in his eyes. I relished the power I felt with the gun in my hand. For months, I had been powerless as I'd watched my father die. I'd felt powerless as Ben snuck off every evening to be with his mistress. No longer. Now, I felt infused with power. I could have turned on the transmitter, put the gun down, and waited for Saldinger to come into the townhouse. I didn't want to. As much as I'd once loved Ben, that's how much I hated him now.

"Why, Ben? Just tell me why?"

He looked up at the ceiling and held his gaze there.

"Answer me!" I shouted.

He looked back at me. "Because I wanted your money. And I didn't want you."

I took a step forward, my head filled with a furious pounding, blocking out the shouts of my sister. I hated him, this man I'd shared my life with, my deepest secrets, and wildest dreams. I'd made him rich, and that's all he'd wanted from me. I held my arms out in front, both hands clasping the gun, my finger on the trigger. I didn't see Mallory run up behind me. I didn't see her step in front of Ben, and I didn't hear her shout, "No, Charly!" until after I'd pulled the trigger and the bullet headed straight for her chest. I screamed when she dropped to the floor.

Ben used the moment to run for the door. I didn't hesitate. I quickly blocked his path but got too close. He grabbed for the gun, but I held on tight as he tried to wrestle it from my hands. Ben had six inches and seventy pounds on me, but it didn't matter. My anger fueled my strength.

"Let go, you bitch," Ben said. The look of fear in his eyes was gone, replaced by a coldness that matched my own.

I remained silent, my only thought getting free of Ben as we each struggled for the gun. I didn't have much time. I knew Saldinger had to have heard the gunshot. I silently thanked my hours in the gym as I made a push to twist the gun upward, then shoved it under Ben's chin and, once again, pulled the trigger.

Ben dropped to the floor, his blood splattering over my beautiful Persian rug, and I briefly thought, *I wonder if that stain will come out.* I pressed the gun into Ben's right hand, then ran back to Mallory. I cradled her body in mine, both of us covered in blood. That's where Detective Saldinger found me when he burst through the back door.

"He shot her. He shot her," I cried, tears trickling down my cheeks. "I rushed him to get the gun away, and we struggled, and it went off. He tried to shoot me, too. Get an ambulance. We need an ambulance. Oh, please, help Mallory. Please help her."

Saldinger called for an ambulance, then gently lifted me up.

"It's on the way." He brought me over to the couch to sit down. "Why didn't you have the transmitter on?"

"What do you mean? It's on." I pulled it out of my pocket and handed it to him. The light was off. "Oh, God, I turned it off when I went back to get Mallory, and I pressed it back on when we got to the den. I must not have pushed it hard enough."

I began crying more steadily, with genuine remorse for my sister. But my anguish over Mallory was mixed with joyfulness. Ben was dead. My nightmare was over.

PART THREE

MALLORY

CHAPTER 47

"What are you doing?" I shouted at Charly when she pulled out a gun. This wasn't our plan. She wasn't supposed to kill Ben. She already had his confession that he was the one who'd hatched the scheme, not me. Now that she'd seen Ben's reaction when he realized she was alive, Saldinger would come in at any moment to arrest him. It was over, all but the trial. Surely, Ben would take a plea, and there wouldn't even need to be a trial. We could both get on with our lives, with the sweet addition of having each other now.

She moved toward Ben, the gun held close to her body.

"Charly, don't!" She wouldn't shoot Ben; she couldn't. If she shot him, she'd be sent to prison, and I'd lose the sister I'd had so briefly. I stood rooted to my spot in the room, convinced Charly was just trying to scare him, urging her to put the gun down.

Charly took another step forward and now extended her arms, the gun held in both hands. "You're going to ruin everything, Charly. Think of us. We finally found each other. Think of our grandparents." She seemed oblivious to my shouts, her eyes fixed on Ben. "If you do this, I won't forgive you," I warned. Her finger began to move to the trigger.

"No!" I screamed as I ran toward Ben, ran to push him away. Just as I reached him, there was a thunderous sound. I felt nothing and wondered why my legs had buckled, then looked down and saw dark-red blood ooze from the top of my chest. I tried to lift my hand to touch it, but nothing worked. I heard sounds of a scuffle, then another gunshot. Darkness overcame the room, and I closed my eyes and drifted into it.

Sounds wafted in from someplace far away. I struggled to open my eyes, and when I finally managed to do so, I discovered I was in a bed in a white room, bright light streaming through its one window. I turned my head and saw tubes running from my right arm to a pole, soft beeps emanating from a screen behind it. I was in a hospital. Why? My left arm was immobilized in a sling, and I felt a throbbing ache in my shoulder.

I strained to make out the voices that I'd awakened to. "Sorry, no one's allowed in," I heard a man's deep voice say.

"But I'm her sister."

"No one means no one."

Charly's voice grew louder, more hysterical. Then I heard a thump and someone call, "Get a nurse."

My head felt so heavy, my tongue so thick. I tried to fight it but couldn't. Slowly, the darkness descended once more.

Voices again. I opened my eyes—it was easier this time—and standing over my bed was a woman, a white jacket worn over her flowered dress, holding a chart in her hands, and next to her another woman in nurse's scrubs.

"Well, there you are," the woman in the dress said. "I'm Dr. Kessler. How are you feeling?"

The pain in my shoulder had lessened, but I still felt groggy. "Okay, I think."

"Well, you're a very lucky young woman. The bullet just missed your subclavian artery. You would have died before you'd gotten here if it were just a centimeter closer."

"My arm?"

"It nicked your clavicle. We've operated to remove the bullet fragments and stopped some internal bleeding, but you're going to be fine."

I knew that wasn't true. I would never be fine again. The sister I'd hoped would become my friend instead almost became my executioner.

"Where's my sister?" I asked.

"She was here earlier, trying to speak to you," the woman in scrubs said, "but the police haven't cleared you for visitors yet. She collapsed while talking to them and was admitted. She's just down the hall. Poor dear, the stress got to her." She lowered her voice and leaned in toward me. "Her husband is dead. After he shot you, she tried to wrestle the gun from him, and it went off. Hit him in the brain. He died instantly."

No. That wasn't what happened. Charly shot me, then she must have shot Ben. I remembered the noise, an earsplitting sound.

"You're lucky you have her. She saved your life," the nurse continued.

Nothing made sense to me. Nothing at all. I closed my eyes and drifted back to sleep.

The next time I woke up, Detective Saldinger was sitting by my bedside. "Well, it's about time," he said when I opened my eyes. It was dark outside the window, and only a small lamp next to my bed illuminated the room.

"How long have you been sitting there?"

"Not long. Maybe thirty minutes. It's the end of my shift. Figured I'd take a chance on you waking up. How do you feel?"

"Like someone shot me."

He smiled. "Glad you still have a sense of humor." He cleared his throat. "Mind if I do a bit of official business?"

"Go ahead."

"First, for the record, what's your name?"

I hesitated. I could tell him the truth, and Charly would go to prison for killing Ben, for shooting me, and I would go back to waiting on tables and squeezing out money and time for art classes. Or I could say I was Charly. My sister would still go to prison, but as Mallory. I would step into her life. I would have her money. I would own her gallery. I had trained for months to be Charly. Either way, Charly would be locked up. She deserved to be. I'd begged her to put the gun down, to put our relationship first. I wasn't important enough for her. She deserved to go to jail. And I deserved to be rich.

"Charlotte Gordon," I answered.

Saldinger looked confused, as I'd expected he would. Charly had to have told him who she was, who I was, and that Ben had been the shooter.

"Your sister says she's Charly."

"She's lying."

"She says Ben shot you, and she struggled with the gun, killing Ben in the process. Is that how it happened?"

"No. Mallory shot us both."

He leaned in close to me. "Damn. It's just what I told you I was afraid of, that Mallory might decide to go ahead and kill you and then take over your life. Just one thing is confusing me," Saldinger went on. "Why did Mallory have the transmitter pen in her pocket?"

"After I got Ben to confess, I came back into the kitchen. Mallory asked to look at it, and I handed it over to her. She put it in her own pocket, but I didn't think anything of it. It didn't matter who was carrying it, did it?"

"It did. She turned it off so we wouldn't hear anything." He stood up. "Okay. I'll let you rest now."

When I was certain he'd left the hospital floor, I buzzed the nurse, and five minutes later she entered my room.

"Need something, honey?"

"Is my sister still in the hospital?"

"She is, just down the hall."

"Is it possible for me to get up?"

The nurse nodded. "You should start moving around. Here, let me help you."

I swung my legs off the bed and carefully stood up. "I'd like to go to my sister's room."

"There's a cop outside your sister's room now. I'm not sure he'll let you see her."

"Let me try."

She unhooked me from the wires that led from various spots on my body to the pole by the bedside, then followed me out of the room. "She's down this hallway, Room 413."

Slowly, I made my way there, careful not to move my arm, which was still in a sling. When I reached her room, I asked the policeman if I could go in.

He hesitated, then said, "Just for a few minutes."

I walked up to Charly's bedside and sat down. "You killed Ben. You shot me."

She turned away from me for a few moments. When she finally met my gaze, she said, "He deserved to die."

"Did I deserve to be shot?"

"You got in the way. It was meant for Ben."

"I begged you to let him be. You didn't care that you'd go to prison, that we'd be separated again. You didn't care about me." I paused, then leaned in to whisper in her ear. "I told Detective Saldinger that I'm Charlotte Gordon, and you're Mallory."

"What!" She looked over at the cop. "So, that's why he's there."

I continued in a whisper. "I came to you to stop you from being murdered. All you had to do was let Saldinger arrest Ben. Now, you're going to prison."

"I won't go to prison if you say Ben had the gun, that he shot you."

I shook my head. I'd thought about just backing up Charly's story, never telling Saldinger the truth, but I couldn't get past the fact that Charly had killed someone. I'd had very little growing up, but one of the things my mother instilled in me was that actions have consequences. It seemed wrong for Charly to walk away from what she did scot-free. "You made your choice. You need to pay for it. Why shouldn't I take over your life? It's no use to you anymore."

Her face darkened. "You won't get away with that. I can prove I'm Charly." She stuck out her hand and pointed to a small scar. "See? I've had that since childhood. Poppy knows it's there."

I stuck out my hand. "Really? You mean a scar like this? Ben told me about your accident. It was really quite easy to cut myself. It didn't take too long for the scar to form."

"You bitch," she hissed.

"I was supposed to be you, in every respect."

She lay quietly for a minute, chewing on her lip. "It's money you want, right? I can make you rich. Filthy rich. I'll give you the hundred million Ben was going to leave for you. Just back up my story to Saldinger. Ben shot you, and then I rushed him for the gun."

I felt tears spring to my eyes. "I didn't want the money. I wanted a sister."

CHAPTER 48

The next morning, after I'd been poked and prodded by the nursing staff, and runny eggs with burned toast had been served for breakfast, an older man, his skin tanned and wrinkled from the sun, stepped into my room and sat in the chair next to my bed. "How are you feeling?"

I recognized him right away. He was Herman Jensen, Charly's grandfather.

"Hi, Poppy."

His mouth turned down to a scowl. "I know you're really Mallory."

"Poppy, how can you say that?"

He moved his chair closer to mine and lowered his voice. "I would have always been able to tell you apart." He cleared his throat. "Charly told me what she did, Mallory. She wasn't herself. Watching her father die, finding out Ben wanted her dead, even you turning up—which was a good thing, she was happy to find you—but all of it together, she just couldn't handle it all. Her thoughts got all mixed up."

He cleared his throat. "She's going to be discharged this morning, but she's under arrest. They'll take her straight to jail, and then she'll be arraigned. You can put a stop to it. Tell them the truth about who you are. Back up her story that it was Ben who had the gun. I've arranged for her to be admitted to a private rehabilitation center. She'll get intensive counseling there. She's deeply repentant about what she did. Please know that."

I squeezed my eyes shut.

Jensen waited for me to open my eyes and look at him. "She wants you to forgive her."

I felt a heaviness in my body. I looked around the room and spotted a large vase of flowers on a table in the corner. Without asking, I knew they'd come from her.

"Please, Mallory, she's genuinely sorry."

"You're her grandfather. Of course, you'd believe her." If I changed my story now, told Saldinger who I really was, I'd probably be in even more legal trouble than I already faced.

I glanced up at the ceiling for a few beats. When I looked ahead, I pinned Jensen with my eyes. "Tell Mallory I don't forgive her."

His nostrils flared. "She's Charly. You know that. I'm going to tell the police who she is."

"You're an old man who just lost his son. They won't believe you over me."

"We'll see about that." As he stood up to leave, he looked like he'd aged ten years over the course of the last ten minutes. He found my eyes and silently implored me to put my family first, then left the room.

CHAPTER 49

I stuck to my story. I was Charly Gordon. The person who'd shot Ben and me was my sister. Charly was arraigned on charges of second-degree murder, and bail was denied. As I'd predicted, my grandfather's protestations that I was really Mallory were dismissed. After all, what reason would Charly have to shoot me? Mallory was the one who had schemed to get Charly's money. Mallory had to be the one to shoot Charly. I had been shot; therefore, I must be Charly. It helped that science couldn't prove otherwise. We shared the same DNA, and since neither of us had ever been fingerprinted, there was no record to compare.

I returned to Charly's townhouse—now mine—after I was released from the hospital, and a few days later went to the gallery. Much as I liked the idea of owning a gallery, my months of dreaming about Paris and studying there were too great a temptation. I offered Sandy the chance to buy it from me, with only a small down payment. I agreed to finance it with very generous terms. She jumped on the offer.

I knew I would have to return for my sister's trial—after all, I was the key witness—but that would be months away. Maybe close to a year—unless she agreed to a plea. I doubted she'd do that. She hadn't wavered on her insistence that I was Mallory, not her. I would need to return for Clark's and Mullin's trials as well, if they didn't take pleas.

Two weeks after I had been released from the hospital, I flew to Paris. I stayed in a hotel rather than search for an apartment. After all, money was no object. At first, I just lost myself in the city. I went to every museum, then started all over and went to each a second time. It seemed like every few streets had artists displaying their work, especially along the Seine, and I stopped to admire and chat with each one. Finally, I enrolled in the Paris College of Art and began taking art classes. The school taught classes in English and led to a US-recognized bachelor of arts degree.

At the end of the day, I'd return to my hotel room and wonder if I'd done the right thing. I had more money than I'd ever spend in my lifetime. I could buy anything and go anywhere. I was finally studying art full-time. But I was alone, with no family and few friends.

Was it worth it? I often asked myself. I didn't know the answer.

Seven months later, I returned to New York for Charly's trial. The assistant district attorney trying her case had scheduled my trial preparation for 2:00 p.m., but before I met with her, I drove to Riker's Island, where Charly was jailed.

When she was brought into the visitor's room, I did a double take. She looked like I had when I'd first met Ben. Her hair color had returned to its natural shade, and her hair was longer and unshaped. She'd also gained weight on the prison's carbohydrate-rich diet.

"Did you come here to gloat?" Charly asked me when she sat down at the visitor's table.

I wasn't sure myself why I'd come. "How are you doing?"

"How do you think?"

I wanted to hate her. I'd wanted her to suffer, for taking away from me the one thing I'd wanted most—a sister to love. How could I love someone who chose revenge over sisterhood? I'd taken her place and her money and sent her to jail. And I was miserable.

I made an instant decision. "I'm going to tell the truth. About who you are and who I am." I think some part of me always knew I wouldn't go through with my deception. I'd been so angry at Charly that I had been willing to pretend what I was doing was justified. But over the months, as I'd lived out my dream, I knew it was unfair.

She stared at me without saying a word.

For months, I had convinced myself that Charly needed to be punished. Now, sitting across from my sister, I finally acknowledged that Ben wouldn't have gone through with his scheme if I hadn't agreed. How could I hold Charly accountable without being answerable myself? "And I'm going to tell them that Ben had the gun."

At that, tears began to roll down Charly's cheeks. "Thank you," she whispered.

I left Riker's Island and headed to downtown Manhattan, where the New York County District Attorney's office was located. I went through security and then took the elevator to Elise Goldman's office. She was ready for me. I sat down. "Before you say anything," I began, "I need to tell you what really happened."

When I finished, she sat back in her chair, tapping her pencil on the desk. After a while, she said, "You can be charged with obstruction of justice, you know. On top of charges for conspiracy to commit murder."

"I know."

"Why are you changing your story now? Why didn't you tell the truth from the beginning?"

"I had spent months becoming Charlotte Gordon. When I woke up in the hospital, I was so confused, I believed I *was* her. And then, when I realized I wasn't, I wanted to be. I didn't want to be Mallory Holcolm, who'd been unhappy most of her life. I wanted to live the life Charly had." I hung my head down and whispered, "I know it was wrong."

Goldman just shook her head. She stood up, then read me my rights. She called for an officer to take me away. Once again, I was trading places with my sister.

Five days later, we were both released from jail. The district attorney still needed my testimony in Clark's trial, so he had allowed me to plead guilty to a reduced charge with a recommended sentence of five years' probation. He could have sent me to jail for a long time, but Charly didn't want him to press charges against me for my lies that sent her to jail. I think the DA felt sorry for me. After all, I'd been shot. And since I now backed Charly's version of Ben's death, he no longer had a case against her.

"We're even now," I said to her once we were free from the prison property.

"I suppose so," she answered, a sad look on her face, before she turned and walked away from me.

Being even didn't mean we could ever become sisters. Too much had transpired. She returned to her townhouse, to her life of wealth. I knew I couldn't go back to The Dump.

I called the person who'd been a substitute father for me since I'd met him—Brian. He brought me back to his apartment and installed me in the guest room. I told him and Stan the whole story, including my ignoble part in it. To their credit, they didn't pass judgment on me. I'd already passed enough on myself.

I felt protected living with Brian and Stan. Each evening, Stan and I would concoct something special for dinner, and Brian would *ooh* and *aah* over how delicious it was. Their kitchen wasn't as grand as Charly's, but it had room enough for two cooks and was stocked with everything a chef would need.

After a few weeks, I began searching the newspaper ads for waitress jobs and a place to live. When Brian caught me doing that, he pulled the paper from my hands.

"Mallory, you could stay here forever, as far as we're concerned," he said. "But from everything you've told me, your heart is someplace else."

He was talking about Jake, and he was right. But I couldn't imagine ever explaining to Jake what I had agreed to with Ben, what I had done in furtherance of that agreement, what I had done both to, and for, my sister. Night after night, Brian and Stan tried to cajole me into calling him. Night after night, I refused.

And so, they called him on their own. I answered the doorbell one day, and there he was, a bouquet of flowers in his hands. I rushed into his arms, and he held me tight. We took a long walk, and I told him about my pact with Ben, and what had happened since I'd left High Falls. I even told him the truth about who had really shot me, something I'd withheld from Brian and Stan. When I finished, he held me again.

"I can't imagine what your life had been like growing up. But I know you're a good person. And you proved that by going to the police. And I know you have a good heart, because you cleared your sister."

I was so relieved, all I could do was cry.

"Come back to High Falls with me," Jake said.

Through my tears, I answered, "Yes."

EPILOGUE

September 2018

I moved in with Jake the day he brought me back to High Falls, and we've been together since. It took me a while to tell the rest of his family what I had done, but they, too, welcomed me into their lives.

I became immersed in the extensive art community in Ulster County and have been learning from my fellow artists. Katy Patel, the first artist I'd met when I'd lived in Ben's parents' house, offered me space in her shop to hang some of my paintings. Three of them have sold, and I guess that now makes me a professional artist.

Jake introduced me to his friends still living in the Hudson Valley, and they've become my friends, too. Of course, they don't know about my past. Still, I'd grown up as an outsider, and now, for the first time, I feel like part of a group.

One of the gardens Jake designed was written up in *Architectural Digest*, and they named him one of the top ten landscape architects in the tristate area. Since then, he's been busier than ever. Now, it wasn't just clients south to Westchester County and east to Putnam County that tried to commission his services—he fielded calls from Connecticut and New Jersey as well. He's had to expand his staff for the eight busy months from March through October. It sometimes takes him away from home for days at a time, but that's okay with me. I'm busy myself.

Today is my birthday, and Jake and I headed to Manhattan to celebrate it with Charly. Although I was the one who should never have forgiven my twin—after all, she'd chosen revenge over me and shot me in the process—it was Charly who had trouble letting go of her anger at me for leaving her in jail for seven months. It hadn't seemed to matter to her that she belonged in jail for killing her husband and was only free because I'd lied for her. For months she wouldn't talk to me or answer my e-mails. Then, a few months ago, Charly contacted me. At her grandfather's insistence, she'd been seeing a therapist three times a week. She asked to see me, and I'd jumped into my car and headed to Manhattan.

As soon as she'd seen me, she'd drawn me into a hug. "I'm so sorry, Mallory. I've been horrible to you, and you don't deserve it." We'd spent the afternoon together, talking and laughing like I always thought sisters would. Since then, we speak almost daily.

I wondered sometimes whether Charly had planned to kill Ben from the moment I'd told her about his scheme, or she'd just snapped, as Poppy had said. Whether she'd taken the gun to commit murder, or for protection from Ben. I didn't know the answer, and it didn't matter to me.

The what-ifs kept swirling around my head so long that I finally had to force myself to stop. I decided I can't go back, only forward.

I've chosen not to condemn Charly, because to do so, I'd have to condemn myself as well. Although I deserve condemnation, Jake's acceptance has helped me forgive myself.

Charly sold her townhouse—it held too many bad memories for her. Instead, she moved into her father's apartment. I've let my hair return to its natural color, and it's back to its original shoulder length, so it wasn't confusing to Carlos, the doorman, when we all walked in, laden with bags. Charly was waiting at the door for us, and as soon as the elevator opened, she ran and grabbed Susan from my arms. My beautiful daughter, named after our mother, six months old now, was all pudgy legs and arms and constant smiles.

"She looks just like us, don't you think?" Charly said.

"Actually, I think she looks more like our mother's baby pictures. Which is good. Two of us is enough."

Charly laughed and bounced Susan up and down, drawing giggles from her. I introduced her to Jake—it was the first time they'd met. "Man, I know you told me you were identical, but it's so crazy looking at you two next to each other," he said.

We walked together into the living room. Herman Jensen was settled comfortably on the couch, but he stood up to kiss me. "Thank you," he whispered in my ear. I quickly introduced Jake to him as well. Charly and I had talked about how we wanted to celebrate our birthdays, and we'd agreed. We wanted to eat lunch at the Modern, the French/New American restaurant in the Museum of Modern Art, followed by a tour of the museum. I could have left Susan at the apartment with Tatiana, who'd returned to work for Charly. But she was likely to sleep through much of the afternoon and was usually cheerful when she was awake, so we took her with us.

The sun was shining, and an autumn crispness had finally overtaken the summer mugginess, so we walked. Jake pushed Susan's stroller while Charly and I strolled arm in arm. We reached the restaurant and were seated by a window overlooking the museum's garden. Once again, Charly and I ordered the same dish. Jake peppered Charly with questions, looking for the similarities between us and cheering when he found differences. When we finished, we sauntered through the museum, taking our time with each painting, discussing what we saw, what we admired, what we didn't. Susan slept through the two hours we spent there.

As we walked through the museum, Charly asked, "When can we meet the Harrises?"

I'd spoken to my father's parents many times but had put off meeting them. I wanted to wait for Charly and me to do so together. "They're just waiting for my call. They're ready to hop on a plane right away. Especially since Susan was born."

Before we returned to Ulster County, Tatiana had insisted we come back to the apartment, where she had a cake that she'd baked for our birthday. As soon as we arrived, Charly's grandfather pulled me off to the side, then withdrew an envelope from his jacket. "This is for you," he said.

I assumed it was a birthday present and opened it. Inside was a check for $10 million. My eyes widened, and I looked up at him. "I can't take this," I said, as I put the check back in the envelope and held it out to him.

He pushed my hand back. "I've thought a lot about this, Mallory. If Charly were born first, you would have been my granddaughter. It doesn't seem fair to me that she has so much, and you so little. I'm an old man with a lot of money. I'd like to do this for you." He reached out and clasped my hand. "And I wanted to show how grateful I am for what you did for Charly." He paused for a moment. "Even if it took you a while to get there."

I touched my hand to my heart. "Herman, I meant it when I said I didn't want money. All I've ever wanted is a family."

"You have your family now. You have Charly and Jake and Susan. I just want you all to be comfortable."

"I *am* comfortable. More than comfortable. I've never been so happy in my life. This amount of money will just complicate that." I slipped the envelope back into his jacket pocket.

He grumbled some words I didn't hear, then smiled. "I'm going to put it in a trust for Susan. That's what I'll do. And if you have more children, I'll do the same for each one."

I was okay with Susan having that money, but I wouldn't take it for myself. I had conspired with a virtual stranger to kill my sister, and taking her grandfather's money would feel like I was benefiting from that one despicable act in my life. Every dollar I spent would remind me of that time.

Just then, Tatiana entered the room, carrying an elaborately decorated cake, topped with whipped cream and two candles, and inscribed, *Birthday #1 for Charly and Mallory together*.

I had started a new life with Jake—a life filled with love and art and nature. And, most of all, it was filled with family. I had all the riches I needed.

ACKNOWLEDGMENTS

Although writing is a solitary endeavor, the final product is enriched by the help of others. My thanks to Elaine Haber, an estate-planning and elder-law attorney, who helped me make sense of what happens to one's money when a billionaire dies; to Sarah Underhill, a hospice nurse, who explained hospice care during the last stages of a person's life; to Dr. Mark Kessler, who helped me figure out how Mallory should be injured, but not killed, by a bullet wound to her chest; and to Susan Posen, for educating me on the art world in Manhattan. Any mistakes in those areas are purely my own.

I am also deeply grateful to my agent, Adam Chromy, who's always the first to read the full manuscript and help steer me in the right direction; my developmental editor, Kevin Smith, whose suggestions made for what I hope is a more exciting book; and to my editor at Thomas & Mercer, Liz Pearsons, whose insights brought the story into sharper focus. Also at Thomas & Mercer, many thanks to my copy editor, Valerie Kalfrin, and proofreader, Jill Kramer. Thanks also to the marketing staff at Thomas & Mercer for bringing my book to the attention of readers. It is to the readers of my books that I am especially grateful—your critiques make me a better writer, and your praise fuels my desire to keep writing.

Finally, I want to thank my husband, Lenny Green, for his unwavering faith in me; my sons, Jason and Andy, who have brought me great joy; their wives, Amanda and Jackie, for being the daughters I never had; and my grandchildren—Rachel, Joshua, Jacob, Sienna, and Noah—all of whom I love more than words can express.

ABOUT THE AUTHOR

Photo © 2014 Darin Back

Marti Green has a master's degree in school psychology and a law degree. For twenty-three years she worked as in-house counsel for a major cable-television operator, specializing in contracts, intellectual-property law, and regulatory issues. She is the author of five legal thrillers: *The Price of Justice*, *Presumption of Guilt*, *Unintended Consequences*, *First Offense*, and *Justice Delayed*. She is a passionate traveler, the mother of two adult sons, and the proud grandmother of five grandchildren. She lives in central Florida with her husband, Lenny, and her cat, Howie. Please visit her website at: www.martigreen.net.